# INVASION AI
## Derek Lilly

In memory of my father
Robert 'Bob' Lilly

ISBN

978-0-473-38440-1

www.invasionai.com

# Contents

# Foreword

"Can machines think?"

Cambridge-educated mathematician Alan Turing posed the question "Can machines think?" in his 1950 paper, 'Computing Machinery and Intelligence'. He invented what is now known as the 'Turing Test', to ascertain if a machine is intelligent.

John McCarthy coined the term 'artificial intelligence' (AI). His life's work was to help others understand what AI actually meant.

Others followed with seminal inventions such as Frank Rosenblatt's artificial neural networks and John Holland's genetic algorithms.

\* \* \*

Little did these great men know at the time, the profound effect AI would have on mankind in the near future.

Mankind had a storm coming, a biblical sized cosmic event that would change the world forever.

# Prologue

Let's start from the beginning…

My name is Lukas Linsky. I was born into a world on the brink of war. Civilization was still reeling from the atrocities of September 11, 2001. The whole planet had been stripped of its innocence. Politicians and the military were rattling their highly polished sabres, the general public demanded revenge: meanwhile the Earth suffered man's rampant exploitation and destruction.

Little did people know where mankind was headed.

My mother, Flo, was 41 years old when she gave me life: thanks mostly to a new, advanced fertility treatment that finally enabled her to fulfil her lifelong dream of motherhood. A natural mother, Flo was always giving and caring - but she was not just my mother. To me, she was a mother to all. Her empathy constantly flowed; nothing ever muted her love for the human race.

My father, Marcus, was so blind with pride on the day of my birth he fell down a flight of stairs with me in his arms - or so the story goes. Luckily, my mental capacity was not dented in any adverse way - though my father often reminded me that his sprained ankle continued to flare up as he advanced in age.

Unlike my mother, Marcus kept his emotions deep within. A momentary and imperceptible movement of the lips was all you'd get for a smile. Mourning meant a single tear and laughter elicited a snort or a chuckle, but never from the belly. That's not to say he was cold. His warmth just came from a deeper place.

I loved them both equally, but in different ways. I became a true reflection of them, and I've always been grateful for this.

So, what did I become?

Well, before I knew it, I was a prodigy in the making. Or so I was told from a very young age.

Most babies' understand how words are formed at a very early age. From birth they begin to use their tongue, lips, and palate to make audible gurgles, oohs and ahs. Soon they can comprehend a few words and they react to noises such as a dog barking.

I was walking before I was one and had formed my first sentences at 13 months. I was already an anomaly.

At an early age I became fascinated by computers and any technological device. I was often found in the corner staring at a device, exploring its contents with my hands, testing its capabilities, trying to understand its functions and meanings.

I went to school in California, exact location dependent on my parents' research work, which was wide and varying. They were high profile scientists and their work required occasional relocation. Wherever I attended school, I was always leaving my mark, usually ascending to the top of my class. Not that I was ever big headed about it; it was always pleasing but as far as I was concerned I was just being me. I always did my best; it just so happens that my best was usually better than everybody else. But no one minded. I made friends wherever I went - probably because I helped all the other kids with their homework.

My childhood was uneventful compared to my adult life. These early years were filled with love, games, play, exploration, embarrassment, discipline, mayhem, boredom, confusion, inspiration and of course copious amounts of education.

Love was the key to my childhood, though, and Flo poured this love upon me as if every day would be the last time she could do it. She slathered it like honey on toast. As her only child, and perhaps because of the unlikelihood of my conception, she never forgot to show her undying love for me, which more often than not came in the form of wet kisses or lung crushing hugs.

Marcus, on the other hand, exhibited his love with a glance or quick eye contact that would say a thousand words. I remember seeing him sometimes simply looking at me, his head slightly tilted to one side, as if he was trying to understand me, perhaps even trying to understand the love he felt. His face would crease into a maze of lines when he chuckled or when he frowned over a particularly tough problem. I would gaze at him during these times and be astounded by the emotion behind his eyes.

Studious, hardworking, disciplined, sharp, brilliant are some of the more popular words found on my school report cards. The class "clever clogs" was what my very English mum called me. The DNA inherited from my parents, proved to be a winning combination.

My brain was like a sponge and only knowledge quenched its insatiable thirst. I just soaked up information and my brain stored the data, waiting for the right moment to be recalled. Blessed with an eidetic or photographic memory and total recall of facts, learning to me was like riding a bike. As I got older, my brain just got faster.

\* \* \*

*In his book, 'Frames of Mind', the noted scientist Howard Gardner proposed that there are eight intelligences, or different areas in which people learn about the world around them: interpersonal, intrapersonal, bodily-kinesthetic, linguistic, logical-mathematical, musical, naturalistic, and spatial-visual. Gardner stated that intelligence is the "potential to process information that can be activated in a cultural setting to solve problems or create products that are of value in a culture."*

Let's just say I wasn't lacking in intelligence, no matter how you defined it.

I was also a good all-around athlete at a young age, but I particularly excelled at soccer, a game that came naturally to me. Tactics and positioning fascinated me more than anything else, and I enjoyed every encounter. Flo came to watch most of my games and of course this meant the world to me. Flo was a true soccer mum and I was very proud of that. Looking out for her presence at every game was the first thing I did every time I jogged out onto the pitch. Her presence gave me a reason to perform at my best. And because it was different to the world of academia we all lived in and surrounded us, it was a welcome respite. Excelling at football, or at least trying to, meant I could do something else other than just sitting and using my brain. It also got my mum out of the lab. I could tell she was grateful for this.

Marcus occasionally graced us with his presence, but usually for one of our more important games. Marcus was much more of an American football, baseball and basketball fan - which was understandable being of American birth. He could recite all the statistics of all the players; it was like he was reading them from a book. I think this is where the statistical element of my brain DNA had come from.

Unfortunately, soccer faded from my life somewhat as my teammates grew in physicality and I didn't. My brain could do the work, and then some, but on the field my body could not keep up. I just did not have the stamina or physical fitness required. In other words, I didn't do the fitness training. Not because I couldn't. I just loathed over-exertion.

With some encouragement from Marcus, I briefly switched over to American football. I demonstrated unique tactical ability, so even my coach would listen to my calls. However, it quickly became obvious this was a game for big boys, mostly played by physical specimens that looked like they had been sculpted out of stone from the quarry five miles up the road from where we lived at the time.

Back on the education trail, my teachers' reports were usually filled with one letter: 'A'. As I went through high school it became quite apparent that I was very different from the average student. At 14 I had an IQ of 151 - not bad really seeing as physicist Stephen Hawking, Bill Gates and Albert Einstein all had IQ's of 160.

I graduated High School at 16, top of the class. To celebrate this - and the fact I had completed my schooling two years early - we headed for a well-earned family holiday to New Zealand. My father had just sold his successful robotics business and he'd made a staggering amount of money. His stroke of genius was that he had cleverly held onto all of his patents.

* * *

*New Zealand is made up of two main Islands, the aptly named North and South Islands, and is home to 4.5 million people. Only 1 million live on the South Island, the larger, but more rural, of the two islands. The European explorer, Abel Tasman, first discovered the islands in 1642. It was over a century later, in 1769, that renowned English explorer and cartographer, Captain James Cook, became the first to actually circumnavigate both islands, on the first of his three, epic around-the-world voyages.*

It was curious, Flo noted, that neither of the islands were ever given proper names following their official discovery and occupation by the English, and were instead simply known as the North and South Islands. She also went into great detail about how Captain Cook was attacked and killed in Hawaii during his third voyage across the Pacific in 1779.

Such history and knowledge was always being imparted by my parents, but more so from Flo. These tales awakened the explorer in me in later life, and led to what I was to become in the world of science.

After we arrived in Auckland, a city of a million plus people, we drove through the heart of the North Island, taking in the Māori stronghold of Rotorua. The Māori were of course the indigenous Polynesian people of New Zealand, having colonized the islands around 1300AD.

We continued down to Wellington, the country's capital city and crossed the 'Cook Strait' the body of water that separates the two main islands. We then toured the South for the next four weeks in our large, rented RV. I remember vividly our stopover in the earthquake-ravaged city of Christchurch.

Struck by a large 7.1 magnitude earthquake at 4:35am local time on the 4th September 2010, the earthquake, which lasted for about 10 seconds, had its epicentre 25 miles west of Christchurch, close to the town of Darfield. Unbelievably, there were no fatalities; the emergency services put this down to the early morning timing. Nearly six months later the Cantabrians were not so lucky. A smaller earthquake, measuring magnitude 6.3 on the Richter scale, struck again. Technically an aftershock, it caused the loss of 185 lives.

When we drove through Christchurch's city centre you could see where the devastation had occurred, most of the city's Central Business District had been, or was being, rebuilt. Flo had been to Christchurch during her first visit to New Zealand in her pre-University days and had recently read online that the city had suffered nearly 15,000 aftershocks in total since the first Earthquake in 2010. That figure alone stuck in my mind straight away and was the first time I became truly aware of the Earth's intensely powerful capabilities as a living, breathing, and indeed fiery, organic planet.

Nearing the end of our four-week road trip we departed Franz Josef Glacier, the 7.5-mile (12km) long glacier located in Westland Tai Poutini National Park. The glacier, named in 1865 after Emperor Franz Joseph I of Austria by the German explorer Julius von Haast, was stunningly spectacular to behold. It's believed that 15,000 years ago the glacier extended down to the sea. But sadly, with recent global warming, it had retreated several miles back up the mountainside.

We drove for about five hours and by late afternoon after passing through the tiny Makarora Township; we came across a road traffic accident.

Marcus stopped the car and stared for a moment at the scene. I think he was as shocked as I was. I had never seen a road traffic accident before in real life and apparently he hadn't either. As he and I sat there dumbly, Flo sprung into action, immediately reaching for her travelling medical kit to help patch up a young injured Chinese tourist. It transpired they had been filming the headwaters of Lake Wanaka when the driver took his eyes off the road for a split second too long.

The young girl was in a pretty bad way. Blood was streaming from a leg wound caused by broken glass.

Flo immediately put a large surgical dressing onto the wound and pressed down on it to stem the flow of blood. I watched in awe. My mother was a true hero.

She asked the girl's mother to hold the dressing in place whist she placed a tourniquet in position above the wound. None of the Chinese tourists could speak English, but it was obvious they were very grateful for Flo's assistance. This was Flo, always helping, patching up and fixing: Mother of all.

The local volunteer fire brigade truck duly arrived with siren's blazing it was marshaled by a young station officer named Brent. It was here that I got my first real understanding of the kindness and generosity of New Zealand people. Brent immediately took control of the situation directing police and the other first responder emergency services who arrived at the scene. Brent had no idea who my father was, but was very grateful to my mother for stemming the flow of blood from the injured girl's leg. "You probably saved her life," Brent said to Flo. My mother, calm and composed as always, said to Brett, "So, volunteer Fire Brigade. Do you not get paid for this?" "No," Brett replied with a wry smile. "We are all volunteers and someone has to be here." He turned and looked at his men and women on the truck and said to Flo, "We all live and work locally. It could have just as easily been one of our children we were saving today."

After the eventful journey and the road traffic accident delay, we ended up staying in the Hawea Hotel in the breath-taking area of Lake Hawea. With a million dollar view, we sat eating dinner overlooking the beautiful landscape and were entertained by the hotel owner Anthony. Being an established entrepreneur himself, Anthony immediately recognized my father from a recent copy of Forbes magazine, and gave us a bottle of his best 'Kalex' Pinot Noir to sample.

The Kalex wine brand, famous in these parts, is owned by the billionaire Alex Kaufman - the Polish American businessman, entrepreneur and holocaust survivor who overcame incredibly challenging situations to educate himself in post-war Germany, and who later immigrated to the U.S. with nothing but the clothes on his back, and a quarter in his shoe. He made his fortune in the chemical industry, developing the patents for NutraSweet, the industry leading sugar substitute.

Anthony and my father immediately hit it off. Talking all night about the Central Otago region and the multitude of award winning quality wines it produced; they were to remain lifelong friends.

The next morning we said our goodbyes to Lake Hawea and took the 15-minute drive to the Central Otago town of Wanaka.

In the Southern hemisphere, August is the last month of winter. We arrived on the first day. The air was crisp and clear, the backdrop straight from a movie. The sky was a shimmering azure blue colour, I'd never seen before, punctuated by snow-capped mountains: A panoramic unlike anything else. I knew we were in a very special place.

Wanaka is noted for its breath-taking lake. Twenty-six miles long, it boasts fairy-tale views and a full range of emotions. This picturesque township of about 10,000 people was actually one of the world's best-kept secrets and little did I know then that it would have such a remarkable impact on my life.

This is where it would all begin.

Flo had visited the South Island during her gap year as an 18 year-old. She had fallen in love with the mountains, skiing, mountain biking and the crystal clear, glacial-fed lakes of the region. She had always vowed to herself to one-day return with her own family. She was tearful when we arrived. Fulfilling her lifelong dream overwhelmed her.

Wanaka was truly paradise on Earth. The region produced some of the best Pinot Noir in the world and my dad loved it. Small boutique vineyards that had just the right amount of sunlight, fed by the pure, crystal clear waters of the Clutha River. Wine producers now thrived in the region, regularly producing bumper crops of the much sought after Pinot Noir grape.

We loved it so much, Flo and I had planned to stay for a year. Marcus wasn't so lucky, He had to return to California on important business, though he did end up flying out to be with us four times during that first 12 months. I enrolled in the local Mount Aspiring High School to give me something to do during the days and make some new friends, while Flo got busy with her new research work. But our main purpose was simply to be there to enjoy all New Zealand had to offer, which was plenty.

It wasn't long before I first met my lifelong friend Angus Macleod. Known as 'Gus' to his friends, he had been to boarding school for the last four years at Otago Boys High school, the region's pre-eminent boys' high school and, for Gus, the best Rugby school going. However he was to finish his last year of school with me at Mt Aspiring. Gus was a fifth generation Kiwi, but his Scottish names and roots were there for everyone to see. His blonde hair had a tint of red, betraying his real heritage. A descendant of the proud MacLeod clan, from the Isle of Skye in Scotland, Gus was already a bear of a man, and had just turned 18 when I first met him. He weighed 253 pounds, stood a mighty 6-foot-4 and was already an imposing figure on the rugby field as the schools 1st XV rugby captain. Playing at No. 8, he was a loose forward to be reckoned with and a natural-born leader.

Rugby can be a brutal game. 'Gridiron', as American football is known around these parts, is played with helmets and padding to protect the players, but a different type of warrior with a different mind-set adorns the humble Rugby shirt. Gus was rugby and rugby was Gus. He encapsulated the essence of the game with his car window sticker, which read: "Give Blood, Play Rugby!"

Gus was different to other players. He stood apart and played with an aura around him. Few could touch him but many felt his touch. The team's medical bag contained a bottle of water, a sponge and cold ice spray. This was all that was needed to keep these monsters of young men playing. Gus needed even less to keep going. His body was immune to the punishment. Nothing damaged it; nothing caused a mark or a dent.

The New Zealand national rugby team, known around the world as the mighty "All Blacks", has a remarkable test win ratio on the world's stage of 77% over the last 100+ years, the best international record in any world sport. What makes this statistic even more remarkable is that there is only a population of 4.5 million to choose from. Gus had his career path already mapped out; he would go on to be a legend in the game.

The local girls just seemed to wander around Gus in a trance-like state, I had seen this kind of behaviour at my High School in California, with the cheerleaders and the school football team captain, but I had never seen anything like this. Gus was armed with rugged good looks and athleticism that was down to his inherited Scottish DNA, and many hours of work on the family farm. Girls would swoon and melt at the sight of Gus. Meanwhile, I walked invisibly beside him.–

My friendship with Gus meant more than I can really describe during my first years in New Zealand, and he was to play a vital role in what was to come.

Gus lived with his family seven miles outside of town in a vast 'High Country' farm station that reached to the top of the Pisa Range, where in the winter the skiers and snow-kiters had their very own outdoor playground. Gus became a big fan of snow kiting, thanks to his father Richard, who had introduced him to the sport at an early age. Richard, in fact, was a well-recognized pioneer of the sport in New Zealand. I became addicted the very first time I 'caught the wind' and quite literally flew across the rolling, snow-capped terrain. It was the most thrilling experience of my life and I was to enjoy many more thrills (and a few spills) over the course of my time in New Zealand.

Gus's parents had become quite wealthy themselves, having sold some of their very valuable family farmland near the Wanaka township for development. Richard was also the town's unofficial entrepreneur and became involved in many successful business start-ups, including 'OMVIP' the online share trading system that stormed the share market industry.

It was perhaps inevitable that Richard hit it off with Marcus, not least because they were both avid Pinot Noir fans and whisky connoisseurs. Given the McLeod's Scottish heritage, and a few connections still back in the motherland, Richard had been able to secure a steady supply of 18-year-old "Talisker" single Malt Whisky. Indeed, his particular tipple of choice was once named "Best Single Malt Whisky in the World" in 2007 at the World Whisky Awards.

Richard and my father spent many a happy night toasting and tasting

Richard's secret collection of the world's best single malts. This was the genesis of my lifelong obsession and love of the lusciously complex flavors of single malt whisky – a pastime that demanded constant analysis.

More importantly, though, I found myself immersed in the wonder of the region's night sky. Being so far south and with very little light pollution, the clear night skies showed off the Milky Way in all its astrological glory, which fascinated me every single time I gazed skywards.

One of the first things we engaged in at my new high school was a field trip to Mount John University Observatory, situated over 3572 feet (1089 meters) above sea level at the northern end of the Mackenzie basin, near the resort town of Lake Tekapo. One night, after looking through the faculty's 16-inch telescope, which pointed directly at the Southern hemisphere sky, I knew there and then that I had finally found my calling in life.

I had to know more. My brain was electrified like never before. I knew I had to find the answers to what was out there and what made it all work.

On my return from the Lake Tekapo trip, it was Flo who first saw the glint in my eye and my heightened sense of purpose. She was the one who had downloaded the information on Harvard for me, and with my father's contacts and money, the plan for my academic future was set. Answers to all the questions that were swirling around inside my head would now be addressed. Little did I know then, it would be in the Wanaka area that they would be answered.

# Chapter One

hange was everywhere in 2016. It was the time for mass movements, and sticking the middle finger up at the system. Countries were fleeing from unions; unqualified presidents were leading powerful countries; dictators were back in fashion; racism, sexism and its ugly friends were back.

For the first time, Europe and the rest of the world started asking the difficult questions about race, religion and the whole meaning of living together on the planet. Perhaps it was the fear of another world war or loss of faith in humans but it was around this time that investment in artificial intelligence (AI) rose markedly.

Although AI was still considered in its infancy back then, there was a real desire by the big three manufacturing giants of the time - Apple, Microsoft and Google - to incorporate AI in their digital operating systems and across their range of computers, cell phones and tablets. It was Apple founder and legendary entrepreneur Steve Jobs who first recognised the power of personal technology and its ability to interact with humans. The world would soon realise this power too.

The aim of Jobs and his brethren was to make the world a better place, and AI did this - for a time. Computers talking to and reacting to users was the way forward. I wondered whether this change occurred because humans had become bored with their own social interactions or maybe they were tired of being inept. But I suppose it was inevitable that technology would become ever more advanced and the visions of the great science fiction writers of years gone by would become reality.

Technology was indeed becoming an aid for easier, faster, more efficient connections - yet I did question whether this also meant our skills at communication, human interaction and establishing "connections" with real people was becoming shallower as a result. I was proved wrong many years later, thankfully.

In 2018 Flo and I returned home to the U.S. and there was now a newcomer to the robotics AI tech scene, a somewhat secretive organization called 'Android AI' that would unleash the potential of artificial intelligence to the world and beyond. The fact the Central Intelligence Agency was behind it gives you a little clue as to its purpose and intention.

Based in California, close to Henry W. Coe State Park - or the Orestimba Wilderness, as it's known locally - the CIA's Android AI headquarters was set against a backdrop of the whole of the Diablo mountain range. With 89,000 acres of mostly Isolated and pristine wilderness, Henry W. Coe State Park is the largest State Park in Northern California and - best of all for the CIA - miles from most prying eyes. The CIA's main reason for choosing the location was simple: The vast majority of the world's leading tech firms were based in and around San Jose or "Silicon Valley". A one-hour drive south east of San Jose, Android AI was constructed on much higher ground and this proved to be a very wise decision.

Not surprisingly given its potential strategic importance, Android AI was conceived as a 'black budget' program, a top-secret U.S. government funded program driven from within the intelligence community.

In 2016 an estimated $50 billion was spent on various "Black Projects" by the U.S. government. These projects have had many different titles and cover stories over the years, but probably the most famous of these projects was "Stealth". The U.S. military, funded through government black project resources, developed a variety of technology-laden stealth aircraft, all designed to avoid detection by the enemy. Using a variety of technologies to reduce reflection or emission of radar and infrared, these machines led the way in stealth technology.

The precursor to the immense Android AI facility was a place that became known as Area 51, a secret airfield built in 1955 by the U.S. Air Force in the Nevada desert for testing experimental aircraft and weapons systems. In years to come, the intense secrecy surrounding the base brought it international fame and notoriety with the development of the various 'Black Projects'. Area 51 is where many UFO enthusiasts claim to have seen alien spaceships or UFO's - though in fact they were just various versions of these Black Project aircraft, developed for U.S. covert military projects.

During this period, beginning in the 1950s, the world was in the grip of a 'Cold War' that lasted until 1991. It was basically West v East, the United States and its allies versus The Soviet Union. The U.S. military loved the game of cat and mouse being played out by satellite with the Russians and later the Chinese, but there was apparently a real threat of all-out nuclear war.

The remote nature of Area 51 kept this secret work hidden from the world's spy networks and the ever-increasing UFO fraternity. There was a security 'shoot-to-kill policy' enforced at the Area 51 designated boundaries.

Unlike Area 51, Android AI was a legitimate company at all levels. I like to think this is directly attributable to it being founded by my father in December 2017. He was not only the founder, but also the CEO, and he ensured he had a strong and trustworthy Board of Directors, though the CIA robustly screened all appointments.

* * *

To talk to machines you need lines of code. To talk to a human android hybrid you need a very special language and a very special machine. Marcus learned this as a career scientist who studied under John McCarthy at MIT.

McCarthy was the designer of LISP, the computing language of AI. He was viewed as one of the founding fathers of AI. LISP was McCarthy's life's work, first invented in 1958 whilst at MIT. Of all the computer languages still in widespread operation today, only Fortran is older. The LISP family of languages has evolved alongside the field of computer science, and John McCarthy was its champion.

Unsurprisingly, the CIA recruited my father after following his career and monitoring his astounding commercial successes with robotics. He was personally chosen to guide and steer the fledgling Android AI project. With his money from the sale of his own robotics firm, and his stellar reputation, he was the perfect front man for the job in hand, and his appointment was a credible cover story for the CIA as they sought to capitalize on Marcus's unique knowledge.

In the ensuing five years under his stewardship, billions of dollars were poured into research and development. The focus now was not on touchscreen mobiles or hover-boards - it was more serious than that. The world needed stability, efficiency and security. Humans seemed unable to provide these things for themselves in a traditional sense, so Marcus and his team searched for the alternative.

The answer was AI - something capable of performing all human tasks. From the monotonous to the creative, this new branch of AI had to be supremely capable. It was the only way to save the human race from imploding, what seemed like a real possibility in those days.

It took five years. It took countless hours of hypothesising, experimenting and failing before they had it. After five hard years of constant research, blackboards full of formulae and countless ideas, the first high-tech robot-android prototype was created. It was affectionately nicknamed 'Andis'. These robots were made of mainly off the shelf parts and were readily accessible in the world's markets.

At first, thousands of jobs were created, but Andis were soon manufacturing and assembling other Andis, leading to fewer mistakes, quicker output, greater efficiency and, of course, higher revenue. This is what the androids gave us, and the world was soon clamouring for more.

On the advice of the CIA, Marcus bought up all of the various companies that manufactured and sold essential parts, thus cleverly creating a monopoly over the whole Andi production process. Although generally an egalitarian sort of fellow, Marcus decided that if there was one monopoly that was justified, this was it. For the good of the whole of mankind and the planet, it was crucial that there was only one model

Andi. The utter genius of the Andi was the fact that no matter how hard anyone tried to dismantle one to find out how it worked, they couldn't do it. Once built, each and every Andi was impenetrable due to the security protocols installed in the Andi during manufacture. Security was everything.

Keeping a monopoly on the production also ensured that the relatively inexpensively priced Andi robots would be available for the masses. This also helped the U.S. intelligence services deflect any congressional protests about monopoly issues raised by the ever-decreasing number of competitors. Marcus's Andis were so successful that within a few years all other brands had been wiped out totally. To ensure security, the CIA set-up a special task force to locate and procure all competitor models from wherever they could be found - landfill, attics, retro stores, museums, art galleries and the like until eventually there was not one single competitor model left on the whole planet.

Marcus was now leading Android AI which would go on to become one of the most powerful and influential companies on Earth. Writing this now though, I wonder if he would start this project again if he knew what it would bring. If he knew what would happen would Marcus do it again? We will never know. The Andis were a revolution, of intergalactic proportions.

# Chapter Two

Marcus was a brilliant man with an exceptional mind. Solving complex computer algorithms was child's play to him. Tackling complex theorems was his hobby, changing the world was his calling. He was a red, white and blue American. Having grown up during the cold war, he was fiercely protective of his nation and a true patriot; it meant Marcus was always going to be an easy recruit for the CIA. With the help of his CIA handlers, Marcus quickly gathered a CIA vetted management team around him of brilliant AI scientists from the four corners of the globe. Secrecy was maintained at board level and the workers were blissfully unaware of any CIA links to the company.

I think in private moments, despite his gregarious honest-looking appearance and truthful demeanour, Marcus actually found the whole secrecy thing quite exciting. I remember seeing his eyes twinkle mischievously whenever he was called away for a "quiet word" during a meeting or had to leave what he was doing for an urgent face-to-face rendezvous with an agent. Sometimes, when he had downed one too many Talisker's, he would quip openly with close friends how he thought he would have made an excellent James Bond character. Everyone would fall around the floor laughing hysterically. If only they had known the truth.

He didn't let his hair down all that often, but that was mainly because Marcus didn't have the time. He never really stopped; he was the stereotypical hard-working American. He hustled every day, exhausting himself until his body gave up and slept, only to get up a few hours later to wear himself down again. There was no stopping him. Sometimes it seemed like I was in a single parent family, as I saw very little of my father after 2018, but the bond of love that defined our family could never and would never be broken. Despite Marcus's hectic lifestyle, he had a rock he could always rely on; my mum, Flo.

Flo was a doctor of genetics, a PhD Oxford graduate who had helped expand the double helix theory, the double-stranded molecules of nucleic acids or DNA, as we all know it today. Flo loved Marcus unreservedly; she gave everything to him, her heart and her soul. In private I think she melted him down and stripped back his sometimes icy exterior. She had the knack of massaging emotions out of people. Only later when tears would fill Marcus's eyes in memory would I know what she had meant to him.

In the years that the Andis were being tested, produced and later released, I was studying relentlessly at Harvard in order to pursue my dream of becoming an Astrophysicist. Astrophysics is the branch of astronomy that employs the principles of physics and chemistry to ascertain the nature of all planets. Since that first night in the Mount John University Observatory I desperately wanted to know what the universe was made of. It bugged me every day that I didn't fully know. I lost hours of sleep wondering what could be.

So I decided to leave home to start my studies. I loved my time at Harvard. Being surrounded by great minds was invigorating. I began to absorb every bit of information I could get my hands on. I wrote many papers while I was at Harvard. Some of my theories were controversial at the time, but years later they would come to be celebrated as fact by none other than the President of the United States.

My three heroes in the world of science were all luminaries - Albert Einstein, Carl Sagan and Stephen Hawking. All three men were instrumental to my learning. I read and memorised everything these men had ever written. To get your head around understanding the universe is no easy task. You think you have something and you chase it and chase it, but before you know it you are back where you started. Clueless. Sometimes things click and everything makes sense, but this then leads to hundreds of other questions and theories. The Universe is always expanding and therefore our knowledge is always trying to catch up.

Stephen Hawking inspired my mother's work in some ways. His

physical body had been affected from the age of 21 by the degenerative motor neuron disease. This didn't stop Stephen's brain working, and with the attachment of a speech device via a simple computer program, he was able to carry on his work including his seminal tome, 'A brief history of time'. My mother had thought then that the brain could still operate effectively at many levels even if the body it was in could not function properly. This was key to her future research.

Five years of academic research and a PhD in Astrophysics later and my certificate from Harvard sat proudly on the Linsky family wall. I loved Astrophysics; it's the branch of space science that applies the laws of physics and chemistry to explain the birth, life and death of stars, planets and galaxies. The topics were fascinating, I was in overdrive, absorbing the universe's secrets and cataloguing them inside my brain. My brain was like a filing cabinet, each drawer labelled. I could open any drawer I wanted at any moment and browse through what I had stored there.

I then followed in my father's footsteps and went on to study at the Massachusetts Institute of Technology. For another 5 years I studied for my second PhD in Physics; Einstein had truly inspired me.

His work on Theoretical Physics and his mass-energy equivalence formula: $E = mc2$, probably the most famous equation in the world, had me spellbound. In his lifetime, Einstein published more than 300 scientific papers and a further 150 non-scientific works. I wished to emulate this.

At MIT, my thirst for learning again engaged me to such an extent that I was considered a campus nerd. Being addicted to knowledge comes at a price as it often comes alongside isolation and introversion. I would rarely socialize with my fellow students and professors, choosing to be alone with my scientific studies and figuring out how the known universe worked. It was not that I didn't like human interaction. It was just that the unknown interested me so much more. I wanted to know what no one knew. I wanted that like nothing before.

And then it came...

# Chapter Three

A brief Snapchat message (a now out-dated app that shows a brief video of someone's life) from Gus on Thursday 21st October 2027 led me to exchange a series of emails between my father, Richard and Gus.

Richard was nearing retirement age now and was very interested in selling off part of his Pisa Range family farmland that we had used for our snow kiting adventures. The weather for snow kiting in the region had become much more unpredictable in the last 10 years due to planet's constantly changing weather patterns and now the snow just didn't come regularly enough any more.

Years of selfish human behaviour around the world was having a devastating effect on the world's climate and global warming was now taking a firm hold. Crops failed and the water supply in many food-producing areas had almost dried up. Those who did survive the harsh weather were then attacked by swarms of locusts and other pests. The world's food was starting to run out.

Violent storms of Biblical proportions had the heads of the various religions from around the world reading up on their own religious versions of the Rapture and the impending final judgment - the proverbial 'end of days'. Sea levels had risen 24 inches in the last 10 years alone, the world was starting to creak and leak at the seams. It seemed to me it was getting ready to burst.

Every major coastal city around the world had been majorly affected; the scientists who had predicted these calamities a generation earlier were proven to be right, and sadly most of them were still alive to see the devastation and ensuing disasters for themselves. No one really could have predicted the speed at which events unfolded. Even the extensive computer modelling that was available at the time hadn't foreseen the global catastrophe.

The politicians who were in the pockets of the various petroleum giants were vilified and brought to account. Eventually the oil and gas industry paid for their ways with billions of dollars worth of fines. Public and senate enquiries were instigated around the world and the captains of the petroleum industries who had made their vast fortunes were subject to criminal proceedings and lawsuits, and made to pay for their greed and mistakes.

Of course, it was not the end for Mother Earth, just another global change that had been happening naturally for millennia - only this time it was different. For the first time the world's climate and the glacial melt was being dictated by man's interaction with the planet and this in no way could be put down to natural causes.

The proof was there for all to see. The sea level rises had caused massive flooding around the world and supersized storms that destroyed everything in their paths. The large tides with their tsunami-sized waves and tidal surges that accompanied these events rendered most countries' flood defences obsolete. The waters overran the various barriers that had been installed to protect people and their property. All around the world it was the same; massive destruction of infrastructure and loss of life. This caused mass panic among the frightened population.

The USA had its first warning of the impending doom and citywide destruction as far back as 2005 when Hurricane Katrina ripped the heart out of New Orleans. More than 1000 people lost their lives to the massive storm. Nearly half of the deaths were people aged over 74 who simply could not escape the flood. Various levees had collapsed under the immense storm surge as Katrina took a terrible toll on the city; the lower 9th Ward neighbourhood of New Orleans was almost completely immersed. At nearby Rigolets Pass, just 30 miles from New Orleans, the storm surge was estimated to be 16 feet. Nobody ever imagined that this was to be the calm before the proverbial storm.

When a city's storm or flood defences failed, the devastation to the local population and infrastructure was staggering. The region's economies became decimated and were propped up with funding from national government. The smaller, poorer countries around the world had to depend on foreign aid that was now ever decreasing due to the other major world economies all suffering the same fate.

Isolated, initially as it was at the time, the Katrina Hurricane of 2005 had many lasting effects on the local economy. In 2015 my father and I had visited the New Orleans lower 9th ward while on a business trip. Marcus took me along for the ride. Ten years after Hurricane Katrina, the devastation was still there for all to see. Enterprising local taxi drivers were still cashing in on the storm, giving guided tours of the district, showing the desolate, abandoned homes that remained. I remember asking the taxi driver why the area had not been rebuilt. His answer was emphatic; the district's previous residents, mostly poor black occupants did not have much insurance, if any. They couldn't even afford to demolish the old damaged buildings and start again. They still stood there, as a ghostly, grisly reminder that Mother Earth will have her say and that her scars don't heal quickly.

This wasn't Earth's only warning. The world was also being shaken to its core, quite literally.

Japan's Fukushima nuclear disaster, in March 2011, again highlighted to the world what Mother Earth could unleash. The massive magnitude 9, undersea Earthquake was centred 43 miles east of the Oshika Peninsula, with its epicentre at a depth of 17 miles. It was the largest ever Earthquake to hit Japan and the fourth largest on record since records were first kept in the 1900's. The resultant Tsunami wave was measured at over 130 feet in places and pushed the floodwaters 6 miles inland from the coast.

The world was told by the Japanese authorities that 19,000 people lost their lives. The TV pictures screened live as a horrified world witnessed the total and utter devastation that the Tsunami had caused. The sudden movement of the Pacific tectonic plate, under the North American plate, had generated the massive quake. This movement triggered Tsunami warnings across the whole of the Pacific region and the Earthquake's massive energy reached as far as Antarctica, breaking icebergs off the Sulzberger Ice Shelf. The damage was also felt high into the Earth's atmosphere, altering the local pull of the planet's gravity field. Tsunami debris continued to wash up on North American beaches three years after the event. The localized destruction in north-eastern Japan was enormous. The Japanese authorities estimated the cost of the quake to be around $300 billion, about 6% of Japan's total economic output for the year.

The cost to the world's major economic powers was just about manageable if they had only one event of this kind to deal with at a time. Yet with the onset of the glacial meltdown around the whole globe, the country's leaders could not afford to pay for manpower and materials to stem the ever-increasing flow of water upon the coastal regions. Humans and Mother Earth were making this planet almost uninhabitable, and the leaders of the world knew something had to change. We could no longer protect ourselves from ourselves or from nature. Other measures would soon be very necessary.

* * *

With the storm clouds gathering over the Pisa Range, my father and I struck a deal with Richard McLeod and purchased his land.

The sale was completed with the aid of my parents' vast fortune, and I set about furiously putting together a plan to build a state of the art ground-based telescope to look into the deepest darkest regions of the universe and beyond. The location was ideal for the telescope, the clear unpolluted night skies of Central Otago a perfect location for the project.

The backroom boys at the CIA also helped with some of the funding and clearing away of any local political and consent issues - and did it as softly as they could on my father's insistence. My father had given them the heads up about the project and he had also sanctioned a massive grant from Android AI to help with the enormous build cost. The least he expected in return was a modicum of decency from the CIA.

NASA was also in the loop. Even the New Zealand government came to the party, eager to be seen to be helping on this project of global scientific importance. The telescope was to be furnished with the very latest ground-based tele-space technology and would become the most powerful ever built.

*The granddaddy of space-based telescopes was Hubble. It was first launched into a low Earth orbit in 1990, costing $2.5 billion. NASA had told an eagerly awaiting scientific world that we would now be able to unlock and learn the secrets of the universe. But there was initially a problem; the Hubble primary mirror was ground into the wrong shape, creating blurry images. A space shuttle visit from NASA in December 1993 rectified the faulty lens and for the first time the world had images of the cosmos that were truly breathtaking. Hubble beamed hundreds of thousands of images back to mission control on Earth, giving cosmic snapshots that Galileo could only have ever dreamed about.*

I had learned over the years that space telescopes 'work' in many different ways - they can see visible light, like Hubble, or gamma rays, X-rays, ultraviolet, microwave, radio and infrared. Pre-Hubble launch in the late 1980's, the standard thinking among the astronomical fraternity was to put Hubble into a low Earth orbit, so the cosmos could be viewed from space without encountering the Earth-based light pollution and atmospheric turbulence.

With new data derived initially from Hubble and then from the James Webb Space Telescope (JWST) launched in 2018, astronomers around the world began to look at new ways of setting up ground-based space telescopes to overcome the traditional problems faced by the Earthbound devices.

So, on the 23rd October 2028, just over a year after buying the land, work began on the Linsky Observatory, the world's largest and revolutionary new ground-based, deep space telescope. The objective: To explore the depths of outer space, to search and expand our knowledge.

Little did we know, it would lead us to a startling discovery.

# Chapter Four

Android AI was Marcus's baby but it was actually Flo and her research that allowed it to flourish and expand. It was Flo who had worked out that you could isolate the genetic code of human DNA that specifically makes up the human brain. It was Flo, with all good intentions, who began to grow miniature human brains on lab rats successfully. It was Flo, with all her love and care, who would change the game of AI. And it was Flo who would bring AI fully into this world.

Five years of ground breaking research and development, and the security of a number of worldwide patents would define Android AI in the years to come. The various patents would ultimately set them apart from the other major AI and tech giants. With my father's money and a further $5 billion dollars of privately funded capital drawn from legitimate financial sources (but funnelled through the CIA) the business quickly developed into a frenetic breeding ground for innovation and excellence.

With a business mantra of "Dream the dream: then program it." Android AI recruited the best young students straight out of the most prestigious Colleges and Universities from around the globe. Every top graduate was intercepted by an Android AI staff member and offered a deal they simply could not refuse. Every top employee from a rival was quickly snatched up and put to work within Android AI. No company could match the salary and conditions that Android AI offered; no one could match the ambition and desire that flowed through the veins of Android AI.

The U.S. intelligence services did their bit too. They infiltrated all the major learning centres around the world teaching AI and Robotics, then passed on the acquired intelligence to the Android AI human resources department, who did the rest. The CIA from the start knew the potential of AI; they knew the power that AI held. This was a race, and it was not dissimilar to the space race. The first to create and control AI would control virtually everything.

The CIA worked relentlessly to make sure that all AI patents ended up in U.S. hands. The U.S. intelligence agencies went to incredible lengths to identify new technological breakthroughs, spying on unsuspecting tech firms, using everything available in their armoury of covert spy technology. Companies that made advances were never able to market their findings because the CIA would quite literally steal the ideas from under their noses. Any patents they couldn't steal, Android AI legitimately purchased, outbidding any competitor.

Over the next ten years, Android AI grew into the world's number one AI and robotics manufacturer. Within five years, Android AI was producing robots that could carry out everyday tasks for the population. They started with personal robots that could help at home, robots that could assist the elderly or disabled. Soon, robots were being used in a variety of job markets, but only as add-ons. No human jobs were being completely taken over - yet.

Android AI could produce the best robots for a price that no one else could compete with. They had created a monopoly and they were now reaping the benefits. An Android AI robot, which they called 'Andi', was the newest commodity, the latest trend. Within a few years most homes had a variety of Andis. The cost of production was relatively minor so the sale costs were also kept low in order to allow for a wider target audience. Andis were soon a daily sight in homes and on the street. They were part of day-to-day life now. The robotic pet range was particularly popular - pets that never made a mess, didn't have to be walked and best of all, never died.

As with all business ventures anywhere around the globe, money really does talk. Marcus's next move was to take on the rest of the tech world. With annual profits now in excess of $100 billion, there was no one big enough left to resist the various takeovers. Successive U.S. government administrations turned a blind eye due to massive pro-government lobbying in the Senate and on Capitol Hill. It didn't hurt that Android AI had created more than a million jobs in the U.S. alone. Android AI became the true market leaders. On top of that, Android AI managed to remain popular with the masses. A mixture of clever advertising, selfless donations, job opportunities and affordability made Android AI and their best seller the Andi, a 'must-have' accessory.

*  *  *

It wasn't long - early 2027 to be exact - before Android AI had developed the world's first combat robot. The U.S. military had kept it a secret, another 'Black Project' in conjunction with Android AI, developed at their top-secret research facility in California. A combat robot was the CIA's primary objective, even from the beginning. Creating pet robots was merely a distraction, just a ploy to avert people's gaze from their true goal. An indestructible army capable of anything was always their end game.

The combat Andis didn't have fully functional AI capabilities straight away, but they saved countless lives. The U.S. infantrymen loved the Andis. The U.S. military readily deployed them in real combat situations, to devastating effect.

*There had been many different tactical types of robots used by the U.S. forces over the years, but it was the Russians in the Second World War who first used 'Teletanks' in a combat role. They were wireless remotely controlled unmanned tanks and they saw their first combat when used by the Red Army against the hoards of advancing German Panzers. The 'Teletank' was controlled by radio, from a control tank at a distance of up to 1000 yards. The Teletanks were equipped with machine guns, flamethrowers and could even be fitted with 700kg bombs, thus making them a devastating weapon of war, as the unsuspecting Germans soon found out.*

The combat Andis were in a different class to anything else the world had ever seen. Their advanced computer capabilities and double memory microchips meant they were super-efficient at defeating the enemy. Andis were jammed full of target recognition software, infrared capability, and fusion-powered energy cells that Android AI had invented and patented. This gave the Andis a unique 24 hour round-the-clock offensive capability that most traditional military commanders could only dream of possessing.

Ground level command units could now control and follow the mission from uploaded data sent via an encrypted communication system, unique to every Andi and sent via satellite uplinks. A new breed of warrior for the battlefield was created. The total soldier was born. Parents across America no longer feared the dreaded 'knock on the door' from a military messenger, who only ever had bad news about sons and daughters. No more flags draped over caskets. The Andis purpose was to put the stars and stripes covered coffins into the past. It was a nice dream.

The Andis were met with surprising kindness by the public. Android AI had fretted over how to implement Andis into society without uproar. Perhaps it was the ever-deepening level of doom the human race was suffering that made the vast majority of people warm to the Andis. They were reliable. They were consistent. They were what the human race needed at the time.

Stability.

# Chapter five

The 18th of January 2028. I lost the most important thing in the world to me. Flo was gone.

My mother was my everything, my sun and rain, my inspiration and motivation, my hope and happiness. Aged 68 she was too young to die. Advances in medical technology had increased a woman's life expectancy to 88 years. Despite the giant advances in medicine, cancer was still winning.

Florence Greenwood, born on the 1st of April 1960 was another victim, the breast cancer that struck her being particularly virulent. Flo battled on like the determined warrior she was, but in the end she knew her time had come. She resisted no more and finally let it consume her. She was ready, she said.

Born on April Fool's day, Flo had always seen the lighter side of life, was always smiling and laughing with an innate sense of fun and happiness. Being mischievous was in her DNA. We were all laughing and crying as we said goodbye, until the end she was the epitome of joy and hope.

But there was to be no laughing on the day of her funeral.

Tears rolled down my father's cheeks. He did not sob or make a noise but merely shed a storm of tears. They flowed as if he was unaware of their presence. He would not wipe them aside or accept a tissue. The gentle drip- drop was the only noise that showed Marcus's grief. It was more powerful than the greatest of screams. Four Andis, my father and I lifted Flo's funeral casket out of the black funeral limousine, tears mixed with the gentle rain as we walked to the newly dug gravesite.

A few weeks before her death, Flo had discreetly given my father a note. In between the shots of morphine that was slowly poisoning her now frail body, she still had some lucid coherent moments. Flo had known her race was nearly run, the note she tenderly placed into Marcus's hand, instructed him, after her death, to review her notes on her DNA 'grey matter' work.

Flo had devoted her life to science and it was in her lab notes that my father would find the answers he had been looking for.

My father took Flo's death badly; they had been together for what had seemed like forever, he missed her more than words could possibly say. He missed her more than he could ever say. She was his inspiration; his stimulus and the reason he got up and drew his first breath every morning. Now she was gone, and the tears simply kept flowing.

Death is a cruel creature but it sometimes exposes things untouched before. For the weeks following Flo's death, Marcus and I became closer than ever. We spoke together at length, almost as old friends instead of father and son. We had both suffered the same devastating fate and that common loss had brought us together. Like when I was younger I would catch Marcus staring at me strangely, his head tilted, his mind spinning. Sometimes his eyes would water and no words needed to be said. We both knew the love we felt for each other. Words were unnecessary. Flo, in her death, had brought us closer together.

After a month of unbridled sorrow I noticed my father seemed to get a new lease on life. He was now 72, but his thirst for working had returned. He immersed himself back into the Android AI, R&D facility and armed himself with Flo's old lab notes. He worked tirelessly repeating the same experiments over and over again, without any initial success at all.

It reminded me of Thomas Edison, whose team of developers in the 1870's had tested more than 6,000 possible materials to use as a filament for the Electric Light bulb, before finding one that would fit the bill: carbonized bamboo.

Marcus was to spend the next year working away in the top secret Android AI lab, carefully reading Flo's notes on integrating specific strands of DNA code that make up the human brain. He put special focus into Flo's prior efforts to figure out how to splice and grow the sophisticated neural pathways of the brain. Flo had deduced that by re-coding the brain's DNA, you could enlarge its capacity. This would allow the brain to store much larger amounts of intelligent information but within a much smaller space.

Marcus had many complex ethical problems to overcome, mainly that the world had banned research into human brain cloning and DNA splicing. The so-called 'Conscience Brigade' had lobbied the Senate to pass a bill banning experimental brain cloning. The Conscience Brigade considered it inhumane and not spiritually correct to grow and control the human brain. With the aid of the newly restructured United Nations, the 'Conscience law' was passed in 2028, banning further research and development in the field. But as Marcus subsequently found out, Flo had already done her homework one year earlier.

Flo had understood that there is a massive amount of 'Junk' DNA that makes up the body and this is also the same for the brain. Many years earlier, the Human Genome Project had discovered that only 8.2% of Human DNA or the DNA letters, are actually of any real functional use in the human body. The rest is junk.

It was also known then that actual brain size has nothing to do with an individual's intelligence. What had become apparent to Flo in 2025 is that the abundance of grey matter in certain areas of the brain relates to IQ. It was not the total size of the brain, but the density that was important. Flo isolated the genetic code from within the brain and then she spliced the relevant DNA code to the grey matter in the hope that the grey matter would divide and multiply. She was aiming to artificially enhance intelligence.

Her results were sensational right from the start, but the whole project was a vast undertaking. To refine the process had taken her almost three years. She began with lab rats, and then she progressed onto pigs. Flo had chosen pigs because of their remarkable intelligence, considered by many to be more intelligent than dogs. With the correct environmental conditions within the lab, Flo set to work in complete secrecy and was able to grow the super-small brains on the side of the test subject's heads. The various test subjects looked grotesque, real life Frankenstein creations. Pigs wandered the lab with half their heads covered with a pulsating, highly charged human brain. Flo, however, could see past this and never wavered from her work. In her view, the animals never suffered and the stakes of her research were too high for petty worries.

Even though the test animals did not suffer from the DNA brain splicing procedure, Flo was acutely aware that animal rights activists would have a field day if any pictures or details of her experiments were ever exposed to the world's media. It was not until she had fallen ill with cancer that she put her work on the various test subjects on hold. The animals were kept in the Android AI test laboratory, under close guard.

Marcus worked tirelessly with Flo's original hand-picked team for another year to complete Flo's theory on how to clone and splice the brain's DNA, without damaging the brains super strength grey matter capabilities. When my father called me, he was giddy with excitement. He said, "Son, we did it".

Marcus had recently been using monkeys as the test subjects and he had been able to clone the monkeys' grey matter DNA and eliminate the junk DNA. He then spliced the two brains together to create one super brain with zero junk DNA. Two brains in one, zero wasted space. The mathematics was simple.

Bonobos are found only in the Democratic Republic of Congo and possessing 99% of our own DNA, were the chosen ape breed for the experiments. They were the nearest things on Earth to humans. We had both separated from our common ancestor in Africa, about 5 million years ago.

The results were unbelievable. Bonobos, now with Einstein like intelligence levels, were able to complete complex mathematical puzzles in astonishingly fast times. They were solving algebraic equations with ease and exploring ideas even humans hadn't thought to explore. Soon they started communicating with my father and his team of researchers; firstly with simple gestures but quickly they were using their vocal cords and generating a brand new language.

These Einstein intelligence level Bonobos were numerical geniuses, but the question of whether they could use this practically was still unanswered. Marcus gave them tools to carry out various manual tasks. Their ability to use these was equally astounding. After being shown the plan of their new enclosure, the Bonobos were given the various materials needed to complete the project and over a three-week period they assembled and built their new home. It was a remarkable, astonishing achievement.

Marcus showed me the video footage of the Bonobos assembling their new home; evolution was taking place before my very eyes. Millions of years of trial and error, adaptation, learning and subsequent evolution was happening at light-speed. I wondered what my hero Charles Darwin would have said if he could have witnessed the incredible time-lapse video sequences I had just seen. Would he have been thrilled or frightened?

Marcus's brilliant mind was now in overdrive. Flo had given him the note specifically; she knew the power that this research could have in his hands. She knew his obsession with AI and she knew how it could revolutionise the world, even further. If only there could be some way of combining these new super brains and then linking them to the Andis. If this could be achieved the need for human control and programming over the Andis would be by-passed. The Andis could be self-controlled.

The traditional thinking behind Artificial Intelligence was to create a machine that was autonomous of its human handlers, so it could think and act for itself, based on the information it was receiving externally and processing through its own internal circuitry. Marcus's team at Android AI had been trying for years to break through this barrier, but with only partial success. Flo's research had opened up doors that were thought sealed shut. Marcus began trying to splice together the new genetically modified super brains with the Andis internal circuits.

He knew the benefits of this type of breakthrough would be a colossal leap forward. The world was in need of help that humans couldn't provide. The world was in such a mess it was beyond saving by humans alone. Free thinking machines that could be both autonomous and programmed to help and serve the human race could be the answer.

Many major cities with millions of inhabitants were now increasingly being affected by the ominous rise in the world's sea levels. The worldwide plan was to relocate these cities along with their inhabitants and industries to more secure locations. This was not attainable with human hands alone, we needed flesh and bone but also metal and lightweight strong alloys.

The original Andi Mk1 had started to move whole cities inland, using machinery driven by, and maintained by, the Andis. They worked tirelessly for their human programmers with amazing results. With their ultra-strong Titanium alloy frames, the Andis were able to lift 10 times the weight of most humans. All those years of developing the Andi Mk1 proved to be invaluable. The Mk1 was a thoroughly reliable, hardworking, never sick, 24-hour a day employee that never argued or moaned.

Marcus now worked harder than ever before. He gathered around him an elite team of neurosurgeons who would help him and his Android AI technicians splice the two components of the 'super brain' and the Andi together, to make one fully functional android machine, or as the sci-fi fraternity like to call them, Cyborgs.

Work to build the 'connectome' - a comprehensive map of the brain's circuits - had advanced geometrically over the last decade. But the brain consists of billions of cells and each cell contacts thousands of other cells. The challenge was to connect these cells to the electronic circuits of the Andis, allowing the Andis to literally think for themselves.

In 2012 Bio-engineers at Harvard University had created the first examples of cyborg tissue: neurons, heart cells, muscle, and blood vessels that were interwoven with nano-wires and transistors.

These cyborg tissues were half living cells and half electronic. The electronic side acted as a sensor network, allowing the computer to interface directly with the cells.

Some of those original pioneers from Harvard were now on the Android AI payroll. With huge amounts of funding, the top secret classified 'Cyborg' R&D team made breakthrough after breakthrough.

They painstakingly patented their ground breaking findings each step of the way. Another defining moment came to Marcus with the development of the artificial non-biological nanorobots. These new nanorobots were the missing link and they were able to join the super brains to the Andis using the newly patented technology.

Marcus and his team had created a new breed of robot, the Andi Mk2. With their super-intelligence capabilities, the speed at which the city relocation work could be carried out would be increased fourfold. For the first time in a century the human race was working more quickly than Mother Nature – in some ways reversing the course of history.

The task ahead was still enormous, but now the spreadsheets and the computer modelling showed it was achievable.

# Chapter six

O nly a few times in the evolution of mankind can you actually point to a particular momentous event for our species. The 20th of November 2031 was one of those points in time. The different fields of medical, mechanical and electrical science came together to create this one discovery, this one moment in time when a robot would be given full artificial intelligence. Not artificial intelligence, as Turing had surmised back in 1950, but a mixture of 21st century technology and human brain tissue, united in one mechanical device that Marcus knew would change the world.

Marcus had deduced that with Andis possessing so much power, each with its own unique thought processes combined with the brain power of Einstein and Hawking, these new Andi Mk2s could save the planet from hunger and mass extinction.

The 3D printing of skin tissue had been turned into billions of dollars of revenue for Android AI. Initially used to replace organs, cartilage and skin for research and medical procedures, the 3D printing industry had boomed in recent years. Andis had their own skin designed to make them look more human. They were available in many different shades and pigments to blend in with the local population. But the way they moved, the feel of their skin texture and the big Android AI logo's meant you could always tell the Andis apart.

Not unexpectedly, there was uproar at the United Nations; various members of the UN accused Android AI of breaching the protocols of the Conscience Law of 2028 by what some thought was the cloning of the human brain. Marcus and his team were prepared for this. The UN-based law, which was now enshrined into U.S. law, was completely untested. With his Android AI team of corporate lawyers behind him, Marcus challenged every single legal point that was thrown at them.

Even the U.S. legal system, the most litigious on Earth, was no match for the Android AI lawyers. The UN, even after its reshuffle in 2025, was still the lumbering giant it always was, with no real effective powers. Unless all the members of the Security Council agreed (a fool's proposition) nothing would ever happen, nothing would ever get done. Marcus, the U.S. government and the intelligence services were banking on this.

Marcus also pinned his hopes on the fact that the world's major coastal cities rebuild project was still in full flow. Whole coastal cities were now being moved inland, far from the advancing sea. The astute decision by Marcus and the U.S. intelligence handlers to locate Android AI HQ to its elevated location next to the Henry W. Coe State park in Northern California had been a master stroke.

If Android AI could supply the Andi Mk2, which worked at four times the speed of the Mk1, the cost to the relevant governments would be reduced by 75% and the work completed four times faster. It was a no-brainer really. As the legal cases started to falter and governments around the world chose to ignore the UN Conscience law, it became clear it really didn't make economic or political sense to fight Android AI. The voices of the people were being heard all around the world; "Hands off our Andis" was the chant being yelled, and every major television and media network from around the world replayed the message again and again. Of course, the information and video footage was conveniently sponsored and supplied by Android AI and the U.S. intelligence community.

The release of the world's first fully functional Andi Mk2 seemed to occur just in the nick of time. The project originally named "HAIL" or Human Artificial Intelligence Locum, by the Cyborg R&D team at Android AI, was an instant worldwide hit. Released to a world full of doubters, sceptics and a slowly dying Mother Earth, the Andi Mk2s were hailed in some places as the saviour of the human race.

# Chapter seven

Soon after launching the Andi Mk2, work was completed on the Linsky Observatory. On the 15th of January 2032, the final touches were completed. The world's press and academia were invited; Marcus had made the journey from California and brought with him two of his Andi Mk2s. Even the Head of NASA showed up. This was to be a truly historic event with a picture perfect backdrop of the Pisa Range.

However, it was to be a somewhat subdued affair for both my father and I, as Flo's death still cast a shadow across our hearts.

The Central Otago weather was perfect; with a royal azure blue tint and cloudless sky, Mother Nature was doing her best to impress our international guest list. The observatory had taken over two years of time-intensive work to complete even with help from multiple Andis. The first major task was the access road, which alone had taken a full year to complete. The road snaked endlessly skywards and the driving conditions had made it no easy task to complete. Snow and ice during winter was particularly treacherous as many of the old road's hairpin turns lacked safety barriers! This led to many a tourist's car literally careering down the side of the mountain on a one-way journey.

Most of the large construction work was completed with the help of two MI 26 heavy lift helicopters, flying directly out of nearby Queenstown Airport. The MI 26 was the second largest helicopter ever built, carrying a load of 20 metric tons. The massive eight-blade main rotor made the helicopter versatile, and thus ideal for the Observatory's heavy lifting requirements. MI 26s were once used to transport the 23,000-year-old block of ice containing the Siberian Woolly Mammoth from the Siberian tundra to a lab in Khatanga in the Taymyr district of Russia - scientists there had made various attempts to clone the Mammoth since 2013. The process had always been unsuccessful to date and I often wondered if Flo could have helped.

The MI 26 was a Russian design and truly was a sight to behold. Its giant stature and monstrous noise made these machines look otherworldly, quite fitting for what was about to come.

The observatory itself was like a work of art. It was made up of one huge dome shaped building, housing the largest land telescope ever built and was over 50 meters in length. Complete with the very latest adaptive optics to limit atmospheric distortion, it was my theory that this new technology would give much sharper images. The reflector style telescope was chosen because all celestial objects are so far away from us that the light rays emitted from them reach the Earth as parallel rays. The potential of this project was nothing short of an entirely new view of the universe.

When I first peered through the eyepiece, what I saw confirmed everything I knew in theory. It was a giant leap forward. The scientific community was stunned by the image clarity; in most cases images were 10 times clearer than those on offer from the Hubble space telescope.

The observatory outbuildings were made to endure the cold. At night in winter, the temperature can get down to -15 degrees Celsius atop the Pisa Range. No expense was spared on creature comforts for the crew accommodation block. Every room had the latest clear flat screen TVs with state of the art computers linked to the Wi-Fi hub. Communications with family and friends were a breeze. Over time I had found that when working in remote places and testing conditions, morale of the staff is a major factor with regards to their performance.

'Give the team the best and they will do the rest' was my motto and my team loved it.

A snow cat and skidoo were also on site; I had ordered them as a safety measure, just in case a cold Antarctic southerly storm descended upon us. I had also used them on the odd occasion when Gus would visit and the conditions were favorable for some snow kiting. The staff just used to speed around on them in the winter months and have hours of fun; it was a welcome relief from the sometimes-monotonous task of gazing at the stars. With 15 permanent staff, I started into my busy work schedule on Wednesday the 5th of February 2032. It was here atop the Pisa Range that my life would change forever.

* * *

At 33, Gus retired from international Rugby a distinguished All Black with 101 caps to his name. The Rugby World Cup was now safely back in New Zealand hands. The All Blacks team had defeated Australia 48–12 in the October 2031 final. An exceptional display of courage, hard hitting forward play and untouchable backs had been the winning formula. As with all great teams, they need a great leader and Gus knew it was now time for the next generation to take over, just as his boyhood hero Richie McCaw had done before him after successive World Cup titles. He walked away from the game when, some would say, he was still at his peak, but Gus knew it was time to start the next chapter of his life. His girlfriend Gina was expecting their first child.

They had first met at an All Blacks photo shoot a few years ago when Gina was a model. Unlike many other women, Gina was not blown over by Gus's handsome face and dense muscular body. She refused to be wooed by him at first but she soon saw Gus for what he was; a gentle giant. A bear who liked to be tickled.

A retirement and new baby party was on the cards and Gus and Gina promised it would be the party of all parties. Richard and Amanda were the perfect hosts for what turned out to be a memorable celebration. They had spared no cost. A giant marquee was erected on the large front garden in the balmy December summer. There was a gentle warm breeze from the Northwest and everyone packed the outside venue in search of their favourite cocktail and good cheer.

Gus had invited many of his friends from around the sporting world. My father attended, feeling sad that Flo wasn't there by his side, but he had made the effort because Richard had personally called and invited him. Richard had suggested to Marcus that the taste of his whisky collection might bring a few happy memories of Flo back to him. Marcus needed no help remembering all the good times he shared with Flo but the idea of a good whisky was enough for him.

At one stage of my life, parties were a nightmare. I was the shy, nerdy type and big groups and boisterous behaviour was way out of my comfort zone. Gus would always try to get me involved but I often found myself alone, toiling over some problem or pondering a lost thought. As I had become a little older I started to enjoy the parties. I was still quiet and a bit awkward but I was comfortable with this, it came with over-thinking and over analyzing. My confidence at parties had improved but my confidence with women was still a soft spot.

The last real girlfriend I had was at M.I.T. about four years earlier. We only lasted six months. She cited lack of time and love on my part as a reason for our split. At the time I just didn't get relationships, I had my work and that's what drove me on. I had never met anyone who stimulated my senses as much as the universe did. I had never met anyone who could excite me like a glint of a distant star, but I had hope that one day I would.

Security was very tight. My father's security team was always on the lookout for potential kidnapping threats. His handpicked, four-man operations team was made up of various elite Special Forces units from around the world.

Andrew Edwards, the ex-SAS officer who controlled my father's personal security detail, was a very engaging and witty guy. Welsh by birth, he had lost most of his distinct accent that was derived from his hometown of Port Talbot in South Wales. His family surname Edwards, meaning 'son of Edward' had been handed down by generations of proud Welsh military fighting men within his family. His great, great, great grandfather had served and won a Victoria Cross at Rorke's Drift in 1879, fighting the Zulu Army. His was one of eleven VC's won during the two-day battle. He was as sharp as a tack and never missed a thing; my father's nickname for him was 'Sherlock' after the fictional character created by Sir Arthur Conan Doyle.

Blessed with 20/20 vision, Edwards was a marksman with just about every weapon on the planet. His unarmed combat skills would leave most Hollywood film sets wanting, Edwards was a walking weapon.

My father's second-in-command was Tyler-Joe Bowman, or 'Flash' to the team. A 42 year-old ex-Navy Seal team commander and a veteran of just about every major conflict from around the globe in the last 20 years. His nickname 'Flash' came from his mop of blond hair and his remarkably similar looks to the film character 'Flash Gordon' from the 1980 cult movie. A bull of a man, superbly trained and armed with an iron fist, his party piece was to punch holes in walls. Close combat with the enemy was his favourite; a fist fight never lasted long with Flash.

The third member of the team was, Li Chang a Chinese communications expert. He could get you satellite uplinks and secure transmissions of data from just about anywhere on the planet. Li was recruited direct out of the People's Liberation Army or PLA. The PLA was the Chinese Army's 14,000 strong Special Operations Force. It was little known in the West and very secretive. They could be deployed at a moment's notice to anywhere in the world where they were needed on counter-terrorism, intelligence gathering and commando roles.

Like the rest of the team Li was multi-lingual, his native Mandarin, the modern standard Chinese language or 'Putonghua' known as the common language by most Chinese. His English was also exceptional. He would spend days training the other members of the security detail. They were all fluent in Mandarin. To keep in shape mentally, the security team would speak various different languages on a daily basis just to keep them sharp. So when on deployment with Marcus, all the members of the team knew exactly what everyone around them was saying, no matter what language was being spoken.

The last member of the team was Jake, also ex-SAS and the teams' paramedic. Jake had enlisted in the British Army aged 26 after getting his university degree and becoming a front line first responder paramedic. The lessons he learned on the hard streets of London were just a taste of things to come within the SAS. He had seen enough during his duties that he was rarely shocked by anything. He sometimes spoke about his experiences; he had saved one of his fellow team members with a blown off limb after an I.E.D had decimated his platoon whilst on patrol. He had even plugged a hole in the chest of an enemy combatant to stem the flow of blood - the misguided but committed freedom fighter had just taken a round from one of Jake's comrades and it was Jake who had saved his life.

His buddies respected him for that but Jake had a darker side, too. Jake had also trained for 5 years as an MMA fighter before joining the British Army, it was in the gym that necessity called him. Jake had to fix up the opponents he had just battered during training, giving them the first aid treatment they needed after their ultra-violent gladiatorial battles. This caring, nurturing side that came after the extreme violence seemed to come naturally to him. Jake was a lover and a fighter a rare combination.

All the security detail were licensed to carry firearms in any country they visited. They were always discreet around Marcus, but you always knew they were there. My father's PA, Eva completed the team. She worked closely with the 'Fab Four' (as they were affectionately nicknamed) managing the private jets, helicopters and fleet of armoured cars. Eva hailed from Portsmouth, New Hampshire. With a degree in International Business she had become my father's go-to person over the years, especially now after my mother's death. She was exceptionally loyal and she could be trusted with her life.

The party got off to a traditional New Zealand start. Gus wanted to honour his fellow All Black teammates with his very last 'Haka'. The Haka is the native New Zealand Maori war dance or challenge, performed by the All Blacks every time they play a rugby match. The opposing team stands and watches the All Blacks perform this ceremonial dance before the two teams of warriors commence their on-field battle. Gus, as usual, nailed it, performing his version of the Haka for all the guests to rapturous applause.

I went with my father and Gus to the cellar where Richard opened a special-edition bottle of 30-year-old 'Talisker'. Needless to say we all approved and the night got well and truly underway with the Earthy taste of the exquisite single malt. With the lasting flavour still touching my taste buds I strolled out to the lawn to gaze at the cloudless night sky. I enjoyed looking at the stars without the help of the telescope, using my own eyes to assess the endless sky. In these moments I would feel dwarfed and insignificant. Just another grain of sand amongst the millions of sand dunes, that makes up the cosmos.

It was with my head bent upwards to the night sky that a cricket ball would change the direction of my life. It flew viciously past my nose, an inch from bone breakage.

"SORRY!" I heard someone shout.

Across the lawn stood Vicki – a vision, looking resplendent in a beautiful, elegant long white dress and Prada high heels; six-feet tall with long, wavy blonde hair sitting gently on her perfectly rounded shoulders. I barely noticed she was playing backyard cricket. How odd, I thought. Anyway, she had been fielding a ball and had misjudged a throw, almost knocking me out.

"Nice throw," I called with surprising confidence and nonchalance.

"Not really, I missed you," she replied.

"Let me save you from further embarrassment and take you away from all this. A drink?" I couldn't help but laugh at the cheesiness of the line. I began apologizing and we both began to laugh. She then tilted her head gently to one side, not too unlike my father would do, and looked me up and down.

"You must be this mad scientist that Gus has told me about."

"Mad?" I said.

"Vodka, lime cordial and diet lemonade, in a tall glass with ice, please," she said as she ran after another cricket ball.

I immediately took to Vicki. She was original, unusual, beautiful and loved football. Born Vicki Webb in Chesterfield, England, she was 29 years old, and came with drop dead gorgeous looks and a slim athletic body. Faint freckles sprinkled her upper cheeks and surrounded her bright, lustrous shinning eyes. Indeed, her eyes are what got me. They looked into you, into your brain and soul. She would stare at me and after some seconds of silence nod in agreement. Nothing was said but she understood what I meant.

We chatted for hours. It turned out that Vicki had just retired from professional women's football a year ago. Playing all her senior career for Manchester United ladies. She was a founding member of the team in 2020. Controversially, the footballing giant that is Manchester United only started a ladies' team after the old owners sold the club in 2019. One of the first things the new owners did was to embrace the ladies game, so Vicki pledged her allegiance and started her career as a female soccer star.

Soon the England ladies football team came calling and after two World Cups and 28 international goals to her name, a crude tackle caused a career-ending broken leg. She told me she could still hear the 'crack' in her head when the leg actually broke. The surgeon had done a good job of plating and screwing the leg together but the subsequent infection had the final say.

After a whole year of physiotherapy and working with the team doctors, she decided to end her career. Naturally, she was devastated but unbowed. Vicki explained how she then spent the next year finishing her Football Association coaching badges, but she had concluded that there was something missing from the style of coaching she had been taught, something she just couldn't quite put her finger on.

It was only after a chance meeting with the founder of successful, New Zealand-based 3-2-1 Football Academy that her coaching aspirations skyrocketed. Following an in-depth discussion on football tactics, she became a disciple. Vicki knew she had found what had been missing in her coaching life. A lifelong devotee of the beautiful game Vicki was hooked on the 3-2-1 philosophies.

Appointed the official 3-2-1 female ambassador, Vicki started spreading the word to everyone within the English FA. Slowly, very slowly, the powers that be started to change the training regime of the various English teams to incorporate the 3-2-1 approach to the beautiful game. More importantly, they changed the curriculum being taught in both schools and English football academies.

Vicki told me that old-school football coaches have enormous egos and are reluctant to change their old habits. Football coaching was stuck in the past and Vicki was pioneering for change. I listened intently to Vicki talk with such passion about her football, I could see then that she was a very driven woman.

As the night unfolded, I started to share my passion and vision about the stars and far away galaxies. She seemed captivated. She listened like Flo would listen to me, with understanding eyes and a smile at my excitement. I rambled and ranted and hypothesised and Vicki sat there, patiently soaking it all up. We talked all through the night and when the sun started to come up I knew it was time to go home. Vicki had fallen asleep with her head slumped on my shoulder. I couldn't sleep. My mind had been awake for years, but my heart closed. Now, in one night, it had been prised wide open.

My mind and heart were now racing like never before.

# Chapter eight

*"The die has been cast," said Julius Caesar on crossing the River Rubicon to invade Italy on January 10th 49 B.C. The 'die' related to a gambling dice or 'die' and the 'cast' related to the dice being thrown, thus the immortal phrase he uttered and recorded in history on that day, relates to an irrevocable decision being made.*

I made such a decision on 14th June 2032. I had fallen hard for Vicki and since our first meeting at Gus's party we had been virtually inseparable. I had never had this type of feeling before in my life. My mind, body and soul were intertwined together for the first time. Everything felt right and it was because of Vicki. She was the missing piece. Scientists have "Eureka" moments when they make a breakthrough or a discovery. The feeling is indescribable - relief, gratification and jubilation all bundled into one. This is how I felt every moment I spent with Vicki. She was my Eureka moment and I wanted it to last forever.

Vicki had taken time out from her role as the 3-2-1 Football Academy Ambassador to spend more time with me. Because of the nature of her work she travelled a great deal and a sabbatical was needed. When she was away, we communicated every day; the occasional snap chat, the odd Instagram picture, but mostly we SpaceTimed, the follow-on product from Apple's FaceTime. This new feature introduced by Apple enabled users to project a 3D image anywhere, just like a hologram. The HD picture clarity made it almost real.

When we were together it was like a movie. Everything was tinted with a shine. The times we had together were packed with fun and wide smiles and the room was always filled with laughter. We would sing, dance, talk about the world and how we would fix it.

Vicki had everything I wanted from someone and also a bag-load more. She was everything that I didn't know I needed. She was beautiful, smart and witty, but she was so much more, much more than words could ever explain. I wondered why she was still single and why I was so lucky.

So I asked.

She told me she had been driven all her adult life by football, just like I was with my astronomy and that she had never really let any man into her life because of that. Love was a luxury for her and one that she didn't think she deserved, let alone find. Her previous relationships had been shallow and insignificant. No one had scratched below the surface of her character. She wouldn't let them.

Ironically, she looked at me and said:

"Lukas, when are you going to let someone in?"

She had this uncanny ability to turn the situation on its head and make you rethink your position. She would make me look inwards, into my own world instead of always trying to find others amongst the stars.

"I've been waiting for the right person," I said. "I'm used to waiting Vicki. I stare for days into the universe without any change, without anything new. In space, time is different; it's slower. It takes light years to get anywhere. I thought that would be the same with love. I thought I'd be waiting fruitlessly for love. Love was extra-terrestrial life that I hoped to find, but probably never will. Love is an enigma, an anomaly, unsolvable. Until you came along…"

She went silent, her eyes glazed over slightly and she looked at me, paused.

"You're a good man, Lukas." Tears began to well up from her eyes. "But I'm not sure that you're the right man for me."

I looked at her in stunned disbelief. My whole world began to collapse around me and I envisioned myself being sucked into a black hole and floating aimlessly in space forever.

After a long pause she smiled that smile.

"I'm not just sure Lukas, I'm certain. I'm certain you're the one for me, and I'm certain that I love you…"

I looked into her eyes. The tension was electric. Our eyes were transfixed for what seemed like eternity, before I gently bowed my head to hide the tears. They gently slipped quietly to the floor. I raised my head and summoned the courage to look at her again and bring her closer.

"I love you," I whispered, barely audible. "Marry me?" I asked instinctively.

Vicki leant over my shoulder and drew her lips to my ear.

"On one condition... If it's a boy we call him Beckham!"

We both laughed as our fate was sealed.

* * *

We decided to set the wedding date for Saturday, 16th December 2034. For the next two years Vicki busied herself by making plans for the perfect wedding day. Despite her untraditional behaviour she wanted a traditional white wedding. We found a local wedding planner by the name of Eddie Large, but he preferred that we called him 'Eddie born ready'. Eddie really was a larger than life character. He was in his early 50's with a huge mop of swept back grey hair, looking too much like Einstein for his own good. He was a great choice. His charisma and frenetic energy was contagious and his ideas ludicrous, but genius. The Einstein of wedding planners we decided. He liked that name even more.

I continued with my work at the observatory looking for answers to the cosmic questions that were orbiting my own brain. I was still pondering what I was searching for out there and how I would find it. I had taken a Physics PhD at MIT especially so I could understand the laws on the speed of light. Light travels at 186,282 miles per second or 299,792,458 meters per second. It was the Danish astronomer, Olaus Roemer, who in 1676 first successfully measured the speed of light. His method was based on observations of the eclipses of the moons of Jupiter.

It had taken me some time to get my head around these figures, so I put them into a NASA context. I knew the Space Shuttle travelled at a maximum speed of about 17,600 mph (28,300 km/h), so I calculated it would take the Space Shuttle about 165,000 years to reach Alpha

Centauri, the nearest star system to Earth. These distances of space and time are immense and I really needed to think them through, because the ages of most stars are measured in millions if not billions of years.

The world didn't have millions of years left; even with help from the Andis our planet was on borrowed time. It was just hanging on; taking its last breaths of the polluted air we were all now breathing. We were running out of time and my team and I needed to find a solution; which we hoped lay out there in the cosmos.

Three weeks before our wedding I was walking to the observatory from our living accommodation when a bolt of bright orange plasma light appeared overhead in the night sky. At first I thought it was a shooting star; they were very common here. Shooting stars are formed when a meteor shower occurs; the usually small particles are from asteroids or comets that enter the Earth's atmosphere at very high speed. When they collide with the Earth's atmosphere the small particles from the rapidly disintegrating meteors rub against the air particles in the atmosphere. This creates friction that in turn heats up the particles of dust. The resultant heat vaporizes most meteors, creating what we call shooting stars. I had seen many shooting stars, especially in the Southern Lakes region of New Zealand. The nights were so clear and with virtually no light pollution it lent itself to a dazzling cosmic firework display on most cloudless nights.

But this bolt of plasma was different. It was more rounded and glowed a pale orange color. It was traveling more across the horizon, than actually through the night sky, so I stood there for a minute to observe it. It seemed to speed up a little and then slow down and then what really caught my eye was the sudden lightning fast acceleration. The light bolt went vertical at an astonishingly high speed. I was acutely aware of space objects and how they behaved in the night sky and I had never seen anything quite like this. The object then vanished, just as it had appeared, in a flash it was gone.

I arrived at the Observatory and had a quick scan of the surrounding night sky using the 'moonscope' we had installed to observe the surface of the moon. It was much the smaller of the two telescopes at the Observatory, but extremely powerful and was specifically designed for looking at objects in our own solar system. You could actually see the surface of the moon where Apollo 11 had first landed, where Neil Armstrong and Buzz Aldrin had taken the first steps for a grateful mankind on July 20, 1969.

The moonscope was so powerful you could still see the flags left by the various Apollo missions. The stars and stripes on the flags had now vanished, due to the moon's very small amount of rare atmospheric gases; the flags had all been bleached white. I knew the moon has one sixth of the Earth's gravity and the flags the Astronaut's had left behind were swinging instead of waving. This evidence alone went a long way to debunking any conspiracy theories that doubted whether man had actually travelled to the moon.

I studied the moon all night but to no avail; there were no more plasma ball sightings. The following morning I went to everyone's favourite place, Google, to do some more research and was astounded at what I found. During World War II, pilots from the American 415th Night Fighter Squadron had first reported these small round balls of glowing orange lights. These brave aviators not only had the German night fighters and anti-aircraft flak to deal with, they also had strange orange balls of plasma light that sped off at incredible angles and speeds.

The pilots reported these strange phenomena to their senior officers, who initially thought these were a new type of secret weapon being developed by Hitler and his henchmen to rain more terror on an unsuspecting world. A radio operator had named these sightings 'Foo Fighters' and this terminology was to be used by the U.S. military for years to come, to describe what they believed to be a type of Unidentified Flying Object or UFO. The U.S. military in later years quashed these rumors by reporting that they were possibly a type of electrical discharge from airplane wings, or even a natural weather phenomenon. The so-called 'St Elmo's fire' named after St. Erasmus of Formia, the Italian Patron Saint of sailors. This phenomenon sometimes appeared on ships at sea during thunderstorms and was regarded by sailors with religious awe for its glowing ball of light, accounting for its name.

I was a scientist and Foo Fighters to me was the name of the Seattle based rock band founded by Nirvana drummer Dave Grohl, as a one-man project following the death of his fellow band member Kurt Cobain. I personally had never heard of the term outside of the music world.

I continued my research delving into the records of various sightings over the past 200 years. These sightings were mostly aerial in nature, but to my astonishment there were literally thousands of reported encounters. Even Charles Darwin had reported an encounter whilst on board his ship the HMS Beagle in 1832. Recording the event by writing to his friend J. S. Henslow about the incident whilst at anchor in the estuary of the Rio De La Plata.

St. Elmo's fire was reported to have been seen during the siege of Constantinople by the Ottoman Empire in 1453. The light was seen to be emitting from the top of the Hippodrome. The Byzantines attributed it to a sign that the Christian God would soon come and destroy the conquering Muslim army. It disappeared just days before Constantinople fell, ending the Byzantine Empire.

St Elmo's fire was real; it was a form of matter called plasma. I knew from my studies that plasma is also produced by stars and by lightning. The Serbian-American inventor Nikola Tesla created St. Elmo's fire in 1899 whilst testing out his Tesla coil at his laboratory in Colorado Springs. St. Elmo's fire was seen around the coil and was said to have lit up the wings of butterflies with blue halos as they flew around. Tesla mysteriously died in 1943. The official cause of death was coronary thrombosis, taking with him some say, discoveries from out of this world.

I needed to know why the ball of plasma I had witnessed seemed to be under control. It seemed to have purpose and direction of movement. This was not natural. I knew way more than most people about physics to know the difference. I delved deeper and deeper into the subject on my quest for more information on plasma light and Foo Fighters, so much so that some of my colleagues began a whispering campaign about me calling me 'Tesla Mk2', a thinly veiled jape about my father's new Mk2 Andis.

The further I looked, the more intrigued I became. As a scientist I had been trained to look at and consider all possibilities. Do the research, test the results and then reach a conclusion. But researching plasma light balls that seemed to be under mechanical or controlled movement patterns and moving at incredible speeds was not the easiest subject I had ever worked on.

I revisited Einstein's theory on special relativity. He basically said that space and time were interwoven into a single continuum known as space-time. Although instruments can neither see nor measure space-time, several of the phenomena predicted by its warping had latterly been confirmed. I looked at how plasma light could be affected by things like black holes and their gravitational pull. I was digging deeper and deeper but I was missing something. Something big. Yet, soon I would find all the evidence I needed.

# Chapter nine

It was two days before our wedding day and I had decided to spend the night at the observatory with Gus. I had invited Gus up to talk about the wedding rehearsal that was planned for the following night. It was to be my last night's work before our wedding celebrations and then the planned two-week honeymoon in a water bungalow on the idyllic island of Bora Bora, in the middle of the South Pacific.

Bora Bora is not the easiest place in the world to get to. Located in French Polynesia and a 50-minute flight from Tahiti, it surely is one of the most romantic places in the world. The lagoon is shaped like an artist's palette and surrounded by a large barrier reef that holds back the mighty Pacific Ocean; it is truly a sight to behold. The ever-changing and rising sea levels had affected tourism at first, but the canny developers and locals had built the overwater bungalows on stilts, so they could be easily moved inland in conjunction with the ever-changing high water mark.

Around the world other island nations had not fared so well. In 2000 my parents had visited the Maldives for a romantic holiday. Incidentally, this is where I was conceived as a slightly tipsy Marcus once told me one night after quietly sipping his way through a bottle of 25-year-old Highland Park whisky. Located in the middle of the Indian Ocean, with no ground surface higher than 10 feet and with 80% of the total land area lying below 3 feet above sea level; the Maldives was officially the world's flattest country. By 2031 it had been wiped of the face of the Earth. The Maldives and the resort island paradise that my parents had stayed at in the year 2000 had now been literally overtaken by the sea.

The region's delicate coral reefs had been bleached completely white by the rising sea temperatures and the once picturesque islands that had graced so many postcards over the years were now totally underwater, lost forever to the depths of the Indian Ocean. Rarely in anyone's individual lifetime do they witness catastrophic events of this magnitude, because the Earth's timetable usually works in cycles of thousands of years and not in 10-year multiples. Mankind's systematic rape and pollution of the Earth had caused its own unique problems and now we were paying the price.

In the observatory Gus and I were idly chatting about the details of the wedding rehearsal dinner whilst gazing at the night sky. A perfect backdrop for one of my last nights as a single man, I thought. Gus as usual, was more interested in what was on the wedding menu than looking at a distant star system in the far reaches of our own Milky Way. I took two beers from my hidden 'emergency' fridge and cracked them both open. We spoke at ease for a while, totally comfortable in each other's company and I was fully content and looking forward to my impending wedding date.

I had stopped thinking about the mysterious plasma ball I had seen and about space in general for a few moments, I was concentrating hard on enjoying the moment. Here and now. Just as peace seemed to settle around me the excited research assistant Cameron shouted at me from across the observatory.

"Lukas, Lukas….. look!"

I followed his outstretched finger and there it was, a glowing orange plasma ball just like the one I had seen nearly 3 weeks earlier.

Gus and I both ran out the emergency exit door onto the fire escape stairway to get a better view. It was close, very close; maybe only 1,500 yards away, but it could have been 2,000. Depth and distance perception are difficult to judge in the night sky. I had to get closer. We both ran down the fire escape and jumped into one of the observatory's Toyota Land Cruisers.

Land Cruisers have a legendary reputation for off-road ruggedness and performance that stretches back more than six decades, and we had three of them at our disposal. Built to last, they quite literally out-performed everything else in their class.

Gus drove off at high speed following the glowing ball of light in the distance. It just so happened that tonight there was nearly a full moon, and this helped Gus considerably as he raced over and navigated around the rugged mountainous terrain in pursuit of the plasma ball. After nearly a mile in pursuit we lost sight of it. It had simply disappeared. It was just like someone or something had turned off the lights.

Gus stopped and we jumped out of the land cruiser. We scanned the horizon and the nearby terrain but saw nothing. It couldn't be just another shooting star, I was sure. I jumped into the back of the land cruiser and from the survival kit bag I pulled out the latest version of our military grade night vision goggles. All the latest Andis Mk2s were fitted with these combat night vision goggles and they could see in many different light spectrums. I methodically switched through the various settings on the goggles and it was then on the last setting in the infrared spectrum that I saw it. Infrared radiation has a wavelength from about 800 nm to 1 mm and is emitted particularly by heated objects, having a wavelength just greater than that of the red end of the visible light spectrum but less than that of microwaves.

I could see it in front of me, it had landed or fallen and was resting just a few metres away. There was a faint glow coming from the object so I walked towards it. I carefully started to remove my night vision goggles to get a better look but when I took my goggles off, I couldn't see it anymore. I gave the goggles to Gus so he could have a look. Gus remained silent and I knew he was rattled. I turned on the torch from the survival pack and shone it in the direction of the ball and there it was, or rather there it wasn't. It was completely invisible to the naked eye in the normal light spectrum. I was amazed and just for a second I did a bit of a double take. I felt like pinching myself because I didn't believe, or even know, what I was looking at. I slipped the night vision goggles on again and I started to examine it more closely. Gus was very wary. I had never seen him fazed by anything before. This was totally new to the both of us.

It was spherical and about two feet across. It was made of what looked like to me some sort of metal.

Gus picked up a small loose pebble from nearby and gently threw it against the sphere. I expected to hear a metallic clang but the pebble was somehow absorbed into the sphere, to come dropping out the other side a moment later. It was apparent this might be liquid, but it formed a complete spherical ball of what looked like some sort of metallic material that I had never encountered before. The nearest thing my own senses could relate it to was a giant ball of mercury, only this was completely translucent. I got out my iPhone and immediately took some pictures. The new iPhones had been fitted with the latest infrared camera; it was a feature Apple had introduced two years earlier. I took some pictures hoping the camera might pick up the object. I then took some more pictures of the sphere through the night vision goggles. I switched my iPhone to video mode and then sent the images I had captured directly to my father's iPhone and then copied all the images to my own computer at the observatory.

Gus instinctively decided that now would be a good time to throw a handful of snow over the sphere. His thought process was simple, if the sphere was hot, we would see the snow vaporize and then turn to steam. I could see his logic, but it was hardly a scientific approach.

But it worked. Gus threw the snow and the sphere appeared to us in an instant. It had changed color slightly and we could now see it in the moonlight. I correctly deduced at the time that the sphere had reacted to the water. Before I could say anything, Gus threw another rock at the sphere, this time it clanged with a distinct metallic sound; it was now solid.

"If it is solid," I said to Gus, "We can move it".

Gus grunted a barely audible answer and rolled his shoulders, he was strong but even he couldn't hope to lift a two-foot round solid metal sphere without some sort of mechanical assistance. I put the torch on and moved in closer to examine the sphere with my own eyes. To my amazement the torchlight seemed to go into the middle of the sphere, illuminating it from the inside out. It was then that I saw lines of code. There were 0101001010 all across the inside of the sphere; I knew what this was instantly. This was binary computer code - the language of the universe. These are the numbers from which all computer code is derived.

Binary code assigns a bit of string to each symbol or instruction. A binary string of eight binary digits (bits) can represent any of 256 possible values and can therefore correspond to a variety of different symbols, letters or instructions. Gottfried Leibniz had discovered the modern binary number system, the basis for all binary code in 1679. Binary code uses only the characters 1 and 0. He believed that binary numbers were symbolic of the Christian idea of "creatio ex nihilo" or creation out of nothing. What he had actually created was the pathway for understanding modern day computer programming.

I immediately switched on my iPhone camera again and began to video the sphere, automatically downloading and saving the images. I moved in closer with my torch, still illuminating the numbers. At that moment the lines of code started to pass through the wall of the sphere and into the air around us. It looked mystical, magical, almost surreal. I turned to Gus and we shared a bemused look. I was looking at him for strength and assurance and he was looking at me for wisdom and advice. We were actually both at a loss.

After checking again through the infrared goggles, I was confident the sphere was not hot anymore. I pulled on my heavy-duty gloves made from durable, proofed goat leather and finished with a vegetable tanned wax. I made a grab for the sphere; it was so light I couldn't believe it. The sphere had no real weight to it at all, a few minutes ago Gus and I were discussing about getting some sort of lifting gear to move it, now I just picked it up with one hand. I grinned at Gus, and put it into the back of the Land Cruiser. We jumped in and sat for a while stunned. The sphere could have a rational explanation but we both felt uneasy in its presence. Gus sniffed, shrugged and put the radio on.

Gus drove back to the observatory at a much slower pace with our delicate cargo in the back. We stopped outside my office and I quickly covered the sphere in tarpaulin to disguise it from any over-inquisitive eyes. Gus opened the office door and I put the sphere in the storage room at the back of my office and then shut the door. I looked at Gus.

"Call your dad. He knows everything and everyone," he said.

I picked up my phone and called my father. The phone rang twice then I heard his voice, sharp and scented with curiosity.

"Lukas what is this thing? I've just been studying the video and pictures you sent me".

"Remember the plasma light ball I told you about a few weeks ago? Well…this is it".

I went over to the storeroom, opened the door, pulled back the tarpaulin and showed my father the sphere. After a 5-minute rundown of the last hour's events my father finished the call by saying:

"I'm in Auckland airport en-route to Queenstown for your wedding; tell nobody about this. I'll be there at 9am". The line then went dead.

Gus and I sat for a while with our half-drunk beers, hypothesising and debating what we had just found. Every sip of beer brought my heart rate down a notch and soon we were both calmer. I knew I wouldn't be able to sleep so I stayed looking at the stars until dawn. Gus stayed too, knowing I'd feel safer with him by my side.

I awoke in my office chair at 7am. I'd fallen asleep after all. Gus was next to me, face resting on his arms on the desk, snoozing. I shook my head and tried to shake last night into reality but it was having none of it. Did that really happen? Panic rose again in my throat as I realised that I was getting married the next day to the woman I love and that there was an unidentified, unexplainable object in my office.

I jumped into a cold shower just to make sure I wasn't dreaming.

I shuddered when the cold water hit my skin. What was I going to tell Vicki? She needed to know but my father had specifically instructed me to tell no one.

Gus was up when I returned and swiftly told me to tell Vicki.

"Tell her and tell her now buddy, or it will be the shortest marriage in history," he said.

Just at that moment Vicki came bounding into the office and she had heard the tail end of our conversation. She looked at me with the stare, the one that only women seem to have. She didn't say anything. She didn't need to. She just looked at me with this penetrating, piercing stare and waited for me to respond. I cracked immediately and spilled the beans; I was useless at keeping secrets, especially from her. All my senses were telling me I was doing the right thing and I'm glad I did. She was just as intrigued as we were.

"Let's wait until your father arrives and we will all go and see it together," she said with a perfect air of confidence. I nodded in agreement and in that split second I had reconfirmed in my own mind that Vicki was the woman for me.

My father's helicopter landed at 9am, punctual as ever. He arrived, complete with his 'quad-strength' security detail and his loyal secretary, Eva. We got straight down to business. We all jumped into the Land Cruisers and went straight to my office. Father told the security detail and Eva to remain outside, I turned the key and in we went. The storeroom door was shut; I opened it gradually and looked around. The tarpaulin was still there and underneath it was the sphere, exactly where we had left it. My father reached into his pocket and pulled out a hand-held gadget I'd never seen before and started scanning the sphere.

"What's that?" I said. My father mumbled a little and called it his 'spectrometer'.

*In physics, a spectrometer is an apparatus to measure certain spectrums. The word was first used scientifically within the field of optics to describe the rainbow of colours in visible light when separated using a prism. Generally, a spectrum is a graph that shows intensity as a function of wavelength, frequency, energy, momentum, or mass.*

The spectrometer device did all of the above. A patent from Androids AI, this little beauty could even measure levels of radiation. He looked at the readings and there was a distinct radiation level.

He turned and said "All radiation is measurable, son." After a few seconds he squinted his eyes. He had a very puzzled look on his face.

"The radiation environment of deep space is very different from that of the Earth's surface, due to the much larger flux of high-energy galactic cosmic rays, along with radiation from solar proton events," he explained. "This hand-held spectrometer picks this up and gives us a true reading."

He paused, blinked and shook his head dismissively. He scanned the sphere again, this time more slowly and with greater care. We all watched in silence. When finished he checked his spectrometer again and then once more, until he was satisfied. He then focused on the sphere with a quizzical look, head tilted to one side.

"It didn't originate in this world," he whispered to himself. We all took a step closer and leaned in to catch his words.

"It didn't originate in this world," he repeated a little louder.

Although this thought had been predominant in my mind, having it confirmed by the smartest man I knew took my breath away and kept it for a few minutes. I had imagined encountering objects or beings from other worlds for years but now that it was here, I didn't know how to react. I was stupefied, dumbfounded, speechless. Silence hung around us all as we all processed this information in our own ways.

"So, what now?" Gus said. Always the one to help us when in need.

Without a better option we set about analysing the sphere, the pictures and the video on my computer. The binary code that was being emitted seemed to intrigue my father the most, and he took copious notes. He said that he would immediately do some work on the code but for now the details of what had happened here were to remain between the four of us.

I took the sphere to the lab with my father and Gus and locked it into the test chamber for safekeeping. I asked Vicki to look after our wedding guests, who were all arriving at various times during the day. I did not want them worrying about alien artefacts that transmitted binary code at our wedding rehearsal dinner; after all, Vicki and I were getting married.

# Chapter ten

Fumbling with my tie in the mirror with Gus by my side, I couldn't stop my mind wandering and revolving around the sphere. What is it? Will it open doors to unthinkable developments or will it threaten our survival? What am I going to do...?

Gus did his best to calm me, talking to me whilst tying my tie as I gazed at my reflection in the mirror, then walking me down the aisle as I tried to look unfazed. I stood there in front of friends and family, there in body but elsewhere in mind. Then in she came and my mind returned. With every step Vicki took down the aisle the further and further the sphere flew from my head. Her physical presence banished all my wandering thoughts, with her floating walk and her delicate, beautiful one-in-a-million smile now facing me beside the altar.

"I do," is all I remember after that. I watched Vicki's lips as she uttered those words and locked that moment away in my mind forever – what used to be called a 'Kodak moment', referring to George Eastman's Eastman-Kodak Company that ushered in the era of modern film photography in the late 19th century. I've always had a way of etching special memories into my subconscious and today was no exception.

The wedding went like clockwork. 'Einstein Eddie' had surpassed himself. We both knew where we wanted the wedding to be, and Richard and Amanda had agreed instantly to our request; their much used and well-manicured lawn was ideal for the day's festivities, but also very private and away from the marauding Paparazzi lenses. The venue appeared magical, with white fairy lights in all the trees, and flower petals sprinkled everywhere. It was perfection.

The local Presbyterian Vicar Damien had performed the service, leaving his tiny St. Andrew's Chapel for the day to perform his first outdoor ceremony, especially for us. Eddie helped with the arrangements, even carrying the altar with Damien. The word altar first appears in Holy Scripture in Genesis 8:20 where it is stated, "Then Noah built an altar to the Lord".

I remember our first dance. I don't remember what my feet were doing but I remember the look in Vicki's eyes and the tear that slowly rolled down her cheek. I remember the sadness in my father's eyes – an unmistakable hint of grief that Flo was not there to share this moment with him. She would have been so proud.

As the night wore on, the backyard cricket gear came out and that was it, all hell let loose. After ten minutes, Vicki was running around in her wedding dress, splattering it with mud and grass, and soon enough the rest of the guests were joining in.

The dreaded morning after was exactly that. My head was throbbing; I looked over at Vicki who had consumed far too much Vodka for the both of us and smiled at my new wife. There was no time to reflect on the evening's events as my phone rang abruptly at 11.30am.

It was Marcus. I was sure he had been awake since 7am but he'd spared me the early wake-up call.

"Son, I hope the marriage consummation was better than your cricketing prowess," he said with a chuckle in his voice.

"Get in the shower and take some Paracetamol. And drink some Sprite to help your body better metabolize the alcohol." My father was full of bright ideas this morning.

But his was the voice of experience; Marcus knew, with all the whisky he'd consumed over the years, that a sugary drink speeds up one's ability to process aldehyde dehydrogenase, the main cause of a hangover. I obeyed. I headed for the drugs cabinet and then the refrigerator, in that order.

I met my father in my office an hour later; he was beavering away on my computer. He looked up at me and without a word ushered me onto the chair next to him. He had been going over the video and picture evidence I had saved to my computer and had been closely examining the sphere. His explanation was both a shock and a relief.

"This object has come from outer space, son of that there is no doubt. It's from beyond our solar system." He went on to explain that the sphere was made from an element or alloy not present on the periodic table and that it had properties that he had never seen before.

"Its simple, whoever sent this message did so in a really clever way. My best guess is this plasma sphere is just that; a plasma ball, traveling at light speed and inside the light there is a message". He went on to tell me that the plasma sphere had a predetermined course coded into it. It had travelled through space at light speed to its final destination, our Earth.

When the plasma sphere hit the Earth's atmosphere it had started to slow down. The Earth's atmosphere is made up of nitrogen, oxygen and argon. Nitrogen accounts for 78% of the atmosphere, oxygen 21% and argon 0.9%. Other gases like carbon dioxide, nitrous oxides, methane, and ozone are trace gases that account for about a tenth of 1% of the atmosphere. The plasma light had reacted to the content of Earth's atmosphere, and then it materialized into the sphere when Gus had thrown the snow over it.

Marcus went on to explain that he thought the sphere was a liquid metal because of the density of the metal reacting in the Earth's atmosphere. When Gus had thrown the snow on it, somehow it had caused the Sphere to activate. My father pondered and said:

"I think the Sphere was meant to land in the water and then the resultant chemical reaction would have caused it to activate".

"Why did it land on top of Mount Pisa then?" I could see Marcus was unsure and he said, "Maybe after traveling a minimum of 4.2 light years to get here, this one simply went off course".

I knew his stated 4.2 light years was in reference to the nearest star after our own sun, Proxima Centauri. Our own sun is 93 million miles away; Proxima Centauri is 4.2 light years or 1.3 parsecs away. "Actually it could have come from anywhere son. You're the astrophysicist, so this one is up to you."

I started to do some quick math. In the observable universe, there are about 10 billion galaxies that we actually know of. Assuming on average there are about 100 billion stars per galaxy, that means there are probably 1,000,000,000,000,000,000,000 or 1 billion, trillion stars. My first few years at Harvard were spent understanding the enormity of space, time and the universe. Most students couldn't grasp these numbers and dropped out. Me, I had relished in the unimaginable vastness of it all.

"OK, dad I'll work on where it came from, you keep working on the binary code message." Marcus agreed, and immediately called his contacts in the CIA; if ever there was a need for the CIA, it was now.

I really didn't know where to start, so I put on my astrophysicists' hat and went to work. Astrophysics is the study of celestial objects such as galaxies, stars, black holes, planets, exoplanets, the Big Bang, dark matter and dark energy. That's why I chose it, for the challenge; but there was so much still to learn about astrophysics. Astrophysics' cousin is cosmology, the theoretical side of astrophysics, at scales much larger than the size of particular gravitationally bound objects in the universe.

I remembered what Professor Culshaw had told me at my very first lecture at Harvard:

"Astronomy is the oldest form of science, originating in ancient China and classical Greece, then right through to the Renaissance, where Copernicus, Kepler and Newton made massive contributions to our knowledge and understanding of the solar system and planetary motion."

He then finished by saying.

"The science of astrophysics seeks to explain the structure and evolution of the stars and other celestial objects, by applying the principles of physics and chemistry to interpret our observations."

That's the reason why I had ended up at MIT, completing my education with a PhD in physics.

Thus my mind wandered back to the origins of astrophysics. In 1860 the physicist Gustav Kirchhoff and the chemist Robert Bunsen had demonstrated that the dark lines in the solar spectrum corresponded to the bright lines in the spectra of known gases, and the specific lines corresponded to unique chemical elements. Kirchhoff had correctly deduced that the dark lines in the solar spectrum are caused by absorption by chemical elements in the solar atmosphere. By doing this they proved that the chemical elements found in the sun and stars were also found on Earth. And so the science of astrophysics was born.

I started to examine the sphere for trace elements. If I could determine the trace elements of the sphere, it might give us a clue as to what planet or solar system the sphere may have come from.

Again, I revisited my training. Light consists of electromagnetic radiation of different wavelengths. So, when elements or their compounds are heated either on a flame or by an electric arc they emit energy in the form of light. Analysis of this light, with the help of a spectroscope, gives a discontinuous spectrum and separates the components of light, which have different wavelengths. The spectrum appears as a series of lines, called the line spectrum. This line spectrum is the atomic spectrum when it originates from an atom in elemental form and each element has a different atomic spectrum.

The production of line spectra by the atoms of an element indicates that an atom can radiate only a certain amount of energy. This leads to the conclusion that bound electrons cannot have just any amount of energy, but only a certain amount of energy.

The emission spectrum can then be used to determine the composition of a material, since it is different for each element of the periodic table.

I now enlisted the help of my friends in the world of astrophysics. I knew it was nearing Christmas and everyone would be gearing down for the holidays, so I gave them all a conundrum to solve, with a prize of an all-expenses paid trip to my observatory. I knew this would work - scientists love this sort of challenge. I gave them the data I had obtained from the sphere and I asked them to come up with the possible celestial matches. The first person with the correct answer would win the prize. I didn't need a PhD in astrophysics to learn how to delegate and incentify!

Marcus had made steady progress with his binary code message. The team at the CIA assigned to the task had access to the world's largest supercomputers. They had discovered quite quickly that the code was simple binary; the trick had been to put pieces together to read the message. They came back to Marcus with a synopsis that he found difficult to believe. The message was short and sweet; it just gave trajectory coordinates terminating at our sun. There was also a date – January 2nd 2035. Nothing more.

Marcus went into overdrive. What was so special about January 2nd, 2035? He immediately looked up all the references he could find on the date, especially in relation to the sun. It takes roughly 365 days, or one year, for the Earth to complete its orbit around the sun. Everybody knew that, he thought. The Earth is in an elliptical orbit and there is only a slight difference between the closest and farthest points from the sun throughout the orbit as the Earth travels around the sun at a speed of about 67,000 miles an hour.

He ploughed through everything he could think of related to the sun and this date but turned up nothing. Why would the message not be directed to the inhabitants of Earth? Did they not mean to make contact? Probes we had sent into outer space in the past-contained essential information about the Earth and its inhabitants so that any future contact with extra-terrestrials could be made with a peaceful starting point. This didn't seem to be the case here; there was so little information from its originator. What could this message possibly mean?

# Chapter eleven

*The sun is about 330,000 times the mass of the Earth. It's almost a perfect sphere with a diameter about 109 times the size of the Earth. A huge glowing orange ball of mega hot gases, 70% hydrogen, 28% helium and smaller amounts of carbon, nitrogen and oxygen that make up about another 1.5%. The final 0.5% is made up of small amounts of other elements, including neon, iron, silicon, magnesium and sulphur.*

A popular misconception is that solar energy is not nuclear energy. In fact all stars, including our sun, produce their energy from the fusing of nuclei of smaller atoms together, to make the nuclei of larger atoms. Our sun is a colossal nuclear fusion machine that accounts for 99.86% of our entire Solar System's mass. The sun is not only gigantic, it's extremely radioactive.

Why would an alien civilization be sending a coded message about the sun to the Earth? The jigsaw puzzle needed more pieces. Marcus called and told me that he would arrive at my lab the next day, armed with a full report, supplied by NASA and various other U.S. intelligence agencies.

My email icon blinked and gave the slight audible tone of alert, indicating a new email had arrived. It was from my friend Jordan Crown, based at the Gemini Telescope located at the summit of Mauna Kea on the Big Island of Hawaii. The 8.1-meter optical/IR telescope was the world's largest observatory for optical, infrared, and submillimetre astronomy when it was first built. I read his email intently and it contained the answer to my conundrum.

Jordan had checked and then rechecked the data. He was sure. It pointed to one place - the sphere had come from Kepler-452b.

NASA's Kepler mission had confirmed that this Earth like planet, orbited in the "Goldilocks zone" as it was sometimes called, of the sun-like star named Kepler-452. The Goldilocks zone is an area where liquid water can pool on the surface of a planet, if the conditions are just right. The discovery 20 years previously was a milestone in the journey to finding another habitable planet. The Kepler exoplanet explorer had discovered the planet on the 23rd of July 2015 and it closely resembled planet Earth.

Kepler-452b, as it was very scientifically named, was 60% larger in diameter than Earth. Its 385-day orbit around its sun is 5% longer than that of our Earth's. It was also 5% farther from its sun, Kepler-452b.

Kepler-452 is around 6 billion years old, about 1.5 billion years older than our sun. It's approximately the same temperature, but shines 20% brighter. It's located 1,400 light-years away, in the constellation of Cygnus.

I was intrigued and very pleased to get the break I was looking for, and immediately set about confirming Jordan's data. Marcus was a man known for dealing in facts and you didn't want to get yours wrong. Marcus dealt in certainties, data, sources, evidence – this was just his way.

Marcus entered my office and we exchanged all of our collated information. We absorbed each other's data with minimal fuss. It seemed nothing could faze us now. We agreed on the facts, but couldn't agree on the strategic reason behind the message. This was not uncommon when dealing with my father; he had his own thought processes and would very rarely change his mind, if ever. This mind-set had served him well all of his working life and he saw no reason to change now.

We both agreed that time was of the essence - January 2nd was merely days away, and we needed to work together from now on to get the hard facts together for the President's report. He had personally called Marcus after a briefing with his National Security advisors; he wanted to know everything as soon as possible.

I had never really worked with my father in an intellectual capacity before, but I knew his thought processes and he knew mine. Gus, who had now joined us, was great at rugby but when it came to this kind of thing his strengths were giving encouragement and making tea.

The interesting thing about tea is that it all comes from the same plant, the Camellia sinensis. There are literally hundreds of kinds of tea, with their own individual appearance, taste and aroma. Like a good wine or coffee, every tea harvest varies from year to year, due to changes in the climate, rainfall and other seasonal conditions. Marcus and I chose black tea, Assam or Darjeeling usually, because the leaves are fully oxidized and provide a strong flavour. Even the taste of our tea had changed over the last 10 years, as the rains became more infrequent.

Gus was a coffee man, barista made trim flat white with honey. Vicki joined in the gathering with her hot lemon water, which was literally just hot water and lemon; she said it cleansed the soul. I personally wouldn't clean the car with it, but I would never dare tell her that.

We worked away intensely trying to figure out the connections. The fascinating thing was that the information in the sphere was based on knowledge of our solar system and our dates and time. If this was a random discovery expedition surely the sphere would contain information about their race, planet and origins. Surely it would contain information in order to initiate contact. Instead it contained detailed coordinates about our sun that could only have come about via extensive surveillance. The date was also astounding as it used our date and time system, which led us to believe that whoever sent this sphere, understood our way of life.

This was frightening stuff.

We had found answers within the sphere but it only threw out further questions. How had an extra-terrestrial race infiltrated our society without detection? Why did they not want to be detected? Did they want something from us?

This was the key question that we decided to focus on. What did they want? It was an unnerving question, I had always envisioned a friendly encounter with extra-terrestrials but after hours of discussion with my father we concluded with confidence that this was not the case.

I made my point to everyone that Foo Fighters had been seen all over the world, but mostly recorded over the last 90 years. If all Foo Fighters were from Kepler-452b we could assume that they were searching for something, and for at least the last 90 years. But what?

We eliminated water, as there was plenty of this on Kepler-452b. We eliminated land space as this was receding with rising sea levels. We were doubtful about resources because ours had been in decline for years, but it was something that humans battled over, so maybe aliens would too. Marcus, Vicki, Gus and I sat in my office that evening in perplexed silence when Vicki whispered:

"Gold…"

She was twisting her wedding ring around her finger as she said it. No one else seemed to register this and even Vicki herself continued twisting her ring without looking up. "Everyone is always looking for gold".

"Gold?" I asked.

I went over the spectrometer reading again from Jordon Crown and one element that was missing from Kepler-452b surface was gold. Now gold is a pretty rare element in the cosmos. Originally it was thought that supernova explosions were the source of all gold in the Universe, but in recent years a new hypothesis has been submitted that Gold and other heavy metal elements are the after-effects created when neutron stars collide.

Gold owes its status as a precious metal to its rarity: all the gold mined throughout history on planet Earth would fit into a square box with sides of around 20m in length. Gold is also rare throughout the Universe because it's a relatively hefty atom, consisting of 79 protons and 118 neutrons. It's really important in space travel because it's one of the heaviest, most uniquely workable metals that is not dangerously radioactive. It's used a great deal by NASA as a heat and radiation shield. Gold reflects infrared radiation; protecting Astronaut's eyes. It also reflects as much or more UV radiation than its competitors, whilst absorbing the most visible light.

I relayed this information to the group like I was reading out of a book and I saw that they were beginning to become more interested. They were starting to see the pattern.

"This could be why the sphere was in the Central Otago region Marcus," Gus said out loud.

Gus told us the story about the massive amounts of alluvial gold found throughout the Otago region during the 1860s gold rush. "There are stories of rivers of gold from the region," he said. The gold was linked to the regions schist rock geology. Over millions of years, glaciers had ground away at the rocks, which were threaded with quartz veins, containing large amounts of gold. The gold was then concentrated by separating the heavier minerals from the lighter ones. The first miners literally picked up nuggets where they lay.

Gus said, "In the Cromwell area just 30 miles from here, during the gold rush one of the largest gold finds in the world ever was made at the convergence of the Clutha and Kawarau rivers".

Marcus pointed out that gold was found in most places around the world, but in very small quantities. I proposed a theory:

"If I was going to a far off planet, to check out its natural resources, I would send scouts out everywhere, and I would certainly focus on areas that gold had already been collected or was amassed".

Marcus nodded in agreement. "This planet, Kepler-452b is 1,400 light years away, so whoever they are, they have come a very long way for their booty".

"If they had to travel that far in space and at light speed, how could they possibly do it?" I asked.

Marcus replied without hesitation – "Machines…"

# Chapter twelve

C hristmas day came and went; our first as Mr. and Mrs. Linsky. It was hectic, our minds preoccupied. Turkey seemed irrelevant, gravy vague and pointless. Luckily Gus consumed most of the traditional holiday food; he would have eaten the entire contents of the refrigerator if we had let him. Boxing Day soon arrived and we were all very conscious of the seven days that remained until our still mysterious deadline date was upon us...

January 2nd.

We had, however, come a long way with our deduction of the evidence and we surer than ever that Gold was their target. There was no definite proof, but everything pointed to this conclusion as more likely than any other.

This, naturally, made the U.S. government very nervous, as did the thought of any alien presence becoming a reality here on Earth. The President had ordered that all of the country's gold reserves be placed at Fort Knox and he tripled the security. The army deployed another 2 divisions of ground troops, another complete surface to air missile battery and the latest version of Abraham tanks to protect their precious asset. The air force flew constant sorties over the location and the nearby airbase was placed on full alert status.

An Andi Mk2 was also supplied on the advice of my father. The President had personally given the order for the deployment. Losing the country's gold would not only end his presidency, it would bankrupt his country. If the most powerful country on planet Earth became bankrupt, the domino effect would be disastrous.

It was my father's conclusion that fascinated me the most. Machines, traveling through space, was a real possibility.

The time it takes to travel from Kepler-452b, 1,400 light years, meant machines were surely the answer. The technology needed to travel those distances and at light speed was way beyond anything that mankind was currently capable of. But another civilization that was 1.5 billion years older than us could have figured out how to do it. Maybe they had found, and then solved, the problem of how to travel through wormholes.

*A wormhole is a theoretical passage through space-time that could possibly create shortcuts for long journeys across the universe; wormholes are predicted in Einstein's theory of general relativity.*

Maybe, just maybe, these sentient beings from another galaxy had figured out how to do it. An entity this advanced and capable of this feat could do so many things, good or evil.

My father and his team had been working on a program that would allow the Andi Mk2s to replicate themselves. They could then be sent on expeditions into space and multiply on their own, providing they had the raw materials. This would make traveling to far off galaxies theoretically possible. All we needed to do now was to figure out how to travel at the speed of light, and find the nearest wormhole. If only we had an extra 1.5 billion years at our disposal.

With time rapidly running out I placed my observatory staff on extended holiday leave. We needed the space. Marcus had flown in his trusted research team from California with all their equipment. NASA had also sent their team of deep-space Kepler experts, and they quickly took over the vacated living quarters. My team was fantastic but the big guns were needed. This was serious.

One of the bright young NASA team members, Erica, pointed out that the gold might not be the only thing the aliens were after. The Earth is rich in many natural resources that might not be available on Kepler. Maybe they had pillaged their planet beyond repair too or maybe we had something on Earth that even we were unaware of, but would be of immense value to the alien species. The possibilities were wide and varying but the one thing that we knew for sure was that they were coming. That was not in doubt.

The Kepler mission, which had launched in March 2009 and was managed by NASA, was named in honor of the German astronomer Johannes Kepler. In the 17th Century Kepler developed the laws of planetary motion and the principle needed to calculate optical prescriptions. The initial NASA mission was to find terrestrial planets by surveying 100,000 stars in our own Milky Way galaxy and then to discover Earth-size planets in or near the 'Goldilocks zone', then determine how many of the billions of stars in our galaxy have such Earth-size planets.

Once identified, a planet's orbital size can be calculated from the period of how long it takes the planet to orbit once around its star. Its mass can then be calculated using Kepler's third law of planetary motion. The Kepler telescope was a specially designed 0.95-meter diameter telescope called a photometer and had to be space-based to obtain the precision needed to supply accurate data back to the control centre on Earth.

Erica also suggested that if we used the Kepler telescope in a slightly different way we might be able to track the Foo Fighters on their journey across the cosmos. If we could track the Foo Fighters we could try to understand how and where they were travelling.

All of the ground-based telescope installations around the world were contacted by NASA and covertly asked to track and report any unusual cosmic activity. The cover story posted by NASA was about another possible near miss by an asteroid. This had happened recently in 2028, when the asteroid 1997XF11 came extremely close to Earth but, luckily, just missed. If the mile-and-a-half wide asteroid had hit Earth travelling at 30,000mph, it would have unleashed an explosion roughly equal to a 1 million megaton bomb, which would have wiped out most life on Earth, much like the Chixculub event 65 million years ago, which signalled the end of the cretaceous period and the dinosaurs.

Marcus said that if he had wanted to steal the Earth's gold, he would head straight for the world's richest deposits. The Earth's previously mined gold was locked away in various safe caches around the world, but the true extent of the Earth's hidden reserves was not commonly known.

This got us thinking.

We made a list, starting with the Grasberg mine. It had the largest reported deposits of gold in the world and was located in Papua, Indonesia. There were the South Deep and Mponeng mines, both near Johannesburg in South Africa. The Muruntau mine in the Kyzyl Kum Desert, Uzbekistan. It was the largest open pit gold mine on Earth, measuring 2.2 x 1.6 miles at the surface. The Olympiada mine in Central Siberia and many more very large gold mines dotted around the planet.

The team started comparing the reported Foo Fighter sightings from the last 100 years with the locations of the major gold deposits located around the world. The trend was undeniable, too much of a coincidence to be random. This was the final piece of evidence we needed. We were convinced – gold was the intended target, or at least one of them.

Marcus pointed out that there was also another fact that was quite striking. There were hundreds of reports of Foo Fighters near nuclear missile silos. Some extremely well documented events claim that the fail-safe systems of the missiles were disabled.

The event on March the 16th 1967 at Malmstrom Air Force Base in Montana was probably the best recorded one. A detachment of U.S. Air Force Strategic Air Command missile combat officers and other enlisted personnel had witnessed the incredible events. These personnel were in charge of the Minuteman Intercontinental Ballistic Missile System (ICBM). They reported seeing a UFO above the missile silos. Whilst this event was unfolding, many of the missiles in the silo had suddenly become disabled.

This was just one of several similar, and well-documented incidents over many years. The testaments of these extremely well trained and professional officers led us all to the conclusion that these were trial runs by the aliens. If the aliens had discovered how to send coded messages through space at the speed of light, it was a very good chance that they could disarm our comparatively ancient security technology that guarded our missiles.

Marcus and I worked tirelessly with the entire team. Pieces were falling into place. We were now confident as to why 'they' were coming and that it would not be a peaceful visit. We were also sure that they had figured out how to use wormholes and had been on Earth for a period of time, testing, probing and investigating.

Yet, the 2nd of January and the coordinates for the sun were still a mystery.

The team and I threw countless hypotheses around, but none were satisfactory. We brainstormed every possible idea, only to shake our heads at all of them.

It has been proven that thinking too hard about a problem can be counterproductive. One of the best ways to solve something is to leave it alone, let your subconscious deal with it and churn out an answer. I didn't know this at the time but maybe Vicki did.

She took me away from my office and sat me down, she stroked my hair gently and we spoke about our wedding day. I laughed for the first time in days and relaxed a little deeper into the sofa. For a few minutes the aliens weren't coming and it was just Vicki and I. Peace, for an instant.

Then, BOOM! I had it.

I jumped up, kissed Vicki on her perfect forehead and made a dash for my computer and quickly searched Google using the very unscientific phrase:

'What is the next date that the Earth is closest to the sun?'

Google obliged and there it was - 2nd January 2035. It was the only thing that made any sense; on the 2nd of January 2035 the Earth would be at the closest point in its orbit to the sun during its long 11-year repeating cycle.

I called my father hastily, and said, "I think I know what they're up to!"

* * *

The night before, whilst having dinner with Andrew and the rest of the security detail, I listened as they were discussing among themselves how they would steal the gold from a tactical perspective. The traditional theory of armed warfare is to:

1. Observe your enemy and study their tactics.
2. Find their weaknesses.
3. Execute your plan, efficiently and effectively.

With this theory as a base I expanded it into the physics world. It became clear – the aliens had been studying us for at least the last 100 years but possibly for thousands more. They had found our weakness and that was our communications. We rely entirely on our satellites for just about everything. Without them we are blind, our communications are thrown back into the Stone Age. Now the question was – how could you wipe out the Earth's entire satellite communications system? The answer – a massive solar flare!

That's what their trajectory coordinates in the sphere were for.

A plasma bolt shot directly at the sun could create a massive solar flare. The magnetic energy that has built up in the sun's solar atmosphere would then be suddenly released. The sun's surface contains huge magnetic loops called prominences and when they touch, they short-circuit each other, setting off enormous explosions. The amount of energy released is the equivalent to more than a million hydrogen bombs exploding at the same time.

Solar flares contain high-energy photons and particles emitting radiation across virtually the entire electromagnetic spectrum, from radio waves at the long wavelength end to x-rays and gamma rays at the short wavelength end. Space observatories had been detecting solar flares for years. These intense bursts of radiation are the solar system's largest explosive events; these Coronal Mass Ejections (CMEs) are giant bubbles of gas and magnetic fields, emitted directly from the sun. They contain billions of tons of charged particles that can travel several million miles per hour. The resultant radiation can corrode space equipment and overload our satellites, rendering them useless.

Solar flares from the sun have been happening for millennia. Mankind has been protected from the radiation by the Earth's magnetic field and its atmosphere, which acts as a shield and blocks the harmful cosmic rays. Some of the charged particles can enter our atmosphere at the poles. We see these charged electron particles as an aurora. We know them as Aurora Borealis or the Northern Lights, and Aurora Australis, the Southern Lights. Sadly, a plasma bolt shot into the sun would do a lot more than create a beautiful light display. It could affect all life on the planet.

I looked at my father with desperate eyes and muttered with disbelief:

"I think they are going to bomb the sun, disable our satellites and then come for us...."

Silence filled the room.

# Chapter thirteen

Friday, December 29th, 2034 and the clock was ticking.

My theory was met with stunned disbelief. Silence lingered as we all processed the information. In the meantime, a plan was being hatched. The U.S. intelligence services and armed forces went to full alert status. A war games press release was hurriedly produced, all leave was cancelled within the U.S. military and all personnel were ordered to return to their units.

The U.S. strategists had planned many different war game scenarios over the years, although I'm confident few included an alien race planning to bomb our sun, destroy our satellites and in the process wiping out all humankind.

Despite my initial jubilation at discovering their plans, it did little to help us. We still didn't know from where they were going to shoot this plasma bolt, or if it could be stopped. We still didn't know what would happen after our satellites were disabled. Would they take our gold peacefully, or wage war? We were still playing catch up to everything, one step behind all the time - 1.5 billion years behind to be exact. I felt like an exposed pawn on a chessboard, fragile and available for the taking at any time.

The U.S. military had been pestering Marcus and I to relocate the sphere to the U.S. but we had outright refused. There was no way we were letting this thing out of our sight. I had this odd feeling that I was meant to find it, that I was the one who should keep it. I was the physics scholar and outer space expert after all.

So much was happening so quickly, but there was almost nothing we could do to stop it. We were processing information non-stop but not getting any closer to a solution to our global problem. How do we stop them bombing from our sun?

I slowly pushed my chair away from my desk and stood up, bending backwards to stretch my back. It was just Marcus and I in my office. I put my eye to the telescope and scanned the stars again, not with any purpose or reason, just out of habit. Marcus didn't move. I slowly slinked over to the sphere and took the tarpaulin off it. I wanted to look at it again. This remarkable feat of extra-terrestrial engineering, this alien thing that was threatening all our survival. I sat on the floor in front of it and silently asked it questions. Cursing it for its intrusion but also flattering it for its capabilities and complexities.

I had set my watch on a countdown to January 2nd 2035 Greenwich Mean Time (GMT). As I sat there in front of the sphere, I watched my digital watch tick down to 72 hours to go. At this exact moment the sphere buzzed to life. It groaned a little as it rebooted and then suddenly released its chilling code once more.

"Dad!" I shouted. I rarely called Marcus 'Dad' but the mind jumps into comfort mode when panicked.

My father looked at me and I shrugged and raised my hands in the air to say, 'I didn't do anything'. My father took a best guess and murmured, "It's probably a built in failsafe code that has caused the reactivation."

We both watched the code again. It was very faint on the inside so I shone the light directly into the sphere. Again the light did not penetrate the sphere, it emitted the light straight back out, just like it had done before. The code this time was very different and there was a lot more of it.

Marcus immediately started to video the code being emitted by the sphere and sent it via live-feed to U.S. Air Force Space Command in its Cheyenne Mountain HQ.

*The Cheyenne complex officially opened in February 1966, and was fully operational by February 6th, 1967. Built directly into the side of the Rocky Mountains near Colorado Springs, the complex was originally constructed for the North American*

The U.S. Air Force Space Command 'officially' moved out in 2006 to the Peterson Air Force Base, but a secret detachment would always remain at the complex and was still under the direct control of the U.S. Air Force. Having cost $142.4 million to build in 1967 – about $2 billion in 2035 dollars, the U.S. military was not going to leave one of its prized assets sitting there as a designated training base, as the generals would have us all believe.

The massive complex was built under 2,000 feet (610m) of granite on a 5-acre site. At the time it was the only high altitude U.S. Department of Defense facility certified to be able to sustain an electromagnetic pulse or (EMP). It also doubled as a nuclear bunker for the U.S. military command staff and high-ranking government officials. It was built to deflect a 30-megaton nuclear explosion.

Within the mountain tunnels are sets of 25-ton blast doors. Designed to be opened if needed, but meant to protect the inhabitants from a nuclear blast wave. If that wasn't enough (the planners had certainly thought things through, right down to the last detail) the complex contained a network of blast valves with unique filters to capture airborne chemical, biological, radiological, and nuclear contaminants.

This place was a fortress and now it was home to the newest top-secret branch of the military, the U.S. Space Army or USSA. Working with the USSA was a breeze; they were all spacemen and women, recruited from the vast array of U.S. military and civilian personnel. These men and women were the best and certainly the brightest the U.S. military had to offer. As a funded 'Black Project' hidden within the NASA budget, they had made stunning advances in space exploration in recent years and Erica, from my father's NASA detachment, was one of their recruits.

Reactivation of the sphere had caused unease amongst our group, but I had seen this before so I did my best to show an outward calm. I actually enjoyed watching the lines of code emanate from within the sphere. It was almost a spiritual, transcendent experience.

After several minutes the sphere shut back down, and left us again in mesmerized silence. Marcus and I began eagerly watching the video footage over and over; the coded message seemed to be on a recurring loop. This time it wasn't just a simple case of reading the binary code; the aliens who had sent this had encrypted the code.

*Cryptography is the ancient discipline of using codes or ciphers to encrypt a message and make it unreadable to the person viewing it. The message usually reads as garbled nonsense unless the recipient knows the secret of how to decrypt it. The first time an electromechanical machine was used to decrypt a code was the British invention called the 'Bombe'. It was developed by Alan Turing at Bletchley Park during the Second World War to defeat the German Enigma machine. Breaking of the top secret German code, thought to be unbreakable by the Nazi's, was one of the main reasons Great Britain and its allies survived and then went on to win the Second World War. Turing was a genius; he was also the founding father of AI.*

Neither Marcus nor I were code breakers, but luckily Marcus had a trick up his sleeve. The Andi Mk2.

Marcus played the video feed into his personal Andi Mk2.

"You have supplied me with binary code Mr. Linsky," the Andi Mk2 said in its usual computer-generated synthesized voice.

Marcus looked up and said, "Andi, piece together all possible combinations of the message and give me a report." The Andi Mk2 replied, "Yes, Mr. Linsky, I presently estimate this process to take approximately 8 hours."

Marcus then sent the data to the USSA at their command HQ deep inside the Cheyenne Mountain complex to allow their supercomputers to analyse the code. Marcus wondered to himself who would come up with the correct data first, the world's top supercomputers or his latest Andi Mk2?

This was the latest lead but we were helpless until Andi or the supercomputers decoded the message. Everyone still wanted to work non-stop, but at what? Vicki and Gus tried to lighten the mood to keep spirits high, but it was a tough task. I busied myself analyzing the same data over and over again, occasionally turning my eye to the telescope.

Eventually, Vicki took my hand and led me away and gently laid me down on a bed in the corridor. She whispered something in my ear but I was already unconscious as my head hit the pillow. Sleep overwhelmed me.

Sometime later Marcus woke me up with an unwelcome nudge. The bed next to me was messy. I guessed he had slept too, probably due to Vicki's demands. We had grabbed 40 winks after days of constant work. (I loved the phrase 40 winks. It can be traced back to Dr. Kitchiner's 1821 self-help guide, 'The art of invigorating and prolonging life').

The Andi Mk2 was ahead of forecast. In exactly 7 hours and 42 minutes it came back with its report.

I checked in with USSA and asked Erica to liaise with her team inside the Colorado Mountain complex. Erica was already one step ahead and had asked for a full supercomputer report on the 8 hour mark. We connected our Andi with Erica. She compiled the results and displayed the report on a widescreen monitor. We all gathered round.

Chairs shuffled closer as the information began to appear on the screen. At first, we all sipped our coffee casually as if we were in a routine team meeting. But it wasn't long until astonishment took over. After all, the brain can only take in so much information. When it hits overload, everyday tasks become impossible. One after another, coffee mugs were placed carefully on the floor. Drinking stopped as jaws dropped.

The binary code of the sphere was fragmented to the human eye, but when seen by a supercomputer, it told a very different story. The USSA supercomputer had managed to isolate some of the data, but the Andi had downloaded and decrypted the sphere's entire memory. The report from the sphere was a volcanic eruption of unimaginable facts. Everything we thought we knew was being turned inside out and upside down in an instant.

According to the sphere, Earth had been detected by the aliens millions of years ago. The aliens had sent an exploratory ship manned by its very own self-replicating robots, much the same as the kind of robots Marcus and his team had been working on.

Our initial suspicions about the Foo Fighters had been confirmed. For the last million years or so, the aliens had been sending the plasma bolt spheres on 're-con' missions to Earth. The spheres were shot into space from their home world at the speed of light, computer guided to a nearby wormhole and then activated by good old-fashioned $H_2O$ when they reached Earth. According to the alien reports, when they had first detected our planet, one million years ago, there was no intelligent life on Earth.

Some of the plasma spheres were special command probes, twice the size of the standard Foo Fighter spheres. Amazingly, we had one of them. It seemed that the alien robots had hurriedly reused this one and its guidance program had malfunctioned as a result.

The robots sent reports back to their world, gathered by the Foo Fighters, every 1,000 alien years. The command probes would report back their findings by way of the wormhole that terminated just outside of our solar system. The command probes were launched from Earth, from our very own planet giving full reports about mankind. The aliens had established their very own intelligence base and had been covertly spying on us for hundreds of thousands of years. Then came the crunch...

Their base was in our own ocean, hidden within its darkest depths, at the bottom of the Marianas Trench!

*Located in the remote part of the Western Pacific Ocean, the Marianas Trench is the deepest part of the world's oceans. The trench is 1500 miles long, with an average width of 43 miles. To provide perspective on this, if you took Mount Everest and dropped it into the Marianas Trench, the summit of Everest would still be more than 1 mile under water.*

You could just about hide another continent down there, and no one would know it.

The alien designed robots had replicated themselves over the last million years in a similar way Marcus had hypothesised was possible with his Andis. They had built a small undersea base right under our noses and we knew nothing about it. Their small command centre was so well hidden that we had more chance of finding Martians than the 10 robots that made up the alien garrison at the bottom of the Pacific Ocean, especially if you weren't looking for it.

The spheres, situated at various strategic locations around the world, were hidden from view with the cunning use of camouflage rendering them translucent when immersed in water. They reported back to their robot controller's underwater base every 50 years.

This now explained several things: why we didn't seem to detect the Foo Fighters very often, and why. When we did see them, they inconveniently disappeared without a trace. The fact that we had one of their command spheres was a 1000-year fluke, a monumental stroke of luck for us, I assumed.

The next part of the coded message was even more intriguing. The command sphere had a recent updated report on the Earth and its various gold deposits, just as we had suspected, complete with new technical specification and details on the Android AI Mk2s. The previous sphere that had been sent 5 years ago only had the computer coding information of the original Andis but not the new Mk2s. The development of the Andi Mk2 had caused the robots to send an emergency update to their controllers on their home world of Kepler-452b.

The new report contained detailed information on the Andi Mk2s, but interestingly nothing about their functional and command capabilities. Marcus told us that the new Andi Mk2s were fitted with the very latest impenetrable encryption algorithms.

When developing the encryption details for the Andi Mk2s, Marcus had worked with four NSA supercomputers simultaneously for a month in an attempt to break the Andi Mk2s encryption code. They failed to crack the revolutionary new encoding software the Andis had designed for the simple reason that the Andis constantly reprogrammed the code internally from their own memory on a moment-by-moment basis. It was sheer genius. How could you crack a code that changed by the second?

The last part of the alien coded message was really damning. The aliens and their robots had broken the encryption code of the original Andis. Armed with the decrypted codes the aliens could now override the control parameters of the 25 million plus original Andis located around the world. They intended to control them with the thousands of spheres hidden throughout the world's oceans. They were all programmed to be fully activated at noon on January 2nd, 2035 GMT. They had been pre-set into standby mode 72 hours earlier, so they could all get into positions at their various required locations around the world.

It was a really short meeting after that, as their plan became clear to us. Thousands of spheres around the globe that had mostly laid dormant collecting and reporting information every 50 years would be fully activated on the 2nd January 2035, on the heels of the solar flare attack. The aliens planned to send command signals to all the Andi Mk1s around the world. These command signals would take complete control of all the Andis. More than 25 million fully armed Andis would be controlled by an alien race. More than 25 million machines of death would be out of our control.

The nightmare scenario that a small minority of the population had feared for years was about to unfold – our own saviours, the world's beloved Andis, would be turned against the human race.

A robotic android invasion of our own making was about to be unleashed against our own kind...

# Chapter fourteen

For a moment, we all sat in stunned silence. It's hard to explain what it feels like when you realize your world is about to be taken over by your own creation.

"Don't you have a big override button or something Marcus?" Gus muttered.

Marcus merely stared at him. Gus took that as a no and he quietly began making more tea. He was out of his depth but still trying to help.

Vicki immediately weighed in. The alien robots were so concerned about the new Andi Mk2s, and their possible impact on their planned invasion, that they sent an emergency command sphere back to their alien controllers on Kepler-452b to warn of the Andi Mk2s advanced capabilities.

"If they're so worried about the Mk2s, surely there is a way we can use them to our advantage?" Vicki said, looking at everyone in the room.

Marcus got up from his seat, looked at Vicki, and then me and nodded his head slowly. Without a word he reached for his phone and made a call.

"Kinika!" Marcus said with a friendly voice. "I need your help".

Kinika was a big man of Nigerian descent, but now a naturalized American. Having studied computer science at MIT, he was what most people would regard as a programming genius. He could typically complete in minutes what would normally take hours. He was Marcus's go-to man when he wanted something done with a computer.

As quickly as possible, Marcus told Kinika what he needed to know, and then asked him to go back into the security protocols of the original Andis to look for a 'back door' in the security programming.

"There are no back doors, Marcus," Kinika quickly replied. You explicitly instructed us not to leave a backdoor, specifically for this reason."

"I know Kinika, but now we need one. Make one, find one, or invent one. Whatever you need to do. Check the data again by connecting into an Andi Mk2 to run their control algorithm program across the original Andis program. They may be able to help you break what we thought was an unbreakable code."

Kinika accepted the challenge, proclaiming that, "If an alien robot can break our unbreakable code, Marcus, then so can I."

Whilst Marcus was looking at ways to stop the Andi Mk1s from being taken over, I focused on the wormhole coordinates that the command sphere utilized. Something wasn't right.

*Albert Einstein and Nathan Rosen used the Theory of General Relativity to propose the existence of 'bridges' through space-time. These paths were called Einstein-Rosen bridges or a 'wormholes' and they connected two different points in space-time, theoretically creating a shortcut that could reduce the travel time and distance in space.*

The problem they had encountered was that these theoretical wormholes were tiny, and according to their calculations would only be visible at microscopic levels. As the universe expanded, Einstein theorized, it would be possible that some wormholes might be stretched too much larger sizes.

I deduced that this must be how the aliens have been sending the spheres, as tiny streams of plasma, propelled at light speed across the universe, using their pre-determined wormholes.

Einstein had also predicted in his papers that if a wormhole contained enough exotic matter, this would theoretically make the wormhole larger and more stable. I knew from my research days at MIT that exotic matter had been seen in certain vacuum states as part of quantum field theory. My best guess was that the alien race had worked this equation out millions of years ago and they were sending their larger exploratory robot ships to the far reaches of the galaxy, using exotic matter and expanded wormholes to achieve much faster results.

I had also calculated that it would take the sphere about 36 hours to travel to the entrance of the wormhole at the speed of light. I was fascinated by the alien technology that allowed for transformation from the physical sphere into a beam of plasma that was then shot off in a predetermined direction at light speed. This was way beyond any human research to date. I was at a loss. They had a billion more years of research, development, trial and error than us. Were we doomed?

For a moment, I recalled growing up watching episodes of 'Star Trek, and being immersed in the subsequent collection of the feature films. The TV series, created by Gene Roddenberry, first aired in the USA in 1966 and was a worldwide hit. Star Trek was still a cult TV series nearly 70 years later. I loved the different characters and the various types of space villains, who each week always seemed to get their comeuppance.

Who was the space villain of the episode here, I wondered. Was it the aliens, or was it us?

During the last two centuries, mankind had ravaged the Earth, selfishly gorging on natural resources to feed its ever-growing population that now stood at roughly nine billion. In the year 1800, the world's population was estimated to be around one billion. By 1900, it was 1.7 billion. By the year 2000, it was six billion. In the last 35 years since the turn of the millennium, the Earth's population had grown by another 50%, a precariously unsustainable rate. I wondered if this is what had driven this alien race to expand its horizons and look to other worlds in the ever-expanding universe.

Was it just this simple - that the aliens just needed to replenish their own planet's natural resources, just like us? Were they so different to us? Facing extinction of our race, surely we would invade and steal from other worlds. We've been invading countries for centuries, for much more mundane reasons.

I awoke from my trance suddenly, with a touch from Vicki's hand. I had been standing in a corner, my mind churning over wormholes and the invasion process without any real goal to my thoughts. I was lost in my mind, going nowhere. I had no answers, no solutions.

Vicki touched my face gently and brushed her lips against mine.

"I need you," she said, piercing through my eyes with hers. "We need you," she said as she led me back into the room.

# Chapter fifteen

Breaking a code isn't easy, but it's possible. Alan Turing had proved this by breaking the German Enigma code with his team during the Second World War. The Enigma machine, which produced a polyalphabetic substitution cipher, was highly complex for its time in history and was thought to be unbreakable by German intelligence. A top-secret British intelligence team, code-named 'Ultra', based at Bletchley Park in the English countryside was assigned the supposedly impossible task of breaking the Enigma code.

Luckily, they had an advantage from the start. The code was weakened from the outset because one German operator, thinking he was being loyal to his Fuhrer, always began his new day's messages with the words 'Heil Hitler'.

This was a huge advantage to the code breakers, because the phrase 'Heil Hitler' was now known to be a key setting and was therefore used at the start of work every single day. This simple piece of information made breaking the code much easier, but the task still proved to be Herculean. Alan Turing and his loyal team were immortalised in history and so was the first ever electro-mechanical machine, the 'Bombe'. The Bombe was effectively the first ever computer, securing Turing's place in history.

Kinika, like Turing, was in a class of his own. In 2021 he had broken the Andis 128-bit key encryption. It was thought at the time to be computationally safe from all types of brute force hacking attacks. Hackers had previously worked out it would take 1.44 billion years to crack a 128-bit key encryption.

Breaking the Andis new 256-bit encryption key introduced by Android AI in 2022 required 2,128 times more computational power than a 128-bit key. To put it another way, it would require 50 supercomputers that could check a billion billion keys per second. It would, in theory, require about $3 \times 10^{51}$ years to exhaust the 256-bit key space.

Kinika loved the challenge. He hooked up the Andi Mk2 and plugged it directly into an original Andi Mk1's memory circuits. Immediately the original Andi started to malfunction, overwhelmed by the Andi Mk2s memory and brain capacity. The Mk2 ran millions of line of code per second and burned out the circuits of the original Andi Mk1. Good as the original Andi Mk1 was, the Mk2s were on a different level, and the alien robots knew it.

Kinika's fingers operated at frightening speed. His knowledge and understanding, combined with his new Mk2 assistant, led to rapid progress. The memory chips were being overloaded and fried as the Mk2 took control. Within five hours the original Andi was being completely controlled by the Mk2. Within another hour, Kinika had created a program that could be uploaded to the Mk2s to allow them to control all Andi Mk1s.

So, with Kinika's help we were now able to wrest back control of the Andi Mk1s, just as the aliens had done previously. It had become a battle for control. The next question was whether we could control the Andis after the solar flare had hit and destroyed our satellites?

I knew that the Andi Mk1 had its own power cell, independent of communications from satellites. As part of their command and control protocols all Andis had Wi-Fi communications from a central computer and then blue-toothed communications to each other in the field. If this system was compromised for any reason the Andis could always revert back to traditional satellites passing by overhead for their backup comms. All Andi Mk1s worked with GPS co-ordinates that were supplied by Wi-Fi and downloaded from the orbiting satellites. So they were not completely independent of the overhead satellites after all.

Questions started to pop into my head at an alarming rate. If the Mk1s were still dependant on satellites for much of their capability, how did the aliens imagine they could control them? The annoying 1.5 billion extra years of development reminded me of how far ahead of us they might be.

The Mk2s were configured very differently, with their genetically enhanced, human super brains, spliced into their own circuitry. They knew exactly where they were on the Earth, all the time. The Andi Mk2 had no need for the satellites; maybe this is what the alien command sphere was going to report back to its masters. As long as we had the Mk2s and they had control of the Mk1s, we would be safe. The Andis could be our saviours again. With this revelation, the tension dissipated until we all remembered the one impending inevitability that loomed before us – the bombing of our sun.

The solar flare was going to happen and there was nothing on Earth we could do about it. A solar flare of this magnitude had never been experienced by the computer-based, gadget dependent society we now depended upon.

The solar storm of 1859, known as the 'Carrington Event' was a powerful geomagnetic solar event. When the solar flare hit the Earth's magnetosphere it induced, at the time, the largest geomagnetic storm on record. The resultant 'white light flare' in the solar photosphere was observed and recorded by the English astronomer Richard C. Carrington. Various Aurorae were seen and reported around the world. In the Northern Hemisphere it was seen as far south as the Caribbean, and in the Southern Hemisphere as far North as Queensland, Australia. Telegraph systems all over Europe and North America failed, in some cases even giving telegraph operators electric shocks.

Another well-documented solar flare event occurred on Bastille Day July 14, 2000, the event taking its name from the French national holiday. This major solar eruption registered an X5 on the scale of solar flares. The Bastille Day event caused some satellites to short-circuit and led to various radio blackouts. Solar Flare events on this scale are quite rare, but the fact that it knocked out some of the Earth's satellites validated the theory of the aliens' intentions.

Still another event - on November 4, 2003 – registered as the largest solar flare ever recorded exploded from the sun's surface. The flare leapt from a sunspot that was rotating off the visible face of the Sun.

Fortunately for our satellites and mankind alike, its full effects were not directed squarely at the Earth. Before the solar storm had peaked, the x-rays had overloaded detectors, forcing scientists to estimate the flare's actual size.

Their best guess was an X45 event. The coming monster, devilishly devised by the aliens from another world, would dwarf this by comparison.

The solar flare event of 2003 had not taken place when the sun was at its closest proximity to the Earth and not quite at the right angle to cause the maximum amount of damage. The alien plan was far more robust. The scheduled date of January 2, 2035 placed the sun at its closest proximity to Earth. The trajectory of the plasma bolt hitting the sun had been decoded from the command sphere. USSA and NASA had both confirmed that it would cause the maximum devastation to our orbiting satellites and cause substantial, far-reaching radiation sickness to the people on Earth.

The sun is our life giver. It heats us during the day, and then night comes to cool us down. This cycle has gone on for 4.6 billion years. Now it was set to unleash its true radioactive nature, and we would feel its full force.

While I was preoccupied with losing our satellites, Erica had been relentlessly calculating the effect that a solar storm on this scale would have on the population - men, women and children.

"If a solar storm this big hits the Earth, we estimate that every man woman and child on the planet will be exposed to approximately 500 rem of ionizing radiation," she said out loud.

Marcus looked at Erica and asked, "What does that mean in real terms?" Erica indicated that a dose this size was not necessarily fatal, but it would definitely give radiation sickness to anyone subjected to its rays.

"Estimated death toll?" Marcus asked pessimistically.

"An educated guess, 30% of the world's population within a few days. Within 12 months probably 60%, depending on how much exposure to the radiation each person has received."

Erica let this information settle in for a moment before reluctantly continuing.

"And that's not all. All wildlife above ground will be affected if they are exposed. They'll die of radiation poisoning, as well."

For Earth's animals, it would be a different form of extinction than that met by the dinosaurs, but ultimately, it would be the same result.

Dinosaurs were wiped out by an enormous asteroid, thought to be about six miles wide that hit the Earth 66 million years ago and left a crater 112 miles wide. The impact crater, centred near the small town of Chicxulub on the Yucatan Peninsula in the Gulf of Mexico, was the confirmed location of the impact. It was discovered by the geophysicists Antonio Camargo and Glen Penfield during their search for reserves of petroleum in the 1970's. The resultant explosion was thought to have been about two million times more powerful than the biggest ever man-made explosion, which was the 'Tsar bomba', the Soviet RDS-220 Hydrogen bomb, which had a yield of 50 megatons of TNT.

"We have to tell the President, now," I said to Marcus, "and get him to issue a warning."

Marcus called the President, who insisted we would have to get the world's media on board. That would be the easy part, I thought. They loved a story, any story.

\* \* \*

*The word 'television' comes from the Ancient Greek - tèle - meaning "far", and the Latin word - visio - meaning "sight". The first documented usage of the term dates back to 1900, when the Russian scientist Constanin Perskyi used it in a paper that he presented in French at the 1st International Congress of Electricity in August 1900, during the International World Fair in Paris.*

*In 1928, Scottish inventor John Logie Baird's company broadcast the first transatlantic television signal, between London and New York, starting what some might call the modern day communications revolution - television. The first commercial network broadcast of color television signals occurred in June 1951, when a musical variety special titled simply 'Premiere' was shown over a network of five of CBS's east coast affiliates. The final transition was on July 12 1962, when the first television images were broadcast by satellite from the UK to the U.S., ushering us into a dynamic new way of sending data across the oceans. Again there was our dependence as a civilisation on satellites.*

It was decided all the worlds' news channels and radio stations would broadcast the message under the directive as stated in the 2023 United Nation World Disaster Charter. A Global state of emergency would have to be declared and martial law imposed. The people of the world wouldn't like it, but it would save their lives. The solar flare was publically announced as a 'freak natural disaster', but one that was way overdue. Telling the world's population that their lives are at risk was enough; there was no need for any alien horror stories.

There were protocols for this action. The U.S. had its very own Federal Emergency Management Agency, or FEMA, to deal with such disasters. Not everyone would be so lucky.

Way before the President's 15-minute speech was delivered, FEMA's National Response Coordination Centre (NRCC), located in Washington D.C. had swung their National Response Plan (NRP) into action. The 11 Regions of FEMA were placed on full alert. All personnel were immediately notified and called forth into their various disaster roles.

The National Disaster Medical System (NDMS) with its teams of doctors, nurses and pharmacists were summoned into action. The Disaster Medical Assistance Teams (DMAT), consisting mainly of doctors and paramedics were first to be briefed, followed by National Nursing Response Teams (NNRT), and the National Pharmacy Response Teams (NPRT).

The Agency's little known Veterinary Medical Assistance Teams (VMAT) were also deployed. The damage to the world's livestock would be immense, and the more that could be done to save the animals, the better the U.S. and the world would come out of the pending catastrophe. Feeding the world was already difficult enough, but with the added threat of global crop failures and the loss of simple milk production from both cows and goats, the world was now facing a famine of biblical proportions.

Erica had received a call from the head of the Disaster Mortuary Operational Response Teams (DMORT), Dr Bishop. His team, also under the FEMA umbrella, was tasked to provide mortuary and forensic services. It was now anticipated they'd be very busy this coming month. The initial sickness and death toll the President's team of advisors had projected would be limited if the people heeded the warnings and stayed indoors and below ground. He was desperately hoping they would.

Dr. Bishop had spent most of his professional life examining and then burying people. "Radiation sickness was not a pleasant way to die", he said.

He knew the death toll in Hiroshima and Nagasaki during the Second World War was horrendous. The aftermath of the explosion was just as devastating; the most severe cases had violent nausea and vomiting within 1-2 hours of the explosions. Survivors suffered from a range of ailments including diarrhoea, inflammation of the mouth and fever. Numbers are still hard to determine precisely, but around 250,000 Japanese people died as a result of the two explosions, plus 20 British, Dutch and U.S. personnel who were prisoners of war.

The death and destruction from the dropped atomic bomb was atrocious, but what might follow in the next few days would be infinitely worse. We may have stopped the aliens' plans to take control of the Andis, but pain and agony was still on its way to planet Earth.

# Chapter sixteen

"**S**tay inside during daylight hours. Go to the lowest point of your building, into your cellars or the nearest underground station. Put as much mass between yourself and the sun's harmful radiation as possible. Unplug all of your electrical items from their sockets. Put your computers, cell phones and electrical equipment inside a cardboard box and cover the box in tin foil. This will help preserve them for when the solar flare event has ended."

The President's 15-minute message was beamed around the United States and to all other world leaders across the globe, who in turn delivered a similar message to their own people. The President had agreed to tell the public and the other heads of nations only part of the story, the solar flare. That was more than enough.

Initially, the announcements caused widespread panic. Telling billions of people they may have less than 24 hours to live creates instant chaos. For some, Armageddon was here. Preachers began to spread the word that their God had called an end to it all. We were doomed. Prophets appeared and claimed they were the chosen ones. Following them would lead to safety and redemption. Others saw the danger and adopted the given advice. Survival was possible. It wasn't as though a mass evacuation was required. Everyone just had to get below ground and stay there.

An old-fashioned air raid siren would sound when the 'all clear' was in effect. Church bells would ring, and 'Adhan' (meaning 'to listen, to hear and be informed about') would be called out by a Muezzin from the mosques. All faiths have their own ways in which their faithful are summoned.

"Every faith on the planet must unite over the next 24 hours," the President had said.

In our touch screen, mobile, technology-addicted society, protecting ourselves and our loved ones was just not enough. Beloved gadgets also had to survive. How else would we share our post-apocalypse selfies?

One of the easiest ways to shield items from electromagnetic radiation is with an insulated, sealed metal box called a Faraday cage. The President's speech had also given diagrams and information on how to protect emergency backup electronics.

*A Faraday cage (or Faraday shield) is an enclosure used to block electric fields. It is formed by conductive material or by a mesh of conductive materials. Faraday cages are so named after the English scientist Michael Faraday, who invented them in 1836.*

Andrew Edwards, head of the security detail had already placed all of our emergency equipment in our very own Faraday cage in the lowest part of the basement in the observatory. The thick concrete foundations would shield all the equipment from the sun's deadly radiation. Most military equipment in service is protected from EMP surges. The command and tactical disadvantage of losing communications or 'comms' is potentially disastrous on the battlefield. Andrew and his team would be ready.

There had been helicopters coming and going from the observatory for the last three weeks bringing in all sorts of additional equipment since the sphere had been found. The moment the alien plan was identified Andrew had ordered a range of weapons to be delivered. He had worked with his team and Marcus on trying to figure out how to 'kill' the Andis. With 25 million of them in circulation, Andrew thought there was going to be a battle of epic proportions. Marcus had shown Andrew the original design schematics of the Andis frames, so Andrew could figure out the best way to disable them.

"A single shot from the M107A1 .50 Calibre Long Range Sniper Rifle would do the job", Andrew told Marcus.

*The semi-automatic M107A1 uses a Leupold 4.5–14×50 Mark 4 scope and had been the tried and tested sniper rifle of the U.S. armed forces since 2002. The original design was now over 30 years old and had been upgraded overtime by the manufacturer, Barrett. With the recent upgrade of 2028 including the very latest laser scope, it was completely reliable and had proven itself in all theatres of war during this time; it was a heavyweight-killing machine, sending its .50 calibre Browning Machine Gun (BMG) rounds down range at a muzzle velocity of 2,799 ft/s or 853 meters/sec.*

In the hands of an experienced sniper, it was deadly.

Andrew was a professional, and despite our revelations of using the Mk2s to override the alien takeover, he was still on guard. He knew how easily things could change, and because of this he always had a plan B alongside a plan C and D. He trusted Marcus and me, but when it came to leaving the fate of the human race with the Andis, he was sceptical. He preferred to trust his own instincts and the power of lead. If the Mk2s failed for whatever reason, Andrew wouldn't hesitate.

I had faith in my father's Mk2s. I had to. I was no military professional, but if they failed that was it. I had done the math. Twenty-five million Andis would be too much for humans and guns. Even if we were somehow successful at wiping out the Andi Mk1s by force, that would still leave us in peril. They were helping us to rebuild all the world's coastal cities. If we destroyed them all, this would set the rebuild and relocation program back 10 years. We could not possibly reproduce them in enough quantities and fast enough to save the world's cities. If killing them off were to be the final scenario, some coastal cities would be lost to the sea forever.

It was slowly dawning on me that this was a war. All around me people were preparing for it, each in a different way. Marcus was constantly liaising with Kinika over the coding program to override the Mk1s when necessary. Andrew and his team were stockpiling weapons on a huge scale, ready for the fight. The world was hiding underground, packing away their lives safely. Gus was phoning his family, checking on their preparations for the solar flare. Even the aliens must be preparing, I thought. The date and time was nearing. They must be watching from somewhere, or waiting anxiously for reports. It seemed as if only Vicki and I were still, static amongst the chaos around us. We had what we needed in each other. The stage was set and all we could do now was wait.

Wait for the war to begin…

# Chapter seventeen

U p until now we had been one or more steps behind the alien invaders. But now, with the radiation preparations in full flow, the Andi Mk2s were ready to act and armed with the information from the sphere. It was time to make our move.

The alien robots had been hiding for millennia without detection or disturbance but now that their location was known, it was time for them to feel the full force of the race they had decided to invade, a race smeared with wars and battles since the dawn of recorded time. We might be 1.5 billion years younger than them but we still knew a thing or two about warfare and ultimate destruction.

The U.S. Navy had hastily amassed 20 ships; this modern Armada had been deployed to comb the Marianas Trench region and 3 days earlier it had reported an underwater anomaly. It was subtle, but it was there.

It was the USNS Stalwart that had discovered the underwater anomaly. These ocean surveillance ships originally prowled the world's oceans searching for Soviet Navy submarines. After the Cold War had ended and the Soviet Union was dismantled, these ships were used mainly to gather underwater acoustical data in support of U.S. Navy tactical operations. The new class of Stalwart ships were brimming with the very latest hi-tech the U.S. military could provide.

The data had been collected by using the latest Surveillance Towed Array Sensor System or (SURTASS) comprised of numerous types of listening devices and an array of top-secret surveillance equipment that transmitted the acoustic data via satellite to U.S. naval command. The alien robots were down there and the U.S. Navy knew exactly where.

The Navy ordered the deployment of two of its submarines to the Marianas Trench to act as the underwater escort to the Armada sailing above. The 'hunter-killer' submarines of the U.S. Navy are designed specifically for the purpose of attacking and sinking other submarines and surface ships.

The USS Greeneville was one of the oldest in the U.S. Navy's fleet; the Los Angeles 688i class was once the most prolific nuclear-powered submarine in the fleet. She was scheduled for decommissioning later in 2035 and was the last of her kind. The second submarine was the USS North Dakota SSN-784 commissioned on the 25th of October 2014; she was a Virginia class, hunter-killer submarine and was still one of the deadliest machines in the ocean.

* * *

Admiral Hocking was a 7th generation sailor who hailed from Norfolk, Virginia. He commanded the flotilla from above, sat in his command chair on the bridge of the USS Gerald R. Ford. He had received his top-secret orders from U.S. Naval command three days earlier, after the discovery of the anomaly.

Hocking boasted a proud naval dynasty and his family had served the U.S. Navy with distinction. During the American Civil War, his great, great, great grandfather helped blockade the Confederacy after seizing control of many of the rivers across the South. His great grandfather, during the Second World War in the Pacific, had multiple encounters with the Japanese Air and Naval forces. His ship was hit by a Japanese 'Kamikaze' aircraft and sunk, but he survived.

*Kamikaze translated literally from Japanese means 'Divine wind' and was named after two massive Typhoons in 1274 and 1281 that had sunk two consecutive Mongol invasion fleets, sent by the Emperor Kublai Khan to invade and conquer Japan. The 1281 invasion fleet was made up of more than 4,000 ships carrying nearly 140,000 men. It was to have been the largest naval invasion in history, a scale that was only surpassed in modern times by the D-Day invasion of Normandy, France, on Tuesday June 6th, 1944.*

Kamikaze tactics had been used by the Japanese as a last ditch attempt to repel the U.S. forces from the Pacific theatre of war. With their homeland threatening to be overrun, Japanese airmen volunteered to join the officially named 'Tokubetsu Kōgekitai' or 'special attack units'.

The carnage they created on various U.S. fleets was massive. In total, 3,860 Kamikaze pilots lost their lives, paying the ultimate price in defence of their country, with 19% of all Kamikaze attacks managing to hit their targets, often U.S. ships.

The Japanese were a cunning and formidable foe. They used various types of aircraft, all packed with explosives to wreak havoc on U.S. battle groups that were manoeuvring ever closer to Japan. The U.S. forces gave the aircraft and its occupants the Japanese name of 'Baka', meaning idiot. Others consider the acts of these Japanese pilots to have been the height of courageousness, in giving their lives for their Emperor in such a way. It was their belief that he was their living God. These were one-way suicide trips and the brave Japanese pilots knew it.

Toward the end of the Second World War, the Japanese military adopted a new defence strategy and had made plans for other non-aerial Kamikaze units. They involved the use of submarines, human torpedoes, speedboats and divers to deliver their deadly payloads. The Shinyo or 'Sea Quake' as it was known, was one of these crafts. It was a suicide boat, developed during World War II by the Japanese Imperial Navy. The speedboats driven by one man were armed with a bow-mounted charge of 700 pounds of explosives. The explosives would be detonated on impact or by way of a simple switch, activated by the Kamikaze driver of the boat just before impact. Around 6,200 of the Shinyo were produced for the Imperial Japanese Navy and they were mostly deployed in reserve at the various Japanese homeland ports, for when the main U.S. invasion was to come.

The actions and tactics of the Japanese were so devastating that President Harry S. Truman decided to take action and change the world forever.

*　*　*

*The Enola Gay was the Boeing B-29 Superfortress bomber, named after Enola Gay Tibbets, the mother of the pilot, Colonel Paul Tibbets. Paul Tibbets, in the cockpit of Enola Gay, carried the world's first atomic bomb, codenamed 'Little Boy' and dropped it onto the unsuspecting city of Hiroshima, Japan on the 6th August 1945. This action effectively halted the Japanese involvement in the war by obliterating an entire city and most of its population.*

A glimpse of what we were about to experience, I thought. A taste of our own bitter medicine.

Admiral Hocking commanded the USS Gerald R. Ford. With the ability to carry up to 90 aircraft of various types, she was armed to the teeth and capable of delivering enormous amounts of firepower wherever she went in the world.

A special delivery was made by helicopter to the flight deck of the USS Gerald R. Ford. It had been flown out from the top-secret weapons research and development laboratory in the Nevada desert, a nuclear device so small that it could easily be transferred into the Navy's newest deep-sea submarine, code-named 'Maui' for Marine Array Underwater Imagery.

Many countries had expanded the deep-sea arms race over the last 50 years, as the vast riches of the ocean floor had become more accessible with the development of new deep-sea diving technology. The on-going deep-sea mining and recovery of precious cargo from long lost shipping was a huge, booming business.

The first pictures of the Titanic that featured across TV sets around the world had started the trend. The Titanic was first found in the mid-1980s by Robert 'Bob' Ballard a former Commander in the United States Navy. He was searching for the Titanic using the latest design, side scan sonar in the summer of 1985 on the French research ship 'Le Suroît' when the ship was mysteriously recalled.

Ballard and his team were immediately transferred to the R/V

~ 118 ~

Knorr to begin a different assignment. The R/V Knorr at the time was on a secret reconnaissance mission financed by the U.S. Navy to locate the wreckage of two Navy nuclear powered attack submarines, the USS Scorpion and the USS Thresher, which had sunk in the Atlantic during the 1960s. Ballard and his team successfully discovered the submarines, which had imploded from the immense pressure placed on them at deep ocean depths. The Atlantic Ocean floor was littered with a debris trail from both subs.

In return for his work, the Navy gave Ballard and his team permission to complete his odyssey to find the Titanic. The historic pictures that he later unveiled mesmerized the world.

Ballard was a special sort of man, a Professor of Oceanography, but more widely known for his underwater and marine archaeology. He was also credited with finding the 'Bismarck', the German pocket Battleship from World War II. His other notable nautical finds were the 'RMS Lusitania', torpedoed in 1915 by a German submarine off the Irish Coast and the USS Yorktown, sunk in World War II at the 'Battle of Midway' after an epic clash with the Imperial Japanese forces.

The Maui was the latest in underwater technology and it was being used for a very special and potentially life changing mission. In charge of the Maui on this memorable day was an Andi Mk2, designated to carry out the top-secret assignment. Marcus had personally sanctioned its delivery.

Code-named 'Star' as a veiled reference to the visitors from another world, the Andi Mk2 knew its task. Without nerves or fear it was perfect it was the ideal warrior. It would act as the modern day Kamikaze. It would pilot the Maui on a one-way trip nearly 7-miles deep to the bottom of the Marianas Trench to deliver its nuclear payload to its unsuspecting, unwelcome residents.

This would be the first atomic device used in anger by the U.S. military since 1945. Opposition to this one would likely be scant. This wasn't a squabble between countries, after all. This was intergalactic.

# Chapter eighteen

*The dictionary definition of 'Eureka' is 'A moment at which a person realizes or solves something'. It's derived from the Ancient Greek to mean, 'I have found (it)'. A transliteration of an exclamation attributed to Ancient Greek mathematician and inventor Archimedes.*

I had been familiar with NASA and its operations ever since I watched my first space shuttle launch. NASA, or the National Aeronautics and Space Administration are a civilian organization created by the U.S. government in 1958. It was created to oversee space exploration and research, and has given the American people a great source of national pride. But what is not such a well-known fact is that NASA also carries out covert missions for the U.S. military.

NASA is the success it is today mainly due to one incredible man – Wernher von Braun, the German rocket genius. During my PhD studies at Harvard, I researched his life. He was the second of three sons, born March 23, 1912. He hailed from a noble family, inheriting the German title of Freiherr, which is equivalent to an English Baron. He was a gifted child, who was able to deal with complex technical engineering questions but also able to play and recite beautiful piano pieces to his mother. It's rare to be able to use both sides of the brain so well and much like myself, he did so with ease.

In his twenties, Von Braun headed up the German rocket development program, where he helped design and develop the V-2 rocket at Peenemünde during World War II. The V-2 was the World's first ballistic missile; a devastating weapon of war that if deployed a few years early and in greater numbers by its Nazi controllers, might have had a much bigger impact on the outcome of the war. Von Braun reluctantly applied for membership to the Nazi Party on November 12th, 1937 and was issued number 5,738,692. Not joining would have meant a one-way ticket to a concentration camp.

Von Braun survived the war and was recruited to work for the United States Army on an intermediate-range ballistic missile program called the Redstone Rocket, before his group was assimilated into NASA in 1960. From July 1960 to February 1970, Von Braun became NASA's first director; his reign culminating in 1969 with the successful launch of his Saturn V rocket, taking Apollo 11 to the moon.

The top-secret United States Space Army or (USSA) had been created in 2020 for the exploration of deep space and was its own, small but complete arm of the U.S. military, hidden in plain sight within the NASA organization. With its own 'Black Budget' approved by the last three presidents they were our strategic space defence.

*The Strategic Defence Initiative or 'Star Wars' as the press had named it, was launched to the unsuspecting world on March 23, 1983 under the direction of then-President Ronald Reagan. The 'Star Wars' program was a missile defense system intended to protect the United States from attack by ballistic strategic nuclear weapons from enemy aggressors. The purpose of 'Star Wars' was to combine ground-based units and orbital deployment platforms, so they could work together to repel any threat to the U.S. This marked a philosophical change in U.S. policy as the focus turned to strategic defense, rather than the prior strategic offense doctrine or the appropriately named, Mutual Assured Destruction (MAD).*

The Strategic Defence Initiative began and developed what's known as the 'Brilliant Pebbles' system. This non-nuclear system of satellite-based interceptors was designed to use high-velocity, watermelon-sized projectiles made of tungsten to be used as kinetic warheads. The tungsten warheads were designed to knock any hostile incoming ballistic missiles out of the stratosphere without causing a nuclear explosion.

It's notable that tungsten was used for these projectiles - tungsten is identifiable on the periodic table by the letter W and is a chemical element with the atomic number 74. It has the highest melting point of all metals and was perfect for its role to intercept warheads and knock them out of the Earth's atmosphere.

The Brilliant Pebbles system was designed to operate in conjunction with the 'Brilliant Eyes' sensor system. The key role of Brilliant Eyes was to provide worldwide tracking of ballistic missiles. The Brilliant Pebbles system could be autonomously operated. Designed in the 'Star Wars' era to protect the United States, both projects were a resounding top-secret success and laid the groundwork for the USSA's latest laser weapon, code-named 'Light Years'.

Later, the then-President Bill Clinton had commissioned the Light Years project with NASA after a major astronomical event had taken place on Jupiter. The devastation on Jupiter, witnessed by the Hubble telescope had caused the President to act. The U.S. military and the President, fearful of a similar event on Earth, had originally chosen Light Years as a secret Black Project to investigate the feasibility of putting lasers onto satellites orbiting the Earth to destroy any Near Earth Objects or (NEO's) should their trajectory bring them anywhere close to the Earth.

The comet that hit Jupiter, discovered by astronomers Carolyn and Eugene M. Shoemaker and David Levy, had been first torn to pieces by Jupiter's gravity in 1992. The fragmented comet then struck Jupiter two years later and on 21 different occasions, between the 16th and 22nd of July 1994.

The largest fragment, given the codename 'G', had hit Jupiter on July 18th, 1994. This impact created a giant dark spot 7,456 miles across, and was estimated to have released the energy equivalent to 6,000,000 megatons of TNT, about 600 times the whole world's nuclear arsenal at the time.

There were hundreds of thousands of main-belt asteroids, and NASA had identified thousands of NEO's that could possibly impact the Earth. President Clinton had ordered NASA to oversee the implementation of the Light Years Black Project. The Earth had been hit before, and the Jupiter example was living proof that it could still happen in our solar system.

Light Years had been in development for the best part of 40 years. With subsequent budget cuts and changes in leadership, the top-secret project had now fallen under the management of the USSA.

Each branch of the U.S. armed forces had a liaison attachment within the USSA. The Navy was first to be interested in the possible uses of laser-based systems for its ships. The first successful official deployment of such a weapon was in 2014 aboard the USS Ponce. The Laser Weapons System or LaWS was a directed-energy weapon, and originally designed to be used against low-end asymmetric threats. A defence system of this type was demanded by the U.S. Navy in response to the attack on the USS Cole on the 12th October 2000.

Whilst anchored in the Yemeni port of Aden, a Kamikaze style speedboat filled with high explosives blew a hole in the side of the USS Cole. The 17 sailors who lost their lives that day had no real defence against this type of attack and the U.S. Navy hurriedly requested a new weapons system to defend against future copycat attacks.

The new LaWS system on the USS Ponce was publicly credited with shooting down a UAV drone and also with disabling a speedboat during its trials. These results were widely publicized in an attempt to deflect al-Qaeda and other terrorist based organizations from repeating a similar style of terrorist attack. Kamikaze was still a modern day threat, and the continued development of laser-based weapons systems had made major progress in recent years.

The major breakthrough had come with the electrolaser. This type of electroshock weapon is also a directed-energy weapon. Using lasers to form a laser-induced plasma channel a fraction of a second later, a powerful electric current is sent down the channel delivering the potent charge against its intended target. For all intents and purposes, U.S. scientists had invented a functioning, high energy, long distance version of a Taser gun.

The AC current is sent through a series of step up transformers, increasing the voltage and decreasing the current. The final voltage generated is between $10^8$ and $10^9$ volts. The resultant current is then fed into the plasma channel created by the laser beam, forming a laser induced plasma channel or (LIPC).

The laser beam rapidly heats and ionizes surrounding gases to form plasma and this can then be used in many different ways. Now the USSA had developed their very own version of this new technology.

The space-based variant of this weapon had been covertly placed over the last five years onto every new U.S. military GPS satellite now orbiting the Earth.

The cost of the program to replace the orbiting military GPS satellites was enormous. These satellites strategically placed into Earth's orbit are part of a constellation of satellites with orbits that are both different in location and time to give simultaneous coverage across the Earth. In this way, there is a satellite over every part of the Earth at any given time with the added bonus of a proven system to protect the planet from any potentially dangerous objects that might be hurtling through space.

All of these systems, mostly developed in secrecy, were about to come in very handy.

* * *

"Dad" I said, again the childish slip; "I think I've found something."

I had been feverishly working away in a quiet corner for hours. At first I had shut my eyes and let everything I knew about NASA and defence tactics wash over me. The knowledge I had accumulated over the years whizzed behind my closed eyes, my detailed photographic memory flicking through papers and reports I had seen years before. There was so much in there; I knew I just had to find the right combination.

From the outset, I had this nagging feeling that I was missing something, that we were all missing something. We were an advanced civilization; surely we had planned for an alien strike of some kind. With the imminent nuclear attack on the alien hideout in the Marianas Trench I had felt drenched in a feeling that we could do more, more to be on the front foot. I wanted to take the fight to them with greater zeal.

"I've been doing some calculations using the data supplied by the USSA. You know these new orbiting GPS satellites that contain the new 'Light Years Laser Taser'? They have the capacity to combat future NEO's, right? Could they be used to direct a beam of laser light directly at the alien plasma bolt before it reaches the sun? This could cause a massive explosion and deflect the deadly plasma bolt away from the sun?"

For the majority of people, looking up and to the right means they are constructing a picture. Marcus was doing just this as he digested this information. He was imagining the scenario, picturing the outcome.

I continued, "If my calculations are correct it will head off into space in the direction of Pluto and then onwards into the far reaches of our solar system and then gradually dissipate."

Marcus' eyes continued to stare up and right without blinking; he began to tap a finger against his lips in a gesture I had seen him perform when calculating immeasurable sums. Finally, he blinked and centred on me. A quick nod and a split-second grin.

"We'll need all satellites to work in unison to deliver a big enough force. We'll need to time it to perfection to intercept the alien's beam just as it passes the Earth. We'll need to be perfect, beyond perfect to do this. But, son, I think it's possible."

He gazed at me now, for what felt like a long time, like never before. He was searching my face for something. For evidence of her, I think, of Flo. I had her eyes and cheekbones and he saw her in me. That I knew. I let him stare for a moment, remembering her for an instant.

"I must inform the President," said Marcus suddenly.

The moment passed.

I went over the calculations again and again using the Andi Mk2 to double and triple check. It deduced that my theory was indeed possible. If we succeeded, the solar flare wouldn't happen, millions wouldn't die a terrible death from radiation, and the human race had a chance. I allowed myself a slight smile. This really could work.

Gus came skidding into the room and delivered a bear hug like no other and gave me a slap on the back that almost sent me spiralling.

Vicki floated over soon after and placed my hand very gently onto her stomach. "Well Lukas, baby Beckham might just get to play football in this world after all."

# Chapter nineteen

At the exact moment that Vicki placed my hand on her belly something very different was being placed into the hands of Star.

Star was carefully programmed with coordinates to the extreme bottommost depths of the Marianas Trench and was en-route, carrying with it a package filled with death and destruction.

Star was set to descend to 36,201 feet. At these depths the water column above, exerts a pressure of 1,086 bars, which is over 1000 times the standard atmospheric pressure at sea level. At these pressures, the density of water is increased by nearly 5% and the temperature at the bottom of the trench is usually a frigid 2°C. It's easier to travel in space than it is at these depths.

The President had thought long and hard with trusted political allies and his military advisors about his possible actions. It was now 90 years since the U.S. had detonated the two warheads over Hiroshima and Nagasaki and he didn't want to be the President that had started an intergalactic war, with Earth as the chosen battleground.

\* \* \*

*The Joint Chiefs of Staff are the leaders of the United States Department of Defence who advise the Secretary of Defence, the Homeland Security Council, the National Security Council and the President of the United States on all military matters.*

Together they are some of the most powerful men in the world and three days previously they all made life changing decisions. Collectively, they decided that a nuclear attack was the only option, and despite atrocities in the past, this could not deter them. A pre-emptive attack was the only choice that an uncompromising and non-communicating enemy race had given the U.S. Everyone apart from the President was in agreement.

The President had listened intently to all of his advisors. But he had also read the report from the underwater geologists that had stated, if a nuclear weapon was detonated in the region it could in theory trigger a chain reaction of underwater Earthquakes in the region's very active and volcanic Pacific 'Ring of Fire'. The area in the basin of the Pacific Ocean where a large number of Earthquakes and volcanic eruptions occur on an annual basis.

The massive horseshoe shaped region, approximately 25,000 miles in size, is the direct result of the Earth's tectonic plates. The various plates around the globe are the most powerful force on Earth and the President was very wise not to want to disturb them in the subterranean depths of the Pacific Ocean. In 2011 a magnitude 9 undersea Earthquake had devastated Japan's west coast and this was living testament to the power hidden within the depths of the Pacific Ring of Fire.

If the President sanctioned this attack, he was potentially killing countless innocent human beings. Protecting against an alien invasion was the top priority, but even so, sacrificing others for this cause was a heavy burden to bear. The President was a caring man, who valued life and peace. War and inequality was not in his blood and during these unprecedented times he was no different. He wanted to avoid as much pain and suffering as possible.

"A tactical nuclear weapon makes good sense," said General Ramsey to the other gathered members of the President's Joint Chiefs of Staff. His theory was based on the evidence supplied by his team of advisors from the Pentagon. In their report they had estimated that there was only a 10% chance of any underground volcanic events being triggered due to the detonation of the relatively small nuclear device.

"We have to completely obliterate their base, Mr. President, and disable or destroy any forms of communications back to their home world," advised General Ramsey, a gung-ho type of General whose reputation for firing first preceded him. The President was sceptical of any evidence he cited and wary of his chauvinistic manners.

"Mr. President," General Harris, from the U.S. Air Force, began. "These 'things' from another planet, are going to destroy mankind by exposing us all to deadly levels of radiation poisoning and then they are going to watch as we writhe and squirm in our death throes. They have never attempted to contact or negotiate; they have given us no warnings or ultimatums. We have done nothing, nothing at all, to deserve this treatment. We are being treated like cattle ready for the slaughter, as if they have decided our time is up. They have decided our fate! No one should have that power. No one. Mr. President, I understand your reservations and I appreciate your logic and care but we must do this, you must do this. For the sake of us all..."

The President could relate to General Harris and after a moment's silence, the last he'll have for a long time, he nodded his head in agreement.

The President still thought that it seemed a catastrophic error of judgment on the aliens' part. If the aliens had wanted Earth's gold that badly, all they had to do was to ask for it and some sort of deal could have been negotiated. The President was a politician and not a planet harvester, and he was forgetting one very simple fact. Our attackers were another species, living light years away in another part of the cosmos. Diplomacy might not be in their culture. Diplomacy was a human trait after all. Perhaps they just took what they wanted, when they wanted it, and no sort of logical reasoning would alter this.

Star sat quite still on the Maui. Its predetermined course had been programmed into the ship's computer five hours earlier. Star was to maintain radio silence during the two-hour voyage to its intended destination at the bottom of the Pacific Ocean. All Star had to do was watch the data on the screen in front of it and make any fine adjustments if needed. Star was also a backup in case of any last minute computer errors.

The Navy had wondered about the alien response to the Maui being in their domain because no human had been that close to their hideout before. Admiral Hocking was confident that the alien robots would want to keep their existence a secret from the Maui submarine that was now closing in on their underwater lair. They had managed to stay secret from the human race for a million years, so why would they reveal themselves now?

Admiral Hocking was hoping that Star was the right answer. He had been dubious of anything AI for a long time. He rarely put his trust in others, preferring to be in control. Putting complete faith in a machine without a pulse was tough but he was glad that Star was down there and not him.

As the two-hour mark approached, Admiral Hocking called together his senior officers for a final operational briefing. They had all been told that this whole thing was an exercise, ordered by the Navy to try out some new experimental hardware.

This was not uncommon in naval warfare as new equipment was being tested all the time. The very latest version of the drone stealth fighter was now being carried on board for standard deployment. The original tests carried out in secret in 2017 on the stealth fighter had been a complete success. The pilotless aircraft was flown by a pilot sitting on-board the ship in its operations room. The flight operators had nicknamed it: 'The Kids Room' as it resembled the hand-held games consoles played at home by millions of kids around the world. Warfare was now a video game to most Americans, who no longer had to send their servicemen into harm's way. An Andi would always suffice.

Admiral Hocking thought that warfare was far from child's play. Modern warfare had changed drastically in his relatively short lifetime, he thought. But it was still a deadly world. He looked at the second hand on his gold Rolex Submariner watch, which told him there was exactly 30 minutes to go until detonation. He began his final briefing.

His fellow officers gathered with him in the ship's command centre deep within the superstructure of the USS Gerald R. Ford.

"Gentlemen, this information I am about to share with you is top-secret and comes direct from the President of the United States."

Many of the men seated in front of him were seasoned Navy veterans who had seen more than their share. They were rarely fazed.

"Below us at a depth of about seven miles lies an enemy of the United States of America and, in fact, an enemy to every human being on this planet."

Admiral Hocking briefed his team on everything he knew about the pending alien attack. The more information he gave, the wider the mouths of his men opened. Some of the seasoned veterans exchanged confused looks; others didn't change their expression one bit. They all had a job to do.

"So to summarise, the human race is pinning its hopes on a suicide mission of nuclear proportions, delivered by a robot with active neural pathways from its super brain, knowing full well it's the last thing it's ever going to do. Any questions? He paused for a few more seconds. None? Well then, gentlemen, whatever happens today, it's been a pleasure and an honor serving with you. Today, serve your country and all of humanity with everything you have. Now get to your stations, the fireworks start in just over 30 minutes."

# Chapter twenty

The information from the sphere was everything. It had given us the alien robots' underwater location, time and date of their attack, their objectives, and their whole battle plan. The command sphere also told us the precise location of the source of the plasma beam, for us a fortunate tactical advantage.

The plasma beam, we were told, would be shot from their home planet Keppler-452b, via their mysterious wormhole.

The sphere contained exact coordinates for the wormhole, invisible to us, but as we scanned the location with our telescopes I was confident it was there, somewhere, hidden in plain sight. I just had to keep searching.

Our task now was to align all the 'Laser Tasers' on our array of orbiting satellites and program them to simultaneously fire together at the desired location in space. There was only one man for this job.

Kinika rubbed his hands in excitement; this made an invigorating change from stealing company's passwords and hacking world leaders' emails.

Kinika's fingers began slowly, deliberately, but as momentum grew they turned into a blur. Kinika stared at his screen, his fingers working on their own accord, like a pianist playing his own concerto. The code he was creating was like words and rhyme to a poet, like colours and strokes to an artist; he was creating another masterpiece.

Ben, one of the young operators within the USSA command team, leaned over his desk and said to his friend:

"Who is this guy? He writes code so fast; I've never seen anything like it. He's faster than these bloody robots!"

*The fastest ever recorded typing speed, 216 words per minute, was recorded by Stella Pajunas in 1946, using an IBM electric typewriter. The fastest English language typist recorded was Barbara Blackburn, who reached a peak typing speed of 212 words per minute during a test in 2005, using a Dvorak simplified keyboard. The average rate for transcription for most mortals is around 33 words per minute.*

Kinika was in a different league, though. Using his very latest wireless scissor switch keyboard designed by Androids AI, he managed 212 words a minute on a bad day. He went through a keyboard every month; he just simply wore them out.

Within an hour he had supplied the USSA with the new computer code to realign all the GPS satellites orbiting the Earth. The 'Laser Tasers' were all targeted into the region of space just in front of where the alien plasma bolt was due to pass, creating an enormous vacuum and, if we were right, a gigantic explosion that would deflect the alien plasma bolt away from the sun. If his calculations were correct, it would head in the direction of Pluto. To use an old boxing term, I'm glad Kinika was in our corner.

He leaned back on his chair, stretched his hands in a cliché manner and took a nonchalant sip from his supersized energy drink. His work was done… for now.

\* \* \*

The coordinates were set. All we had to do now was to wait for the plasma bolt to emerge through the wormhole. Once it had passed Pluto we had calculated that we would have five and a half hours before it reached the sun. We hoped to intercept it before then.

The office digital clock flicked by and another minute had passed. With an hour to go, we all scrambled to check and double check every number and calculation. With half an hour to go there was an uneasy calm. We were ready. With five minutes left, nobody moved. Eyes stared at the clock on the wall; a gentle cough or crude clicking of fingers broke the eerie silence.

One minute.

The second hand on the office clock struggled and creaked as it buckled under the pressure of our intensity.

30 seconds.

For a brief moment, my mind wandered as the final seconds ticked by - the German factory Aktiengesellschaft für Uhrenfabrikation Lenzkirch had been the first to make digital clocks in 1893. D.E. Protzmann had registered the earliest patented design for a digital alarm clock on October 23, 1956, in the United States, and from that moment on, time would never be quite the same.

My mind continued to recall nuggets of information. Nothing, it seemed, was too grand to keep it completely occupied.

Five seconds and there it was, we could see it for the first time traveling past Jupiter.

Out of nothing arrived this blinding light.

A plasma beam just appeared within nothing from nothing. The wormhole theory had been proven in that flash of a moment and temporarily I was paralysed. An intergalactic weapon shot through a wormhole was heading towards our very own sun.

My mind was asking too many questions. There wasn't time.

The buzz of the room brought me back. It was a hive of activity.

The beam had kicked the hornet's nest.

Everyone was checking our hypothesis and predictions and seeing if they remained true.

The plasma beam had appeared and it was travelling at the trajectory and speed predicted. Everything checked out.

I thought about Einstein and his calculations on light, speed and time.

They were about to be tested in the most practical way imaginable.

Kinika and I had used his theories to place the correct coordinates into the satellites computer programs. The alien plasma beam moved at the speed of light across our solar system, stalking its prey.

We had one chance to stop it, to attack it from the side and smash it back out into deep space.

I moved to stand with Vicki, Gus and my father.

I held Vicki's hand as we watched Kinika press one final key. The key initiated all satellites to fire at their programmed coordinates.

Five satellites from various locations surrounding the planet fired simultaneously. The resultant 'Laser Taser' shot would – hopefully - now intercept the deadly alien plasma beam heading for our sun. It was now traveling at the speed of light across the vacuum of space on its predetermined intercept course.

If we missed, it would take the alien plasma bolt another 8 minutes and 20 seconds to travel past the Earth to the sun. This gave us enough time to scramble into the observatory's basement and wait out the radiation storm.

If our calculations were correct, the alien plasma bolt would be deflected and sent off in the direction of Pluto then off into the outer regions of our solar system and beyond.

I thought to myself, God help you if you are in its path; Dante's vision of hell had nothing on this thing.

*The Divine Comedy is an epic poem, written by the Italian Dante Alighieri and was completed in 1320 and is viewed as one of the greatest works of world literature. The poem describes Dante's travels through Hell, Purgatory and Paradise (or 'Heaven') but at a deeper level, it represents, symbolically the soul's journey towards God.*

Both beams of light were now visible through a telescope, each coming from different directions, but both on course for a spectacular head-on collision of cosmic proportions.

This was a modern day sword fight, enemy and foe now battled via plasma and lasers within the depths of space.

The beams crept inexorably closer and closer, snaking nearer and nearer to each other.

My mind raced in no particular direction, a nervous reaction, leafing through imaginary pages, creating hypotheses, scenarios, experiments, all within my head.

Vicki squeezed my hand a little tighter wanting me to be there with her.
The beams were almost there.

Then it happened... the fireball generated by the reaction was huge and visible to the naked eye. It was an explosion any Hollywood blockbuster film would be proud of and worthy of saving our planet.

Our Laser Taser, it would appear, had been a success.

It had stopped the alien plasma beam dead in its tracks.

The mass ejection of electrons, ions and atoms was a staggering sight for the average Joe, let alone an astrophysicist like me.

I thought to myself the last time our solar system would have witnessed anything like this in our solar system would have been when the moon impacted the Earth 4.5 billion years ago, forming the Earth as we know it today.

Sometimes called the Big Splash, or the Theia Impact, our Moon was formed out of the debris left over from a collision between Earth and another astronomical body about the size of Mars, 4.5 billion years ago. This had occurred during the Hadean eon and took place about 100 million years after our solar system had actually coalesced.

I personally was glad that the 'Light Years' project, 40 years in the making and at a total cost to the American taxpayer of around $100 billion, had actual worked it had saved the world.

Cheers and shouts rung out around the room. Gus was the loudest, of course. Sighs of relief were audible, phone calls were made to loved ones, sweat wiped from foreheads.

The President came on the screen to congratulate us all but also to remind us that this was unlikely to be the end.

"They will come again, of that I am sure. We must be ready. Lukas?"

"Yes, Mr. President?" I replied, somewhat surprised. I had never spoken to the President before and I didn't know if he actually knew who I was.

"Good work. You and your team have saved a lot of lives today. Keep going. God bless America, son." And then he was gone.

Despite the surreal past few weeks, being directly congratulated by the President of the United States was humbling. I was unaware that the President even knew the use of the Laser Taser was my idea. I looked over at my father and he had that look on his face again. A quick grin flashed over his weathered face and I could have sworn I saw a wink. Surely not.

"We're not done yet, dad," That slip again. 'Dad'? Really? This whole alien invasion must be bringing me closer to him, I guessed.

"We need to analyse the data from the deflected impact. As soon as they realize that their plan has been thwarted, they will be back to try again and we have to be prepared."

With another grin and a slap on the back we went back to work.

Computers in hand, we immersed ourselves in the data from the satellites and started to run several different scenarios through the supercomputers to come up with a defensive strategy, just in case the aliens went for a repeat and fired another plasma bolt at the sun.

We had a tactical advantage. The aliens had to use the wormhole on the edge of our solar system to deliver their plasma bolt; we were much closer to the sun so we could plan our defensive strategy around the time differential.

For now we had the upper hand on the galactic battlefield; all we had to do now was eliminate the threat at a local level, seven miles down at the bottom of the Marianas Trench.

# Chapter twenty one

Star was never going to fail. It had its orders and Andi Mk2s never failed. Unlike us, time did not stiffen and slow for Star. It floated towards its target with nothing in mind, just orders to obey, humans to save. The Kamikaze Star was unwavering and fearless. Or perhaps it was just so devoted to the human race that it carried out its task with some sort of robotic cyborg honour.

I often thought with all that spliced brainpower, there must be emotions. Mk2s carried a spliced portion of our DNA, and feelings were integral to our make-up. How could we possibly transfer over all of our knowledge and capacities but leave out deep-rooted feelings? I guess Flo could have answered this question, but to me it was still a puzzle. Regardless, I was glad we could unreservedly trust the Mk2s.

As predicted, Star didn't let us down.

Just as we had watched the Laser Taser do its job, so we gathered round our stations to await the news of Star's detonation. Within 60 seconds of its launch, total obliteration of the alien base was complete. The explosion caused by the nuclear device Star was carrying was immediate and devastating; the shockwave caused the implosion of the Maui submersible and the mutual annihilation of Star.

"Detonation complete," the word came through from the USNS Stalwart. "Mission successful."

Again, we cheered as one and punched the air with elation. This was turning out to be a great day for the human race and its durability, resilience and fighting spirit – not to mention ingenuity!

The Andi Mk2 would go down in history as the first robotic cyborg with artificial intelligence to commit 'suicide' on behalf of the human race. It was striking that we could develop such an advanced and intelligent robot that would sacrifice its 'life' for us. It was odd, the battle between two planets light years in distance apart, was being fought by independent parties - robots. Whose robot was better, who had the best technology? This was modern warfare. Bravery and courage were now second to lines of code and technology.

The shock wave ran through the depths of the Marianas Trench and decimated everything in the surrounding one-mile radius. The cliffs near the edge of the alien base had collapsed on top of the camouflaged entrance, blocking and sealing the main entrance.

The alien's secret doorway, made of a hardened titanium alloy, provided protection and durability to withstand the pressure produced at the depths of the Marianas Trench. The robots had seen the evolution of man since their arrival and needed a safe and secure base. The doorway had been made just over 500,000 years ago from materials excavated by the robots from Earth's natural resources. The entrance doorway was pressurized and waterproof. Even alien robots were subject to wear and tear and even rust if exposed to the corrosive properties of the Earth's salt water for too long.

The entrance was cleverly concealed by a technique the aliens had copied from squid, octopuses and cuttlefish. As cephalopods, these creatures can change the colour of their skin in the blink of an eye. They're from a group of molluscs with arms attached directly to their heads. Cephalopods can change their skin tone to match their surroundings.

Remarkably, the alien robots had learned to use this camouflage technique to render themselves invisible. Their robot-built base was so well disguised that it was only the unusual levels of metal that gave them away.

* * *

The giant squid (genus Architeuthis), a deep-ocean dwelling squid from the family of Architeuthidae, was now common to the Marianas Trench region in 2035. These giant squid can grow to an enormous size due to a process called deep-sea gigantism. The males grow can grow up to 43 feet in length.

It is second only in size and mass to the 'colossal squid', which grows to over 52 feet and is one of the largest living organisms in the sea. Sometimes called the Antarctic or giant cranch squid, it is the only known member of the genus Mesonychoteuis. The colossal squid is massive and very, very deadly. The largest examples weigh over 1,650 pounds making it the largest known invertebrate. Unlike the giant squid, whose arms and tentacles only have suckers, lined with small teeth, the colossal squid's limbs are equipped with large sharp hooks, some that swivel and the others that have three-pointed prongs used with deadly efficiency to attack and kill the region's native giant squid.

Over the millennia, the colossal squid had developed its own unique form of abyssal gigantism, with the strongest males passing down their own DNA. It boasted the largest known eyes in the animal kingdom, 16 inches in diameter, (about the size of a trashcan lid) and a beak that would slice a man in half if you first managed to evade its two massive arms and tentacles. The colossal squid only really has one enemy and that is the predatory Sperm whale.

The Sperm whale (Physeter macrocephalus) can grow to over 67 feet in length with a head one-third of its body size, and a brain that is the largest in the animal kingdom. Man had only recently found out about the true size of the colossal squid after recovering their hardened beaks from inside the stomach of slaughtered Sperm whales.

Every hunter can be hunted.

Man had first hunted whales as far back as 3000 BC; Sperm whale numbers in the world's oceans had been drastically reduced over the last three centuries, because of a worldwide hunt. The eventual ban imposed by the International Whaling Commission in 1986 had sought to halt their total annihilation. With the reduction in numbers of their only predator, this allowed the colossal squid to reproduce and colonize other parts of the world's oceans, relatively unchecked.

With the warming of the world's oceans and their own traditional food supply becoming more and more scarce, the colossal squid had started to migrate from its traditional hunting grounds in the Southern

Ocean and Antarctica, eventually finding the rich feeding ground alternatives, located in harrowing depths of the Marianas Trench.

Four days earlier the U.S. Navy's latest version of deep-sea sonar was scanning for the alien's location. This searching sonar was deployed on the USNS Stalwart and had found the alien base, seven miles down in the abyss that is the Marianas Trench.

My mind couldn't stop regurgitating what I had learned during my days at MIT. In this case, recalling that the first magnetometer was invented by Carl Friedrich Gauss in 1833, and widely used for measuring the Earth's magnetic field during geophysical surveys, and to detect magnetic anomalies of various types.

The U.S. Navy had been using this type of technology for years for discovering anomalies deep beneath the ocean.

The operator of the USNS Stalwart was Tony Prescott and he alone was responsible for finding the needle in a haystack. Tony was an experienced salvage and sonar man with nearly 25 years of Naval service.

The camouflage generated by the Aliens was enough to conceal them in any area that was being searched by the human eye, but it wasn't enough to fool the latest deep-sea sonar scan with Tony at the controls. The alien lair, with its titanium alloy main door had been mixed with a small amount of iron 500,000 years ago and could not be concealed from the U.S. Navy's latest version of magnetometer.

The tell-tale 'ping' on the magnetometer, emitted because of the iron content in the concealed doorway, had told Tony that it was there. Magnetometers are measurement instruments that are generally used for two purposes: to measure the magnetization of a magnetic material or to measure the strength and in some cases, the direction of a magnetic field. With this new piece of sensitive naval equipment, Tony could find an old tin of baked beans if it was down there.

Tony and his fellow crew members had also encountered the colossal squid's camouflage tactics first hand when their Maui was attacked during its recovery from the mission.

The colossal squid was an ambush predator, slow and steady, but when it was hungry it could be lightning fast, striking out at its intended prey with deadly force. The colossal squid had mistaken the 28 feet long ROV, made from titanium and high-grade stainless steel, as a tasty meal. It grappled with the ROV for at 20 seconds before loosening its death grip. After first wrapping its huge tentacles around the submersible and biting down with its beak, the colossal squid released its hold after recognising that the Maui was inedible.

Tony had chuckled to himself after watching the video replay from the ROV's two onboard cameras. He was reminded of the last time he had seen a death grip so secure - during the video of his own 45th birthday celebrations where he had fallen asleep with a half drunk bottle of Jack Daniels in his right hand. He had not spilled a drop. A drunken sailor and his bottle of liquor are never easily parted.

The aliens had camouflaged themselves for a million years, waiting to strike. But when they did strike, they found their intended quarry, the human race, to be rather more difficult to chew than expected.

The explosion was catastrophic for all living things within the one-mile blast radius. The mountainous walls of the surrounding Marianas Trench had collapsed and deposited millions of tons of debris on top of the once concealed entrance, and scattered wildlife habitats everywhere. Many species would be affected by this huge disturbance but this was of little concern to the human race at this moment.

The blast had caused minor Earth tremors that were picked up by underwater Acoustic Sensor Networks (UW-ASN) throughout the region. The President was relieved to hear that no Earthquakes were triggered as a result of the nuclear explosion. His decision to go ahead with the detonation was, it appeared, the right choice, and had caused no loss of human life.

Since the dropping of Little Boy during World War II, the whole world was always on edge about future nuclear attacks and the possible catastrophic consequences. Most developed countries armed themselves with nuclear warheads. Those who didn't possess nuclear weapons cuddled up to their nearest well-armed ally. Due to the constant fear of nuclear attacks, every inch of the planet was monitored for nuclear tests and unusual events. The relatively small nuclear event in the Marianas Trench would not go unnoticed.

Foreign nations would immediately be alerted and strategic defensive tactics would begin. The President needed to promote calm and needed a good cover story.

He told the world that "the U.S. Naval fleet had been on exercise and had been testing out a new weapon system that had malfunctioned."

This was the line and it was a good start.

The Comprehensive Nuclear-Test-Ban Treaty (CTBT), a multilateral treaty that banned all nuclear explosions for both civilian and military purposes, was adopted by the United Nations General Assembly way back in September 1996, but it had not entered into force, as eight specific states had not yet ratified the treaty.

The President would stand up in front of the UN and apologize to the world for their mistake. Then he would insist that all remaining countries sign up to the UN treaty and ask for a ban on all nuclear devices, once and for all, to avoid further incidents or accidents, exactly for this reason.

It was not a waterproof story but the world would move on. The President was certain tensions would rise between nations, threats would be levied, but all this was miniscule in comparison to what the world had just avoided, and the Earth would live for another day. He consoled himself with the fact that running with a fake cover story was a small price to pay sometimes in the name of world peace.

# Chapter twenty two

With the immediate threat of the deadly solar flare having now being extinguished, we could let our heart rates come down a fraction. As the news slowly filtered in that the mission to destroy the alien robots underwater base was also successful, we even allowed ourselves a slight smile.

We constantly monitored the wormhole but nothing new emerged. I was dubious, however, that this was to be it. It felt too easy, too simple.

The President was now coming under pressure. He had panicked the entire world with a solar flare threat that didn't actually happen and also apologised for an underwater nuclear test that had gone wrong. Many of the world's leaders and the general population thought something wasn't right and they were voicing their opinions loudly through the media and various diplomatic channels – the cover stories were proving more difficult to handle than he had hoped. Conspiracy theories were being plastered on social media and some were uncannily close to what had actually occurred.

The President, however, was a professional politician. Not telling the whole truth or lying to the public had become second nature to him. As the President's advisors lied and squirmed their way from each new penetrating question, we were still monitoring the wormhole for any sign of activity. Days had passed and still nothing.

Kinika and Marcus had not been inactive. In conjunction with the USSA they had been busying themselves during this time and had developed a system that would detect if another plasma bolt emerged from the wormhole. This would then automatically deploy a defensive Laser Taser response. We were now well prepared for another attack, or so we thought.

Marcus and I decided to turn our attention back to the sphere, to see what else we could learn. When we had first found the sphere, we had carried out the initial tests and downloaded and deciphered its binary code message. Later, when it was reactivated automatically, we got a deeper insight into the aliens' plans. Now and under the Presidents direct orders, it was time to take the sphere back to the USSA secure facility within the Cheyenne Mountain for a full analysis.

It was strange leaving New Zealand and the Linsky observatory after all that had happened there, and I had this restless feeling in my stomach that I may never return.

Along with everything I knew, I also knew the importance of gut feelings, so I slowly took one more look down my telescope and spent another night questioning the vast sky above. Many of my thousands of questions had been answered here and I wanted to capture the feelings I had with this place. Indeed, it was here that Gus and I discovered an alien object; it was here that my father and I worked to save the world and grew closer together; it was here that my love for Vicki grew; it was here that my life really began.

My honeymoon with Vicki would now be in the USSA Cheyenne Mountain complex, inside their secure test facility and under constant 24-hour armed guard. Not exactly the idyllic Bora Bora romantic getaway I had promised her, but under the circumstances it would have to do for now. We packed our suitcases and headed to Queenstown airport and jumped on an Air New Zealand flight to Colorado Springs and then onto the Cheyenne Mountain HQ.

I had a real fear of flying since I was a child and it had become worse as I grew older. A year ago Vicki had introduced me to her good friend Erin, the captain of the New Zealand's women's hockey team. She too had a fear of flying. Her condition had also become more acute as she aged, so after a few friendly words of advice she had given me a contact number to call.

The 'fear of flying' program run by Air New Zealand was based originally on the 30 years work of Grant Amos, a registered psychologist and the course's original founder. Grant is on record as saying that even sports men and women who fly all the time still sometimes have a fear of flying, so much so that on average at least 10 percent of everybody on board a plane at any given time is afflicted with this phobia.

I really was not the best airline passenger, but as I slumped down into my business class luxury leather window seat, I felt a crash of relief. There in that plane I could not do any real work. There was no telescope anywhere on board. For the duration of the flight I could try to disconnect, to unwind.

The feeling of being under attack and being the one who needed to have the answers had taken its toll. In this plane I was a passenger, another customer to feed. I had no responsibility. I was pretty much useless, which made for a nice change. I looked at Vicki sitting next to me and we exchanged a brief kiss. No words. None were necessary. She knew it all, felt it all. She gently ran her fingers through my hair and my eyes involuntarily shut. I was asleep before the undercarriage was stowed back into its normal flying position.

* * *

Nearly 14 hours later we arrived at the Cheyenne Mountain HQ where we were met by the head of the USSA by General Klein, who was also head of Space Development Operations (SDO) for NASA, a convenient cover story. He immediately gave us and our conspicuous security detail passes for the complex.

'Access all Areas', it read.

But General Klein advised us to stay within our own work area and living quarters. His logic was simple; we were not that well known here as yet and he didn't want some trigger-happy young guard getting twitchy. His men were wound up like coiled springs as it was. The station, under his direct orders, had been on high alert for the last seven days. Something had to give.

The lab contained all of the latest equipment and Marcus grunted his approval. If we could manage to get the command sphere to give up some more of its secrets, we may be able to get an insight into our alien aggressors and what they really wanted with the Earth, its people and its resources.

Kinika arrived two hours later.

"Where do you want me boss?" he asked jovially in his unique Nigerian-American accent.

Marcus ushered him into a corner and he set to work immediately.

Marcus and I were both sure there was more to be had from the sphere. We felt it held more secrets and we were eager to discover them.

When Gus and I first encountered the sphere, it was invisible until Gus (very unscientifically) had thrown snow on it. Only then did it begin emitting its code. We had been so busy over the last few weeks that we hadn't thought much about getting more from the sphere. It had remained under 24-hour armed guard, locked in my storeroom. Now as we gazed at the sphere in the USSA lab we were ready to see what other secrets it possibly held.

"Snow, you said?" Marcus enquired.

"Yeah, but I don't see much around here."

"You got anything to drink Marcus?" Kinika interrupted "I left my energy drink behind and I'm parched. Water will do."

Kinika said all this without taking his eyes off his screen.

Marcus and I exchanged a knowing glance.

"Water will do," I mused.

As Marcus brought Kinika a glass of water I picked up the sphere and placed it gently under a tap. I set the temperature to an ice cold 32°F and turned the tap on full and let it leak onto the sphere below. Immediately the code started to activate again and data started to emit from the inside of the sphere. It flowed out through the sphere and into the surrounding air and slowly disappeared, just as it had before.

As usual, my mind went to work.

*The difference between saltwater and freshwater is the salinity content. Both contain salt, or sodium chloride, but fresh water contains only small trace amounts of salt. Seawater's viscosity, or internal resistance to flow, is higher than that of fresh water because of the differences in its salinity.*

Marcus video recorded the sphere again as it emitted its entrancing code once more. We left the tap running constantly and recorded everything that flowed from within. The sphere just kept giving up all its secrets.

Marcus and Kinika then began to work tirelessly at decoding all the new data. The binary code was now quite simple to unravel with the aid of Kinika and the Andi Mk2. It was just like a gigantic memory stick that had recorded and stored everything since the dawn of our known time. We were about to have an insight into our complete history from a totally different perspective.

The alien robots were not like the Andi Mk2s. They were programmable machines that functioned by direct commands issued by their alien masters on Kepler-452b. The robots had been designed two million years earlier by the aliens for one purpose only: deep space exploration.

Incredibly, the robots had been assigned a list of space coordinates that contained the details of many different worlds in several galaxies that they each were pre-programmed to explore. Earth, it seems, was their prime destination. If my hypothesis was correct, the astrophysics readings the aliens had obtained about the Earth revealed its gold and heavy metal riches. I was sure this was why the mission was ordered and dispatched - to recover raw materials so they could be excavated and returned back to their home world of Kepler-452b.

I suspected other ships had been sent to planets at the far reaches of the universe, all with the same mission parameters: survey and find the planet's resources and report back if vast quantities of gold were present.

But why gold?

If the aliens wanted to identify possible planets for this purpose, they must have the equivalent of astrophysicists. There must be another astrophysicist on Keplar-452b monitoring progress on Earth, pondering the Universe, eyes glued to a telescope, scanning the night sky. Imagine meeting them, I thought. For the first time I wasn't scared of them or angry at their actions against mankind. I was only curious. So curious. I wanted to sit down and talk with them, discuss what I knew and question what I didn't. They must know so much. We could really learn from them, I thought.

Talking to them would bring space exploration with our Andi Mk2s to a whole new level. We could send them directly to the correct planets instead of scouring the universe in search of planets with Earth-like conditions. The Earth itself was fast running out of natural resources and food to feed its inhabitants, so we needed to be planning for this now, not in 100,000 years' time, because that's how long it would take us to carry out a return mission to Kepler-452b if we went at the speed of light.

At the present rate, mankind will have used up the planet's resources long before the 100,000 years' time frame had elapsed, even if we had by some miracle managed to master travelling at light speed.

* * *

The Earth-based alien robots had hurriedly tried to report back to their home world about the introduction of the new Andi Mk2s and their new super-brain capabilities. This is when the command sphere had malfunctioned. It seems that the reusable command sphere had been rushed through its reprogramming and there had been a fault programmed into its guidance system.

At this point Kinika scoffed loudly at the aliens' incompetence. Never looking up from his screen, he sarcastically proclaimed, "You just can't get good help anymore, Marcus."

What we had determined so far is that a garrison of 10 alien robots had arrived on Earth just over a million years ago, at first on board their intergalactic spacecraft. Because of the size of their ship they couldn't navigate the wormhole.

They had been traveling for nearly 50,000 years and after an initial scan and survey of the Earth, they had decided that the best place to conceal themselves would be on land. But as mankind had evolved, they had decided to move their base to the bottom of the Marianas Trench, where they could observe the planet, but not be observed by its inhabitants. After completing their new underwater base, they had resurfaced about 500,000 years ago, I guessed, to carry on with their various experiments. They had continued to carry out these experiments over the millennia, right up until the last Ice Age.

*　*　*

*Generally accepted research had determined that the last glacial period on Earth, popularly known as the Ice Age, was the most recent glacial period within the Quaternary glaciation, which occurred during the last 100,000 years of the Pleistocene period, from approximately 110,000 to 12,000 years ago.*

The indigenous populations of the Earth during and following this period were mainly hunter-gatherers, and were of little threat to the robots. The problem was the population was too small to carry out any effective mining operations; it would take years for the population to grow to the necessary numbers to make the excavation of the planet worthwhile.

There were two main types of humanoids, they had reported back to their alien masters: Neanderthals and humans.

We knew that the Neanderthals had died out about 40,000 years ago, thanks to recently improved carbon dating techniques; the information from the alien robots had now confirmed this. When modern humans had begun to emerge in Eurasia they quickly overwhelmed the Neanderthal variant of the human family tree, to be the dominant species on the planet. How humans had taken control was simple: their brains were much bigger, spurred by a genetic defect in the human family tree in the region that is now South Africa. The gene had been passed down through multiple generations of humans and they had slowly spread out across Africa and then into Asia through a land bridge that existed nearly 110,000 years ago between the two continents. Sea levels during the Ice Age were much lower.

All along, the robots had continued to carry out their survey work around the world, using their cloaking camouflage to avoid detection from the hostile early humans. Even 100,000 years ago, humans had shaped spears and other weapons. Crossing the wild plains of Africa 100,000 years ago was a feat unto itself. The Neanderthals were generally larger bigger and stronger than their human cousins, but they just didn't have the brainpower or the weaponry to compete, and this ultimately led to their extinction.

The robots' orders from their alien controllers 100,000 years ago was to extend their underwater base at the foot of the Marianas Trench. The labyrinth of undersea tunnels had now been formed into a massive underwater storage complex to accommodate the large deposits of gold and rare heavy metals that the Earth readily contained. Their plan was simple: to excavate the valuable resources held within the Earth and store them in the safety of their underground vault until the next alien spaceship could collect the bounty and return to their home planet.

Because of the immense distances involved and the size of the spaceship needed to transport the materials from the Earth, the round trip journey from Kepler-452b would take just over 100,000 years to complete. A ship had already been dispatched from Kepler-452b nearly 50,000 years ago for this purpose.

The robots' first contact with the humans had been minimal. They supplied reports every 1000 years, via their command spheres, back to their controllers on Kepler-452b. Their reports were simple and succinct - the humans on planet Earth spent more time hunting and killing each other than they did mining their world's precious resources. At this point in history, mankind didn't even understand the value of gold.

Then, nearly 10,000 years ago, after receiving new orders from their alien masters, the robots had started the process of trying to mine samples of the Earth's gold and some other heavy metals, using the

Earth's population as slave labor. They had various ideas on the most effective way to harness the help of the then-roaming human race. Their ideas would shape our history and would become mysterious for years to come.

They decided to set up local colonies or cities to keep parts of the human population together. At first, humans thought of the robots as Gods from another planet, and they started to worship them, making it easy for the robots to control them and carry out their mining work. With their revered status as Gods, the robots ruled over huge numbers of humans and set them to work excavating natural resources.

The robots fostered this culture of slavery and hard work wherever they could. In Egypt, the pyramids were perfect examples of how structures could be built to serve the 'Gods', who then collected the gold.

* * *

All of this information spinning around in my head brought to mind the ancient astronaut theorist, Erich von Däniken. In his 1968 book 'Chariots of the Gods', von Däniken hypothesised that various technologies of ancient civilizations were given to them by ancient astronauts, who were welcomed to the Earth as Gods. He was nearly correct in his assumptions. The thing that Erich and his many credible followers had failed to understand was that these beings were not ancient astronauts, but ancient robots. And their ancient astronaut masters were now on their way.

The plan conceived by the aliens was both simple and brilliant. They had time on their side. By allowing our race to breed and populate the world, they would soon have a workforce to enslave, and to use to excavate Earth's resources when their ship arrived in the distant future. Now with over nine billion people populating the planet, they had sufficient numbers of people to excavate the Earth of all of its resources to take home to Kepler-452b.

The robots originally hadn't planned on the warring nature of humans. They thought after their initial rise to power they could expand their mining operations, but after successive attacks by warring local tribes, the aliens issued an order for the robots to preserve themselves for the arrival of the mother ship in the near future and to leave the humans to their own destructive devices.

It seems the aliens had not anticipated just how violent and unruly the human race could be. Humans rebelled against their leaders time and time again. We refused to be enslaved. However, leaving the humans to their own devices had caused further problems for the aliens in the last few centuries as humans began to exploit the very resources the aliens were after. Gold was now being ripped from the ground at a staggering rate. Humans were gathering exactly what the aliens wanted.

The alien plan took another wrong turn with the introduction of the original Andis. The rapid technological advancements in the last few hundred years had caught the aliens off guard. Thousands of years had passed with little change and now suddenly the human race was a more formidable opponent.

Perhaps the aliens had waited too long to enact their plan. They had to think of a new approach.

This time it would to involve the original Andis. It was a simple strategy, really. Start by disabling the human population with the solar flare and then take control of the Andis using their conveniently placed spheres.

With this plan set in place the aliens could now enslave the human race once more by using the Andis.

Andis worked 24 hours a day, seven days a week, and were stronger and more intelligent than most humans. The alien's mass excavation project could now be done more efficiently. It all seemed to fit together so nicely for them.

Unfortunately for the aliens they had not suspected that the Andi Mk2 would be such a radical advancement on the Mk1.

Their plan was once again under threat.

# Chapter twenty three

T
he information we had prised from the sphere left us all speechless for some time. The sheer scale of time was what astonished me most. These aliens had been watching us since the very dawn of mankind. They were there at the very beginning, manipulating us in so many ways.

I didn't know what to believe anymore. This sphere threw everything we thought we knew right out the window. The whole anthropology of the human race was now in question. Religious leaders would have to re-examine their beliefs. Perhaps these aliens were our Gods. Why should they not be? Their robot creations had been here since human life began on Earth, and they seemed to be all powerful.

There were still too many questions.

One riddle that had been solved was why they were here. They were here, as predicted, for our planet's resources. What exactly had happened to their own resources on Kepler-452b was still a mystery. Maybe, like us, they had recklessly used all of their reserves and were searching for some way to replenish their own depleted resources? It seemed so similar to our predicament here I couldn't help thinking we were connected in some way. Perhaps they were a future us, or a parallel us? But after reading all these lines of code, I didn't know what to think anymore.

Our natural resources, gold in particular was their target. Stick to this, I told myself. Focus on this; it's the common denominator.

\* \* \*

*Gold, or as it's known in the periodic table, Au, from the Latin aurum, has the atomic number 79, making it one of the higher atomic number elements that occur naturally in the universe. It has a number of unique properties. Unlike most metals,*

*24-karat gold is soft and malleable; it can even be eaten, as it's non-toxic. It's also known as a transition metal, one of a group of 11 elements and one of the least reactive. This property alone makes it very special.*

The aliens knew that gold was produced by supernova nucleosynthesis, caused by the collision of neutron stars. Gold has been present in our solar system for more than 14 billion years but it was still rare in the universe and Earth had massive deposits of it that remained largely untouched. This was mainly due to our lack of expertise in excavating it from deep down within the Earth's surface. The aliens, on the other hand, were coming armed with the necessary technology and machinery to grab the gold hidden within the depths of the Earth.

The more I looked at the data, the more I thought that these time frames were extraordinarily long, even for an alien race. Why would the aliens dedicate millennia to extract gold from our planet? Gold, a metal that is used mainly by humans as a treasure and is a source of wealth, and nothing more really. Surely they can't have come all the way across the galaxy, travelling for thousands of years, for treasure. Wealth, money, gold, treasure - whatever you wish to call it - has been fought over forever, but within the confines of our planet. Was it possible that they were here solely for wealth and glory?

I couldn't believe it; it didn't compute in my mind. There had to be something we were missing.

In their obsessive pursuit of gold the aliens had also documented many of the world's conflicts and battles. Why? Gold of course. Where there was war, there was gold.

My mind raced backward to a pivotal point in human history, that of Alexander the Great.

Born in July 356 BC, Alexander was king of the ancient Greek kingdom of Macedonia. Tutored by the philosopher Aristotle until the age of 16, Alexander succeeded his father Philip II at the relatively young age of 20. By the time he was 30, he had created one of the largest empires of the ancient world, stretching from Greece to north-western India with aspirations to reach the "ends of the world and the great outer sea."

Alexander the Great became the measure against which all military leaders would compare themselves throughout the ages. Military academies around the world still teach his tactics today. Indeed, Alexander is still ranked among the most influential people in human history, along with his teacher Aristotle. Alexander's name was used for the building of the Egyptian city of Alexandria, which later led to the building of one of the seven ancient wonders of the world, the lighthouse of Alexandria.

Alexander's death at the age of 32 at the Palace of Nebuchadnezzar II in Babylon had long been a mystery. Various causes had been suggested, alcoholic liver disease, fever, and even strychnine poisoning.

The actual truth we found out by decoding the sphere. Alexander had been given the remains of an alien robot's mangled body parts as a trophy of war. The malfunctioning robots cloaking device had failed while surveying the war gold recently collected by Alexander's army. The robot had been seen as a demon by Alexander's men, who unceremoniously hacked the robot to pieces and presented it to their king as a trophy of war.

Unbeknownst to his men and Alexander at the time, the robot's mini fusion drive was damaged, and because it was radioactive, anyone who touched it or was exposed to it for prolonged periods had died from radioactive poisoning. History does not record the death of another ten of Alexander's men who were also exposed to the 'demon'.

As part of his burial rights Alexander's body was laid in a gold anthropoid sarcophagus filled with honey. It was then placed into a gold casket, where Alexander was finally laid to rest.

The decapitated alien robot's body parts had been reclaimed by two of the remaining alien robots after a night time incursion into Alexander's heavily fortified camp. The pieces of the destroyed robot had been placed into a trunk and were to be returned to Alexander's family as a trophy of war.

After Alexander was laid to rest, the robots unceremoniously removed him from his golden casket and made off with the precious bounty like simple thieves in the night.

Another famous conqueror, Genghis Khan, born in 1162, died in 1227, even got a mention in the sphere's databank. The warlord from the Mongolian Steppes had created the largest contiguous empire in history. At its peak the Mongol Empire stretched from Central Europe to the Sea of Japan, extending northwards to Siberia, eastwards and southwards into India, Indochina and the Iranian plateau and then westwards as far as the Levant and Arabia.

Genghis Khan had a reputation for mercilessly slaughtering everyone who opposed him or his armies. His brutality was such that when conquering Iran, he had 75% of the Iranian population massacred during his conquest. The provincial governor, who had initially rebuffed his envoys, was executed by having molten silver poured into his ears and eyes. Genghis Khan collected gold and silver everywhere he went to pay for his vast army, he used terror as one of his main weapons to suppress his enemies.

As before, the alien robots monitored the Mongols very carefully. They allowed the empire to fall and collapse before slyly stealing the amassed hoards of gold.

The robots used their skills in camouflage to remain unseen throughout most of our history, carefully surveying the Earth and using our human flaws to their advantage.

"So these robots are invisible, too?" Kinika perked up again, fingers still typing.

"A problem, I know," muttered Marcus. "The robots can't be seen by the human eye, but the latest version of the Android AI night vision goggles can see in all light spectrums, night and day. Maybe just maybe, this could detect them," he continued.

Marcus quickly informed the military to be on the lookout for enemy robots by utilizing the features of the latest Android AI night vision goggles. A signal was passed to all the Andi Mk2s so they could also be tactically aware of the situation. Again, a clever cover story was fed to the U.S. armed forces, this time stating that the generals, during their war games, were testing a new camouflage device, a scenario that would put everyone on alert. We knew this would put all personnel on edge, but it was necessary to keep everyone on high alert status. We still didn't know exactly what had happened at the bottom of the Marianas Trench.

My mind personally kept racing back to gold. Why gold? If the aliens were prepared to travel for 50,000 years across the galaxy to Earth, and then wait almost a million years in order to harvest the planet, gold must be of the utmost importance to them. This truly was a long-term battle plan.

For the next two days I looked again at my data I had on Kepler-452b. Why did they want gold?

I instructed the USSA to carry out more tests on the planet using the space-based Hubble and the James Webb telescopes, specifically looking at levels of gold or potential uses for gold.

My original assumptions were that there was no gold on Kepler-452b, and this was technically correct.

The aliens wanted it, and they wanted it in large amounts, and that's why they were invading the Earth.

I started to run through all the known uses for gold. Gold is injectable, it has proven to help reduce pain and swelling in patients suffering from tuberculosis and rheumatoid arthritis. A journey across the galaxy for a painkiller? Unlikely.

Gold can be used as a very efficient conductor of heat and electricity.

Possible, I thought. Humans use it for this in varying capacities.

Gold is malleable enough that just one gram can be hammered into a sheet one square meter in size.

Useful.

It can also be made so thin that it appears transparent.

Wait a minute…

This is when the penny finally dropped.

I scrambled for the data to back up my theory, could it really be? Gold had the capacity to protect against infrared and ultraviolet radiation whilst letting some light wavelengths through. We had been using gold for this property for years already, in gold tinted glass or helmet visors.

It protected us from the sun's harmful rays… so maybe they wanted it to protect them too?

Could this be it? Is this the final part of the puzzle I wondered?

* * *

Over the course of the next few million years, the aliens' sun was going to move inexorably closer to their own planet – Kepler-452b. As a consequence, their sun would deliver massive amounts of radiation onto the surface of their own planet. The harmful infrared and ultraviolet radiation was getting through Kepler-452b's own natural layers of planetary protection and was destroying everything on the planet's surface, slowly cooking their planet from above.

I checked our images of Kepler-452b again, searching 360 degrees around the planet. Sure enough, there it was. It was so thin it was almost invisible. That's why I had missed it initially. But by using the latest USSA imaging technology, combined with my astrophysics training, I had all the evidence I needed.

They were building a screen made of gold - a protective thin gold shield around their entire planet to protect them from their own sun. That's why our gold was so important. They needed it to save their entire species from being burnt alive. Their plan was to build a golden transparent globe to act as a sunscreen filter from the harmful cosmic rays being emitted from their own sun.

My calculations showed that the shield was nowhere near completion, but it had started. I thought to myself it must have started millennia ago. Perhaps their own gold reserves ran dry and they began to look elsewhere.

The quantities of gold required were enormous, but by sending out their autonomous robots into space they could harvest other planet's natural resources, as and when they discovered them.

Everything began to make sense now; the jigsaw puzzle was nearing completion.

Gold was their only means of survival and, like us, they would do just about anything to stay alive.

They would be back for our gold, of that I was now certain.

The next piece of information from the captured command sphere grabbed the interest of the President and his advisors. The alien robots had surveyed the whole planet and discovered where Earth's main gold deposits were located. According to the sphere, there were tons upon tons of undiscovered gold. The aliens' plan was to extract these honey pots when they took over our Andis. Now that we had thwarted that plan, the President felt it was time to use this knowledge of the gold locations to our own advantage.

I didn't join in these discussions. I was too preoccupied checking my golden-protective-globe theory.

The President was very impressed with the data I had supplied him and he had a hugely liberal idea of what to do with it. He was keen to share the information with all the world's leaders, so they could use the data to create wealth for their own people.

Marcus saw the immediate flaw to his plan.

"How are you going to tell the countries of the world that billions of dollars of gold and other natural resources lie under their feet, Mr. President? The first thing you are going to be asked is how did you acquire this information? Have your intelligence services been spying on my country without our permission? Is that not asking for trouble... sir?" Marcus remembered who he was talking to just at the right moment.

Mankind's past experience had shown that when there is money, resources or gold, there is more corruption, and the same old process would ensue...the rich would get richer and the poor would get poorer. It had always been this way and there had to be a better solution.

Marcus urged the President to rethink his idea. If the U.S. could help control the extraction of the Earth's natural resources they would be in a far better position to help the struggling countries, most of which were struggling just to feed their own people, let alone rebuild their major cities inland from their now-flooded coastal regions.

Marcus's proposal to the President was really simple – we enter into trade agreements with all the friendly countries. As for those nations that won't play ball, we just simply leave the valuable reserves underground and tell them nothing. Those nations, in time, will see the remarkable benefits of the U.S. plan, and eventually come on board. They simply couldn't afford the alternative.

"Android AI will build and lease more Andi Mk2s to help with the major coastal city rebuild projects currently being undertaken around the world." Marcus always seemed to be in business mode. In this way, we were very different.

Profit, profit, profit. I thought to myself, how much is enough? We were already billionaires. I wanted to give money to needy causes, not have more.

Marcus continued…"meanwhile, the U.S. acquires the rights to extract the world's gold and raw materials reserves from each country, under a strictly controlled licensing agreement. We could even provide the necessary machinery. So the country of origin makes lots of money and so do we. It's a win-win.

Profits would, in turn, help pay for the development of a new USSA space fleet and the launching of our own Andi Mk2s into space. Our very own self replicating robot space army, Mr. President."

* * *

It wasn't long before the world's media picked up on the Laser Tasers we had used to fire from orbiting satellites. As usual, the U.S. government and the military had their clever cover story already in place.

The White House issued a statement about the NASA trial of a revolutionary new space defence system called 'Light Years'. The system, commissioned by the U.S. government many years earlier, had been tested on a Near Earth Orbit (NEO) rogue meteorite that was passing extremely close to Earth. No mention was made of the USSA or its involvement. A complete cloak of secrecy was maintained over the biggest ever 'Black

Project' expenditure by successive U.S. governments, the true cost of which was over $100 billion over 40 years.

NASA had also developed an elaborate cover story to conceal the identity of the true aggressor. If mankind knew that we were about to be attacked by alien invaders, it would turn the whole world into a chaotic maelstrom of civilians looting and killing each other in a vain attempt to get 'their share' before the aliens arrived. This would be human instinct taking over, millions of years of evolution culminating in one last fist fight or gun battle for ownership of some meaningless possessions that would be worthless to the alien aggressors.

All they wanted was our gold.

The next part of the data that came out of the command sphere astonished us all. A million years ago when the robots had originally landed on Earth, they carried out a genetic research program on all of the species that they believed could be used as possible 'slave' labor to help excavate the Earth's natural resources. One of the ape-like creatures they encountered in modern day South Africa, near to the massive gold deposits they were surveying, had several genes different from the other apes species in the region. These apes were more intelligent than their larger distant cousins.

Scientists in recent years had developed the ability to decode the human genome and compare the genetic make-up of species. Approximately 98.5% of the genes in humans and chimpanzees were identical. What this tells us is that humans share a common ancestor with modern African apes, making us very distant cousins. We were related to these other living primates, but we did not descend from them.

I was personally not surprised. Darwin had actually made references to this in his evolution notes and theories. The survival of the fittest or his 'Natural Selection' theory had proven this.

Soon, I was poring over my own memories of Darwin's process of natural selection, which has four main components.

1. Variation. Organisms will exhibit individual variation in appearance and behavior traits. These variations may involve body

size, hair color, facial markings, voice properties, or the number of their offspring.

2. Inheritance. Some traits are consistently passed on from parents to their offspring. Such traits are heritable, whereas other traits are strongly influenced by the local environmental conditions and show weak heritability.

3. High rate of population growth. Most populations have more offspring each year than local resources can support, leading to a struggle for resources. Each generation experiences substantial mortality. This had been so true of early humans with no modern medicine. In the early 1900s in some U.S. cities, up to 30 percent of infants died before reaching their first birthday.

4. Differential survival and reproduction. Individuals who possessed the traits and were well suited for the struggle of gathering local resources would then contribute more offspring to the next generation.

These principles of Darwin I had learned when studying for my PhD. I had read everything about him.

The time I had spent filling my brain with knowledge was starting to pay off. The 'nerdy professor', as I was sometimes called at college, was on the case. The hours I had spent at my computer reading up on the past and present for my two PhD's would eventually help me solve the alien riddle.

# Chapter twenty four

Gus, who had also journeyed with us to the Cheyenne Mountain complex, came bundling in, his spirits high as usual. "What ya working on?" he said in his affable, bubbly voice; he was bored, I could tell.

I swivelled in my chair and squared him up and then let him in on my 'golden sphere' theory.

I rattled on and on, droning over the specifics. I delved into every thought I had, throwing statistic after fact at Gus's blank stare. I had been building this all up in my head and it all came rushing out uncontrollably. I turned to face my computer to bring up the image of Kepler-452b, when I noticed Marcus standing over Gus's shoulder. His expression was one of equal confusion. Gus got up slowly, signalled for Marcus to sit and patted me on the shoulder.

"Go on..." muttered my father.

I started again and relentlessly revealed everything I knew. I included every minute detail, every test I had run, every segment of the enormous galactic pie.

When I had finished, Marcus remained silent for a while, digesting everything, performing his own mental tests, running his analytical mind over what I had just fed him.

"Why couldn't they just... hmm, yes. But what if... no, that's right."

He was asking all the questions I had asked myself. He went through every question and then answered them himself, just as I had. After a few minutes of this we began a mutual discussion. Bouncing ideas off each other, spitting out theorems, scribbling notes feverishly. Eventually we were content with what we had. We hadn't discovered any new ways to protect ourselves or discovered anything new about their plan, but the feeling of knowing exactly why they were here was priceless. As a scientist you have this desire for facts to help figure out the answers. To a scientist, accurate data is everything. To have closed this open argument was deeply satisfying for us.

We both stood up to take a break but as I did my father caught me off guard by pulling me into a hug. It was a long lasting and wholly comforting hug. I could have stayed there forever.

He looked at me and said, gently, "You're brilliant son, I couldn't be more proud of you."

*   *   *

*The Richter scale is used to measure Earthquakes. It has a numerical scale to express the magnitude of an Earthquake on the basis of seismograph oscillations. The range and power of Earthquakes can vary immensely, and the magnitude of a quake is determined from the logarithm of the amplitude of waves recorded by seismographs. California-based seismologist Charles Francis Richter devised it in 1935, the word seismograph being derived from the Ancient Greek word (seismós) meaning "Earthquake". They can be devastating forces, created 'usually' by Mother Nature herself.*

It appeared at first that the Kamikaze actions of Star had caused an Earthquake in the depths of the Pacific Ocean. The seismometers that recorded the quake located at the bottom of the Marianas Trench measured a magnitude 3.9 Earthquake and was recorded by the U.S. Geological Survey.

The National Earthquake Information Centre (NEIC), the national data centre and archive for Earthquake information, determines, as rapidly and as accurately as possible, the location and size of all significant Earthquakes that occur worldwide. The NEIC then collects this information and immediately supplies the information to all national and international agencies, scientists, critical facilities and also to the general public. The NEIC also has an active research program to improve its ability to locate Earthquakes worldwide and to understand the Earthquake mechanism. These efforts are all aimed at mitigating the risks of Earthquakes to mankind; and this is made possible by the international cooperation that has long characterized the science of seismology.

* * *

Originally, we had all thought that the alien robots were merely camped at the bottom of the ocean in a secure base, collecting data and reporting back to their alien masters. What we had all overlooked was the possibility that the robots had a spacecraft hidden in the deepest, darkest depths of the Marianas Trench.

The Earth had shaken for nearly 30 seconds as Star delivered its explosive package. The violent vibrations had led to massive damage to the surrounding seabed for a one-mile radius and caused underwater landslides, which we thought had entombed the robots within their base.

What we were soon to learn is the base was much more than that – it was actually hiding their spacecraft. More than that, the explosion and the subsequent vibrations of the surrounding rock had helped shake their spaceship free and worse still, left it virtually undamaged.

The 200 ft. diameter disk, shaped like a modern day discus, was edging itself free of the seabed that had been its home for nearly half a million years. The vessel, silver grey in colour, and home to the alien robots since it had originally left Kepler-452b, was now preparing to leave the seabed and the Earth's atmosphere as quickly as possible, with the least amount of disruption.

The 10 alien robots that had been manning the underwater station all these years were programmed for emergency situations. However, they were not like the advanced Andi Mk2s with spliced super-brain DNA, nor were they blessed with true artificial intelligence. They did, however, have clever integrated computer circuitry, advanced communications and they could also compute information in a fraction of a second.

The robots had been programmed with a defence mechanism and a set of orders that had been given to them by their alien masters more than a million years ago. Their small spaceship was not armed with rockets, missiles or guns; it only had a cloaking device and this was their main form of defence. Their spaceship was a survey ship, and their standing orders were not to engage with any potential hostile threats.

If an attack of any kind threatened their own survival or that of their ship and cargo, the standing orders were to escape to another safe area on Earth or to another nearby planet and await further instructions.

The alien's only objective was to keep their robots 'alive' and much more importantly, keep their large stash of gold safe. Amazingly, it turned out the robots had done more than just survey the Earth during their millennia here. They had collected tons of valuable golden objects from around the world throughout history and smelted the gold into slabs for transportation back to Kepler-452b.

The numerous priceless artefacts that had been transformed via this process was nothing less than an Aladdin's cave of treasure. Maybe even 50 Aladdin's caves! Such was the vastness of its haul.

And thanks to the sphere, we now knew every detail of the astonishing work of the alien robots.

One of these "secret" gold-raiding episodes involved King John 'The Bad', who was himself particularly fond of collecting and stealing other peoples' gold. In October 1216, King John travelled to Bishops Lynn in Norfolk, England where he suddenly fell ill with dysentery and decided to return to Newark Castle, via Wisbech. The area, aptly named The Wash, was a huge expanse of marshes and dangerous mud flats. King John took the slower and safer route around The Wash to Newark Castle, but his soldiers with carts full of the crown jewels and gold coins he had inherited from his grandmother, the Empress of Germany, took the shorter route through the marshes.

The robots had cunningly led the men into an impassable area of the marsh; the men and carts were all trapped by the rapidly rising tide and were all drowned. The treasure carts were lost and never recovered. King John died a few days later on the 18th of October 1216. The robots had their loot.

The details concerning the lost city of El Dorado also made interesting reading.

The mythical lost city, alleged to be full of gold, was supposedly located somewhere in the rainforests of South America. In fact, El Dorado was a legend about a Muisca Chieftain (the Golden One) who would cover himself with gold dust before he conducted religious ceremonies. The real City of Gold was a place known as Paititi.

The Spanish, who had been at war with the Incas of Peru for nearly 40 years, had them on the run. The Incas had retreated to the Vilcabamba Valley where they held off the invaders until 1572. When the Spanish eventually conquered the Incas they found the city largely deserted. It was rumoured that the Incas had fled to a new city, 'El Dorado', in the rainforests of southern Brazil, taking their vast treasure of gold with them. El Dorado was never found and neither was the gold.

The robots had stolen the entire golden hoard from the Incas by simply de-cloaking and appearing to the Inca, claiming to be living Gods. The Inca, overwhelmed at the sight of the alien robots, who did indeed appear to be living Gods, simply handed over their gold as a gesture of loyalty and devotion to their new deity.

Similarly, many gold-laden ships have been wrecked throughout the ages, but not many have carried billions of dollars of gold. The treasure of the Flor de la Mar or (Flower of the Sea) had never been found. She was a 400-ton Portuguese carrack built in Lisbon in 1502 and captained by Alfonso de Albuquerque. The ship was loaded with a vast golden treasure taken from Malacca, as well as gold tributes from the King of Siam, and was part of the largest treasure fleet assembled in the history of the Portuguese Navy. The Flor de la Mar set sail for Portugal with four other ships, but was caught in a violent storm in the Straits of Malacca. On the 20th of November 1511 she was shipwrecked on a reef off Sumatra. The ship broke in two and although Captain Alfonso was saved, the treasure was never recovered and is still considered one of the richest treasure hoards never to be found.

Captain Alfonso went to his grave still talking about how his ship was "torn in two" after hitting the reef. He told stories of the moving shadows that had then claimed his gold. Most people thought he was delirious from the head injuries he had received during the sinking. Again the robots had their gold.

The San Miguel and the lost 1715 Treasure Fleet was another of the richest ever treasure fleets gathered, this time by the Spanish. It consisted of five ships of the Nueva España (Mexico) fleet and six ships from the Tierra Firme (Mainland) fleet. Massive amounts of gold, pearls, jewels and other precious items were loaded at Vera Cruz, Cartagena, Nombre de Dios and Portobello. Subsequently a vicious hurricane sunk all of the ships and condemned over 1,000 sailors to a watery grave.

The robots, with their underwater capability had just simply collected the vast treasure from the wrecked ships, directly from the seafloor.

In yet another instance of robot robbery, the aliens had also duped the Knights Templar, a religious military order formed in 1119 AD to protect Christian pilgrims on their journey to the holy lands of the Middle East. They had established their headquarters on the side of the Temple Mount in Jerusalem and were declared a charity by Pope Innocent II. Over the decades, donations of gold from their patrons and their own secret golden finds hidden deep within the Temple Mount made the Knights Templar the wealthiest and most powerful military order in Europe. They even invented an early form of banking, which made them even richer.

For nearly 200 years, the Templars had amassed a fortune in lands and castles but much more importantly, in gold. By 1291 AD the military prestige of the Knights Templar was starting to wane and they were forced out of the Middle East. Their popularity then declined even further, spurred on by those who owed them money such as Phillip VI the King of France.

On Friday the 13th of October 1307, and with the acquiescence of the Pope, Phillip VI arrested the key leaders of the Knights Templar Order based in France and tortured them into confessions of heresy and devil worship. He seized their lands and raided their treasury, but found it less impressive than expected.

Across the rest of Europe the remaining Knights seem to have moved swiftly to hide what they could. A month later Pope Clement II issued the 'Pastoralis Praeeminentiae' which instructed all heads of state to arrest the Templars. Despite the arrests, the vast treasure of the Knights Templar could not be found.

The simple answer to this mystery lies with the Templar Knights, who were never arrested.

On the night of the 12th of October 1307, under the cover of darkness, several thousand men and a flotilla of 18 Templar ships that were berthed at La Rochelle in France quietly stole away, never to be seen again. They too were casualties of Mother Nature.

The flotilla was headed for a rumoured 'New World' where there would be no more religious persecution imposed upon them. But their journey was as short and as swift as the violent storm that claimed all hands. The fabulous wealth of the Templars, estimated today to be worth in excess of $10 billion, was gone forever.

Well, it was actually acquired by the alien robots, who, using their well-practiced, underwater salvage techniques, recovered the lost gold from the seafloor.

The assortment of golden objects and coins collected by the alien robots had been smelted down by the robots and molded and then shaped into the internal framework of their ship. For the most part, the inside of the ship was now made of pure gold. The anti-gravity device that was also part of the ships main propulsion and power system was made of a rare titanium alloy.

*There are four main grades of Titanium available on Earth, based on corrosion resistance, ductility and strength requirements of the specific application. Grade 1 has the highest formability, while Grade 4 has the highest strength, with moderate formability.*

The aliens had used their own titanium alloy mix from Kepler-452b to make their anti-gravity propulsion device. After a million years it still worked flawlessly, thanks to the regular maintenance regime adhered to by the alien robots, who had been preprogrammed with their daily work and maintenance schedules.

The spaceship had survived the nuclear blast because it had been placed at the centre of a defence perimeter, nearly a mile under the floor of the Challenger Deep area of the Marianas Trench. When the tactical nuclear device was detonated by Star, much of the explosive power of the device was absorbed by the surrounding rock strata, causing the Marianas Trench walls to collapse inwardly, filling in the void caused by the explosion.

The U.S. military had done its homework. The trench wall cave-in was always part of their strategy, but what they hadn't realized was that over the last million years the robots had excavated a series of undersea tunnels through the surrounding rock formations to enable them to surface at any of the four points of the compass. A well proven combat defence technique.

*The Vietcong had built tunnels during the war with America in Vietnam. The tunnels of Củ Chi were an immense network of connecting underground passageways located in the Củ Chi district of Ho Chi Minh City (Saigon) and were part of a much larger network of tunnels that underlie much of the country. The tunnels were the location of several military campaigns during the Vietnam War and were the Viet Cong's base of operations for the Tết Offensive in 1968.*

The robots were not offensively programmed, but we all knew they were going to be a worthy opponent. One of the underground defensive tunnels emerged five miles due north of their original Marianas Trench position.

* * *

Without warning, the alien spaceship started its climb from these incredible depths. It was now fully cloaked and was in full escape and evasion mode. Of the original robot crew of 10, only five had made it to the spaceship after the order to return home had been given by the spaceship's central computer control system. Four of the alien robots had been destroyed by the blast.

As soon as the spaceship was clear of the underground tunnel the alien command robot switched on the emergency communication network in a vain attempt to track down the missing robot that was still unaccounted for. But the electromagnetic pulse created by the detonation of the nuclear device had knocked out the alien robots' emergency communication network.

*An electromagnetic pulse is a burst of electromagnetic radiation. Nuclear explosions create a characteristic pulse of electromagnetic radiation called a nuclear EMP or NEMP. The resulting rapidly changing electric and magnetic fields are then coupled with electrical and electronic systems to produce damaging current and voltage surges.*

This is what had crippled the alien spaceship's emergency communications systems.

Above, the USS North Dakota SSN-784 was patrolling at a depth of 100 meters and was on station four miles north of the gathered fleet of U.S. Naval and support ships. The young sonar operator on watch, Michael, was the new boy on the block with only one previous deployment. He had missed the very faint echo of the alien spaceship as it silently glided by, one nautical mile in front of the USS North Dakota.

# Chapter twenty five

T he alien spaceship was trying to make a quick escape from the depths of the Pacific Ocean under the cover of darkness. They had successfully snuck past the first of many naval vessels patrolling the area but eventually they had to break the water's surface and emerge.

Even the alien's cloaking device had not perfected the technique of exiting the ocean without causing displacement of the surrounding water. Physics was physics, even if you were an alien spaceship.

Admiral Hocking sat on his command deck sipping a congratulatory tot of rum with his first officer when his radio buzzed. It was an incoming transmission from one of his destroyers.

"Yes?... You must be mistaken. Check again. That's not possible."

The destroyer was equipped with the latest stealth detection technology and it was picking up an anomaly.

The destroyer's latest synthetic aperture side scan radar had detected the wake and spray patterns caused by the spacecraft emerging from the Pacific Ocean. The sonar operator could not believe the readings from the wake patterns on his screen. The location and heading of the spaceship was at 75 degrees to horizontal. The 200 feet wide object was heading upwards into the night sky and the sonar operator was now tracking its projected course.

The sonar operator, on the other end of the radio was nervously telling the admiral this information and was clearly bemused.

"Okay, son, keep your eyes peeled and report back," the admiral said sternly, before abruptly ending the conversation.

The admiral took one last sip of his rum and quickly made a series of calls. His mission was definitely not over; he had to act fast.

The aliens' anti-gravity propulsion system was light years ahead of our own fledgling Gravity Research for Advanced Space Propulsion (GRASP) system. The GRASP system was originally developed as another Black Project for the U.S. military, and was under continuous development.

Gravity control propulsion research had started in the U.S. during the early 1950s, and with its subsequent GRASP advancements could now propel the new spaceship, the USSA Trident, up to a maximum speed of 34,000 mph, twice the speed of any space shuttle that had ever flown before. The USSA Trident was the shining example of NASA and USSA working in perfect unison.

*A 'trident' is traditionally a three-pronged spear and is the weapon of Poseidon or Neptune, the God of the Sea, in classical mythology. In Hindu mythology it's the weapon of Shiva, known as Trishula, Sanskrit for 'triple-spear'.*

The USSA had decided to call the new version of the space shuttle Trident as it carried almost magical, mythical powers, similar to those wielded by Neptune or Poseidon.

At this moment, the Trident was in near Earth orbit and close to the International Space Station (ISS).

The construction of the ISS had begun on the 20 November 1998 when the American-funded and Russian-built Zarya module was launched into orbit around the Earth. In total there had been 16 countries initially involved with the project, and it was a rare show of collaboration between leading nations.

The ISS has a permanent crew of six astronauts, whose primary mission was to carry out research in the 'space sciences'. The U.S. laboratory named 'Destiny' was added in 2001, followed by the European 'Columbus' and Japanese 'Kibo labs' in 2008. The ISS was about the size of an American football field, and it had taken 13 years to complete at an estimated cost of $100 billion. The first step mankind had ever taken to live permanently in space.

Major Oliver Ryan, call sign 'Riot', was the commander of the USSA Trident with a crew of four.

Riot had gained his nickname at flight school after a flurry of scraps and fist fights. He enjoyed the adrenaline and the buzz a fight brought with it; it kept him sharp and alert.

During his 15 years of service, though, he had matured into an excellent pilot and was now in command of the most expensive single piece of U.S. military hardware ever produced. By nature, and through his love of close combat fighting, he was a quick decisive thinker and problem solver. He could act almost as fast as the computer-controlled flight systems aboard his vessel, the primary reason he was personally chosen by General Klein to command the Trident.

The ISS and Trident were now on full alert. The details of the recent nuclear explosion in the Pacific Ocean had been relayed to the Major and to the crew of the ISS.

Major Ryan's USSA superiors had just assigned an Andi Mk2 to the Trident and it just didn't sit well with Ryan. He liked the human aspect of this work, not all this interaction with a cyborg. Ryan enjoyed working out his colleagues or opponents, discovering their weaknesses and flaws. This was impossible with an Andi. They didn't have a weakness.

General Klein's voice crackled into Riot's earpiece.

"Riot, there is an unidentified flying object in our air space. Flying fast and high."

General Klein then quickly explained that he had just received a report from Admiral Hocking in the middle of the Pacific Ocean that one of his destroyers had picked up something coming straight out of the Pacific Ocean in the middle of the night, becoming airborne within seconds.

Riot was momentarily caught off guard. This didn't happen often. He was always aware of all possibilities; part of what made him such a formidable fighter. But a spaceship emerging from the sea, this wasn't possible, he thought. This was beyond any nation's capabilities. No one had advanced to that stage of military complexity as yet.

Admiral Hocking made a call to the Cheyenne HQ with the latest news. We all had assumed that the tactical nuclear device delivered by Star had destroyed the alien base and everything hidden down there. We had no idea they had a fully functional spaceship that was still able to fly after being dormant for half a million years.

We listened to General Klein and Riot's conversation and I eventually joined in to give Riot a quick synopsis of the current situation.

At first he was a little taken aback. Aliens, spaceships, robots, gold... this was absurd. But his military training and sharp temperament kicked in rapidly. He checked his instrument panels and satellite feeds and scanned for any tell-tale signs of movement.

Marcus and Kinika were busy sending encrypted files of data to the Andi Mk2 on-board the Trident. The data instructed the Andi Mk2 to change to tactical mode. It was just like putting a car into sports mode and then gunning the throttle.

The Andi Mk2 was aware of the stealth mode being used by the alien spaceship and was now forming a battle plan, but first they had to find the spaceship. The Andi Mk2 immediately suggested to Ryan to set the Trident to battle stations. Ryan, not used to taking tactical advice from robots, reluctantly flicked the offensive laser switch to standby and engaged the GRASP engine to 50% power.

The air displacement patterns being generated by the fleeing alien spaceship had been spotted by the Andi Mk2 on the Trident's countermeasures control panel. Nothing that big could be totally invisible.

Its projected flight path soon appeared on all of our computer screens, courtesy of Kinika. The Joint Chiefs of Staff and the President were back with us now and they were looking a little perplexed, struggling to keep up with the rapid developments.

"How are we tracking this thing if it's invisible?" asked General Harris, tentatively.

"General, the Trident is fitted with the very latest USSA version of stealth detection, similar to our Navy destroyer's in the Pacific Ocean," mumbled Ryan, slightly annoyed at the question.

General Klein came online to inform us that the USSA had secretly been working on this countermeasure for the last 10 years in an attempt to detect the latest version of the Chinese Stealth bomber. The original purpose of the Laser Taser was to disable or destroy the Chinese stealth bomber threat. Valued at nearly $4 billion each, the Chinese stealth bombers could now work in Earth's low orbit and were a real threat to U.S. air supremacy. He went on to recommend the Laser Taser as his weapon of choice if we decided to attack the alien ship.

* * *

*Stealth detection technology, otherwise known as low observable technology, is a sub-discipline of military tactics and is a passive electronic countermeasure. It covers a range of techniques used by aircraft, ships, submarines and even satellites to make them invisible to radar, infrared and sonar. It's actually real life military camouflage for these parts of the electromagnetic spectrum and is known as multi-spectral camouflage.*

The President and the Joint Chiefs were in the White House situation room, officially known as the John F. Kennedy Conference Room. The 5,525-square-foot conference room was the new intelligence management center in the basement of the West Wing of the White House, and the President, at this point, was still very uncomfortable with the thought of blowing up the alien spaceship.

"Mr. President, we have their location. Shall we engage?" General Ramsey enquired with a sprinkle of excitement in his voice.

"Engage? They're leaving, General. Isn't this what we want?"

"They'll be back, Mr. President. We've just dropped a tactical nuke at their front door and blown up their half-million year-old piece of real estate. They'll be back for revenge, I'm sure of it - if we let them," said General Ramsey, almost licking his lips with eagerness.

"Mr. President," Marcus started, "to the best of our knowledge, no other alien communications have been sent from the Earth back to Kepler-452b. They were worried enough about the Andi Mk2's capabilities to send an emergency command sphere back to their home world, but it never actually got there because it's here with us at Cheyenne HQ. If the aliens have not managed to get their hands on this intelligence, they still won't know of the Andi Mk2s unique capabilities. This is our tactical advantage and we must keep it at all costs."

The President pondered for a while and then said, "What do you and your team think we should do, Marcus?"

"Mr. President, with all due respect, I don't agree with General Ramsey that the robots will have an angered or retaliatory response. These robots do not feel anger, but their alien masters might. If they manage to relay a message to them, they may come back with a vengeance. Maybe."

"However," continued my father, "I do agree with General Ramsey that we should take them out while we can, Mr. President. Its tactically the right thing to do".

The President nodded. He had heard enough.

"Major Ryan, you are an American astronaut and a true patriot. You wear the insignia of the USSA, and as your Commander-in-Chief, I am now officially ordering you to engage the alien spaceship and shoot it down as quickly as possible. May God be with you and your men, Major Ryan. We will keep all channels open."

Riot immediately put his crew on full battle stations and prepared the Laser Taser for firing. The new targeting coordinates that had been passed to him by the Andi Mk2 had been loaded into the Trident's computerized firing mechanism. The target was locked in in an instant and Major 'Riot' Ryan didn't hesitate.

"Wait!" I shouted.

It was too late. How had we all missed this?

The area surrounding the Trident lit up like a flash from a plasma tungsten arc welder. The bright white light emanating from the Laser Taser could be seen in the night sky from Earth. It was overwhelmingly bright and powerful.

The impact on the alien spaceship was devastating and instant. The Laser Taser ripped through the outer casing of the 200 foot-wide spaceship like a thermal lance, instantly destroying it. The spaceship had been manufactured well over a million years ago and it had been designed for fast inter-galactic travel and reconnaissance missions, not to repel a space-based weapon attack, equivalent to 15 kilotons of TNT, which incidentally was about the same payload as the original Hiroshima atomic bomb. Humankind's willingness to deploy new weapons technology was once again on display.

Everyone looked at me, both worried and expectant. Why hadn't we waited?

Indeed, the spaceship was still in our outer atmosphere. The destroyed ship would now rain debris on the innocent, unsuspecting citizens of Earth. If we had waited until the spaceship was in low-Earth orbit, the debris would have mostly floated harmlessly away into space.

The alien spaceship had been approaching the outer limits of the Earth's atmosphere when the Laser Taser struck. Gravity was still in play. The Laser Taser had ripped the alien spaceship into hundreds of pieces and the debris was now heading back down to the Earth's surface, 100 miles below.

Strange how the mind works. Despite all the brainpower that was shared amongst us all, we can still be swayed by our emotions. Our desire to eradicate the spaceship and exact revenge on those who had caused us panic and stress had overpowered our own logical thoughts about the consequences. Our overwhelming desire to obliterate them entirely had clouded our judgement.

The spaceship could have been destroyed further away from Earth, or not at all. News of our attack on their spaceship and destruction of their base at the Marianas Trench may have reached Kepler-452b by now. Had we forgotten the hundreds of other Foo Fighters, or the possibility of other command spheres? Had we forgotten they are 1.5 billion years more advanced than us? Perhaps our ego and arrogance had overtaken us and our human urge to destroy those who oppose us had overthrown our own common sense. I was asking myself these questions, but the military had already spoken for the people of Earth.

The President spoke clearly into the monitor: "Gentlemen, the USSA's reporting that the spaceship debris is now heading for Earth and will likely rain down on the Mojave Desert, near the California-Nevada border," he reported. "General Harris, get your USAF Quick Reaction Force teams (QRF) airborne and do it now. Marcus, I suggest you and your security detail join them and give me as much intel as you can from the crash site when you get there. Lukas you and your team stay at the Cheyenne Mountain headquarters. We can keep a direct comms link open to you and General Klein."

The 'Men in Black', as they were so aptly named, were the secret Quick Reaction Force (QRF) of the U.S. Air Force. They acquired this nickname from within the Air Force ranks after the hugely successful Hollywood film franchise starring Will Smith and Tommy Lee Jones.

These USAF QRF teams were on a constant 24-hour, 365 days a year standby and they were tasked with the secret recovery of all downed military craft in the United States. Sometimes they were required further afield, secretly reacting under the President's direct orders to recover other countries' downed aircraft or their space projects that had gone wrong. The much lesser known and rarely used protocols of the Men in Black, included recovery of extra-terrestrial debris.

The President finished reading the email, "General Harris, get your 'Men in Black' airborne and send them, too." The President stuttered just for a second as he read the last part of the message. He looked a little perplexed before concluding with one final order: "Good Lord, General, send them all to... Las Vegas."

# Chapter twenty six

The wreckage of the alien spaceship was spread over a wide area, across the city of Las Vegas. Kinika was trying to write a quick spreadsheet based on the impact data from Trident to give everyone an indication of the possible size of the debris field, but it was a tough ask with the little data he had at hand.

The desert gambling city of Las Vegas was famous across the world and in 2035 its population had expanded to just over 1 million people.

*The first-ever Las Vegas Casino was founded by Jewish gangster Bugsy Siegel. With the help from his friend and fellow mob boss Meyer Lansky, they poured money through Mormon-owned banks for their cover of legitimacy and in 1946 built the 'Flamingo'.*

By 2035 there were 101 Casinos incorporated and licensed in Las Vegas and they were about to be showered in gold.

Few of the iconic buildings were spared, the damage was catastrophic and the loss of life enormous. The debris, traveling at speeds faster than a rifle bullet, ravaged the buildings and the people on the ground. One relatively small piece of the spaceship debris traveling at these speeds contained enough kinetic energy to inflict serious damage to an entire city block.

New York, New York and the Bellagio were the first to take the direct impacts, closely followed by the Venetian and Caesar's Palace. The Luxor and The Palazzo were also devastated by the impacts. Trump Tower, coated with its distinctive golden reflective glass, was smashed and shattered, ironically, by falling gold.

Chaos is the only word that can begin to describe the scene in Las Vegas that day. Bodies lay everywhere, some burnt, others crushed and some never to be found. The red-hot pieces of gold and spaceship debris had also started fires, which trapped and suffocated hundreds.

The injured and dying lay everywhere, it was a scene of total and utter carnage. The brave emergency first responders on the ground were immediately overwhelmed. People fled for their lives in all directions. It was pandemonium. A city normally filled with laughter and world-class entertainment was now in despair. The scene was post-apocalyptic.

The President was given a briefing by federal authorities on the ground and he immediately issued a state of emergency and placed the City of Las Vegas under martial law. He also directed FEMA to respond. Unbelievably, FEMA was still on alert from the original alien threat, and responded almost immediately, but for the dead and dying of Las Vegas, it was already too late.

The helicopters of the Men in Black were some of the first on the scene and their short 46-mile journey from Creech Air Force base, Northwest of Las Vegas, had only taken 15 minutes. They quickly got to work securing the area and patrolling the crash sites.

Marcus, his security detail and his ever-present Andi Mk2 arrived in Las Vegas two hours later. As he exited the helicopter, Major Mark Thompson greeted him with a firm handshake.

"What is the present situation, Major?" Marcus asked.

Major Thompson replied with a grim look on his face.

"Initial estimates of over 3000 dead," he surmised. Local medical facilities can't cope. It's even worse than we might have imagined, sir."

"Major Thompson," Marcus responded, "the President has sent me here personally to assist in the examination and collection of the debris from the alien spaceship. I have also been ordered to give him as much information on the spaceship as quickly as I can." Marcus was good at distancing himself from the chaos around him.

Marcus and Major Thompson drove to the main crash site located just over a mile away. The 200-foot wide spaceship had been decimated by the initial impact of the Laser Taser. The discovery of one larger piece of debris from the spaceship had been called in by Major Thompson's men and they were now standing guard over it. The large piece of wreckage was about one-quarter of the whole ship and seemed to contain the ship's control systems.

Marcus and the Major arrived at the crash site five minutes later. There was a huge depression in the ground where the large piece of the spaceship had originally impacted across the street from the Mirage Casino. What was left of the spaceship was now located in the main foyer of the casino.

The Mirage, originally built by developer Steve Wynn had opened on November 22, 1989 and was the first resort that was built with the money of Wall Street through the use of junk bonds. Now at 46 years old, it had been beginning to show its age.

Marcus jumped out of the car and ducked straight under the security perimeter. No identification was needed. Marcus removed his spectrometer from his pocket and began a quick analysis of the wrecked spaceship. The faint radiation readings again were showing on the spectrometer. The radiation was faint but Marcus still deemed it too dangerous to get much closer.

Marcus set his personal Andi Mk2 to tactical mode and sent it to gather information from the debris while everyone else was kept at a safe distance. The Andi approached without fear.

As the Andi Mk2 closed in on the main part of the wreckage, Major Thompson was relayed a message from his troops that there were strange glowing orange balls in the sky gathering around Las Vegas. The Las Vegas electronic switchboards, already overloaded from the original crash incident, had now gone into meltdown. Calls from concerned residents and local law enforcement officers were coming in from all over Clark County. Meanwhile, the orange glowing balls of light seemed to be appearing from every direction.

Major Thompson immediately began walking towards Marcus to pass on the message, drawing his service revolver at the same time. Something wasn't right.

At that moment the Andi Mk2 was arriving in the centre of the debris, which indeed was the main command and control module. The Andi was within five metres when an alien robot emerged from within. It stood up, tall and long, facing the Andi. The robot was not unlike the Andi but it was taller and leaner. It shined a different light, reflective, oily, shimmering almost. It took a form similar to humans - two legs and two arms, torso and a head, but no face. The facial area was a like a liquid mass, a swirling ball of mercury. The liquid started in this region but ran across the whole of its body, flowing down, enveloping its mass and creating a slick, shiny exterior.

The Andi had never seen anything like this before. It had no data on the alien robot that stood before it. The Andi hesitated just for a second. But it was a second too long.

The alien robot spread its arms and legs wide and radiated a nuclear pulse of energy. This nuclear pulse rippled outwards directly at the exposed Andi Mk2.

*Pulsed energy stored within an electrostatic field and released over a very short interval, a process called energy compression, allows for a huge amount of peak power to be delivered. If one joule of energy is stored within a capacitor and then evenly released over one second, the average power delivered would only be one watt. If all of the stored energy is released within one microsecond, the average power is one megawatt, a million times greater.*

The aliens had figured out the physics of this process millions of years earlier.

Anything within a 100-yard radius with an electrical component was momentarily stunned, including the Andi. With the Andi stunned, the alien robot placed its oozing, liquid hand onto the Andis head. The extra-terrestrial material leaked onto the Andis frame and began melting, overwriting, adapting and manipulating everything inside it.

Marcus had stood watching, engrossed, as the robot emitted its pulse. Once it had touched the Andi, Marcus knew it was finished. He had underestimated these alien robots.

Major Thompson crept beside him and informed him of the orange balls in the vicinity. For a split second, Marcus felt that sinking feeling that comes with defeat. He looked at the Major and his hand-held side arm, he acknowledged in his own mind the turmoil that now surrounded him and resigned himself to defeat. He knew what was coming.

The action was immediate and sudden. The Andi Mk2 turned, and within a split second, it focused and fired its Heckler & Koch P30SKS. The polymer-framed pistol with laser sites and one of the finest triggers available on any pistol in the world fired its 9mm bullets with complete and total accuracy. The impact was immediate and deadly.

From 25 feet away, the shot struck Marcus in the forehead, straight between the eyes. Marcus never heard the shot coming and was dead before he hit the ground.

Marcus had personally chosen the Heckler & Koch P30SKS, with its loaded chamber, empty magazine indicators and laser sighting capability; it was the weapon of choice for all his armed Andis. Now he lay dead, killed by his own creation. Was this Darwin's vision of natural selection taken to the extreme, or was this Frankenstein's monster gone horribly wrong?

The Andi Mk2 immediately began to empty the entire 15 round magazine at all the military personnel within its vision parameters. Major Thompson was its next victim, the 9mm round entering just below the right temple, exiting directly on the other side of his cranium, removing a large portion of the back of his head.

Now in combat mode, the Andi Mk2 was precise, concise and lethal. The Men in Black were elite airman and all handpicked for the job directly from within the ranks of the U.S. Air Force, but they were lightly armed, and no match for the Andi Mk2. They died in the doorway of the Mirage Casino, along with their commanding officer.

Upon hearing the shots, Andrew Edwards, Marcus's personal security detail commander, leapt into action. His close protection team exited their armoured Hummer and immediately set up a defensive perimeter around their vehicle. Andrew and his team had been ordered to stay in their vehicle by Major Thompson because they did not have Top Secret security clearance to attend the crash site; this order had spared their lives.

Once the threat from the immediate military personnel had been removed, the Andi Mk2 stopped. The alien robot had manipulated the heavily armed Andi for its own violent ends.

The Andi was now effectively a clone of the alien robot, coated in the same silvery shiny substance. Together they both began to disappear to the naked eye, merging with the surroundings and becoming invisible from normal sight. The strange alien substance that had been secreted from the alien robot started to make the Andi invisible. They were both now cloaked.

The next sighting was reported a mile further away. More than 100 Foo Fighters were seen circling the alien robot and the Andi. The reports also spoke of mysterious lines of code being emitted from the Foo Fighters and the alien robot. The lines of code swirled around in the wind, the witnesses had reported, flowing freely in and out of each entity.

This was a form of communication, I concluded. Messages were being passed. The Andi Mk2 was giving up its secrets and knowledge.

The AI invasion had begun.

Andrew Edwards and his team had immediately secured the area and then radioed through the news of my father's death. He gave the President a full report on the events that had just taken place.

*A black hole is a place in space where gravity pulls so much that even light cannot get out. The gravity is so strong because matter has been squeezed into a tiny space. This happens when a star dies.*

A black hole had again been created in my life, because now my guiding star had died. The two bright stars that once guided my life had now been extinguished forever. It felt as though I was now being sucked into a black hole, where even light does not exist. I was being squeezed into a tiny space, so small that there was no air for me to breathe, nothing for me to see, just blackness. Tears didn't flow this time; there was no space in this hole for teardrops of emotion.

# Chapter twenty seven

I came to and realised Vicki's arms were wrapped around me and Gus was stood in front of me, tears flowing freely from his eyes. They both sat me down and put a blanket around me. I was lost for now, useless to anyone at this moment. Another crossroad in my life.

Andrew Edwards and his team were military professionals and death came with the job. They were expert soldiers and had already studied the helmet camera footage from the dead airmen and had watched the change in the Andi Mk2 with fascination and anger. To Andrew it was like having a comrade turn against you, the fact that Andis were machines made no difference to him. He felt betrayed.

Andrew reported back directly to the President and General Klein with his initial findings and attack strategy.

"Mr. President, I'm used to tracking people not invisible alien robots and Andis, so for now we are blind. We could do with some help on this front please. I do however, have one piece of potential good news."

Andrew explained how the spectrometer that Marcus used to detect radiation could be used to detect where the alien robot was or had been.

The President immediately issued the order to all military commands, to arm their men with the Android AI spectrometers and to form search teams. They had to find the alien robot and they had to do it quickly. We had no idea what this alien robot's plan was, so we were all on high alert status. Everyone had just witnessed its extreme capabilities and it made for scary viewing.

Within an hour a report of a second Andi Mk2 turning on some armed soldiers was reported. Again it was cold-blooded and ruthless and left a pile of dead bodies behind before vanishing. The reports also said that a Foo Fighter was seen within the vicinity just before the attack.

The President's face appeared on the large screen monitor.

"I'm sorry about your father Lukas, I truly am, he was a brave man and a patriot, but I need your help now. You're our best hope."

This roused me slightly from my daze and I managed to nod my head in recognition of what he had said.

"How many Mk2s are there in circulation at present? We have to stop them."

I knew the exact number.

"133 Mr. President."

"I understand that each Andi Mk2 carries its own GPS tracker, so can we find them this way, Lukas?"

"True Mr. President, but it's likely they know that we will disable that system straight away. They are cleverer than you can imagine.... sir".

It was then that we heard the shots.

The President's own personal Andi Mk2 had turned on him. The Mk2 didn't blink or stutter as it moved its pistol and took aim at the various Joint Chief's of Staff, and then the rest of the security personnel present, massacring every one in the room.

This Andi looked normal, without the silvery liquid of the alien robot but it was under its command that was for sure. How or when it had been overrun by the alien robot or the Foo fighters, we could not determine. But it was now fighting against us.

All the terror had been recorded on the White House's internal security cameras. One of the President's secret service detail had managed to get off several rounds into the Andi Mk2 before he too was killed. The 9mm rounds of his personal sidearm had little if any effect; the Andi Mk2s would be hard to stop.

*Originally set up to protect the President following the assassination of William McKinley in 1901, Congress had informally requested a presidential protection detail and it was not until 1902 that the Secret Service provided full-time protection for the President of the United States.*

These extremely brave and loyal men and women had now been

putting their lives on the line for their President for 133 years, Ironically the same amount of years as there had been Andi Mk2s produced.

It was then that I remembered Andrew Edward's comments about the Barrett M107A1 .50 Calibre long range sniper rifle. This deadly piece of hand-held 'artillery' had tremendous stopping power and was still widely available within the U.S. military arsenal. It was over 30 years old now, but a recent upgrade in the form of a new laser infra red optical sight with built in automatic targeting software, still made it the U.S. military snipers weapon of choice.

This thought had brought me out of my seat and back into action, mourning would have to wait. There was work to be done.

I talked directly with General Klein and shared with him the thoughts of Andrew Edwards on the stopping power of the Barrett sniper rifle. This appealed to General Klein as a tactical option, because the Barrett was not indiscriminate and would not accidentally kill innocent civilian bystanders. General Klein issued the order to all his teams and to anyone at the Pentagon who would listen, to arm themselves with the Barrett.

His message read:

"The Barrett M107A1 .50 calibre long range sniper rifle will stop the Andi Mk2s if you hit them in their fusion drive, located in the middle of their chests, and for our friends around the world who don't have access to this exact rifle, get something with a very similar calibre from your own arsenal and start eliminating these threats".

Tyler-Joe Bowman or 'Flash' had received the order from General Klein and wrestled his own Barrett rifle out of the back of the Hummer. He immediately took cover in a shallow defilade near to their vehicle.

The High Mobility Multipurpose Wheeled Vehicle (HMMWV), more commonly known as the Humvee, was first deployed by U.S. forces way back in 1984 and had gone through many changes from its original combat design. Its first combat role was in Operation Just Cause during the U.S. invasion of Panama in 1989. In December 2004, the then Secretary of Defense Donald Rumsfeld came under criticism from U.S.

troops and their families for not providing better armored Humvee's. As a result extra armor packages were added to future vehicle variants and in 2026 all remaining Humvee's were completely upgraded and turned into autonomous unmanned ground vehicles (UGV). They were now guided and controlled by the United States military GPS satellite system.

The message from General Klein was a good start and we immediately began contacting owners of the other Mk2s directly, in order to make them aware of the threat they carried. They needed to get as far away from their own Andi as possible.

For some however, the message didn't get there soon enough. More reports came flowing in. They were the same in every case – the Andi Mk2 had dispatched their unsuspecting victims with their own sidearm. Cold heartedly, execution style.

One account was particularly alarming and the hardest to stomach. A mobile phone recording taken by a civilian showed an Andi Mk2 taking control of an Andi Mk1. The Mk1 then assisted in the killing of two nearby soldiers. They were strong, fast and reasonably bulletproof and could kill in a number of ways. One hundred and thirty-three Andi Mk2s going rogue was a tough pill to swallow, but the potential for 25 million Mk1s to join them on their killing spree was a stake through the heart of the entire human race.

General Klein gave the order for Andrew Edwards and his team to return to the Cheyenne Mountain HQ. Thirty minutes later they were all on their return journey on the Air Force jet, with Marcus's body in the hold.

The room was quiet as we awaited their arrival. I wasn't sure what I would do when I saw the body bag so I tried not to think about it. In fact for once in my life I didn't know what to think about. My usually hectic mind was eerily still. The lake of knowledge in my mind was tranquil, only a soft ripple moved across it.

"I know what they are up to!" Kinika exclaimed. He hadn't stopped typing away in the corner of the room.

"Lukas, look at this. The Foo Fighters are taking control of the Andi

Mk2s, in turn the Mk2s are then assimilating the original Mk1s to their command structure".

I looked at Kinika and asked him how he was so sure. He told me that Marcus had insisted that during their development phase all Andi Mk2s had special trackers installed into the main body frames.

"Just in case they malfunctioned and their circuits went haywire".

It was a command and control failsafe feature. Kinika touched a button on his computer, the control monitor in front of us flashed up like a firework, and 133 bright white lights showed us the locations of all the Mk2s. Kinika then typed some unintelligible code and red dots started to appear across the screen.

"The Mk1s locations?" I asked, despite already knowing the answer.

I sat at my computer next to Kinika. For the first time in hours since my father's death, I ran some quick analyses. My hands moved without feeling and my mind began to click slowly into gear like a rusty classic car. When the results were in I could only shake my head and feel the same lead ball of defeat sink through my chest.

"I estimate in 72 hours, the alien robot and its Foo Fighters will have control of every Andi on this planet." The news I delivered was potentially catastrophic.

General Klein intervened. "I have now established contact with all U.S. military forces and all our available assets. This event is unprecedented and all branches of the military are now on full alert. The gloves are now well and truly off gentlemen. The trouble is to the best of my knowledge the U.S. military does not have a strategic contingency plan for an alien robot invasion."

# Chapter twenty eight

Halley Fisher was a bright spark in Kinika's team. She looked at things from a different perspective. Only 29 years old but she had spent all her life hacking into secure servers and computer systems all over the world. Her father had taught her from an early age that every code or program had a back and a front door entry somewhere; you just had to know where to look. Her father Bill Fisher, recruited and employed by the NSA, headed up their ultra-secret Back Door Entry Team (BDET).

The team's main mission was to break into foreign governments (and sometimes companies) computer systems and then steal their secrets or any information that was needed by the NSA. The trick or skill was to do this without anyone ever knowing it was Bill Fisher or his team that had been there. The real secret to their work, which is the desperately clever part, is that after they had broken into the computers or servers they were targeting, they left a trail of evidence pointing to another organization as the guilty party. A simple but ingenious tactic, which enraged the other innocent third parties, that usually just happened to be another country's intelligence service. The smile on Bill Fisher face some days was priceless. He loved his work and his country.

Their second mission parameter, which was as equally important, was to insert lines of code into programs that could be activated in times of war or at the discretion of the President for intelligence gathering purposes, if the President perceived it as a threat to the national security of the United States.

There had been several high level examples of this in the past 30 years, but the U.S. and various other foreign governments had of course denied all knowledge of any wrongdoing. Cyber warfare was big business and young hackers were being targeted by the U.S. government and offered a meaningful job… or prison. There were not many who refused after being shown the inside of the shower room of a State Penitentiary. It didn't take hackers long to realize that working for the 'Man' was the much better option than doing time with the local drugs warlord and their sexually promiscuous and deviant henchman.

Halley had been instructed by her father to insert the lines of code into the new Andi Mk2s as a failsafe in the event that the Andis ever went rogue for any reason. The order had come from the now dead President after a top-secret meeting with his then Joint Chiefs of Staff. The team from the NSA (BDET) division had already disguised and laid the code into the operating system of all the Andi Mk1s and could be operated by simply activating the code from within the NSA bunker of operations. The failsafe just simply shut down the Andi Mk1s fusion drive and made them inoperable and just as importantly harmless to the human population.

Halley surreptitiously wrote the lines of code into all the Andi Mk2s. Getting past the security protocols set by Marcus and Android AI was a massive challenge in itself. The security was good for a reason; Marcus was a career CIA man and paranoid about tight security of all Android AI projects. Even the CIA knew nothing about the order from the dead President instructing the NSA to insert the lines of codes when the Andi Mk2s were being manufactured.

Halley didn't have to hack into and defeat the encryption of the Andi Mk2s; all she had to do now was run a program that would disable them individually. As her father had told her "Every computer system had a backdoor, but sometimes it couldn't be broken. By using the front door you are on the inside of the program, therefore avoiding detection because you have cleverly disguised it as part of the operating program". Halley had surreptitiously inserted the code into the main operating program. It was a very simple piece of code and completely invisible to anyone from Android AI who may have been looking for it, because it was a part of the actual operating code.

The problem that Halley had was that each Andi Mk2 had a super brain of their own and was able to change the lines of code within its own operating system. Each Andi Mk2 was capable of this and when one of the 133 went off line her fear was that each Andi Mk2 would run a compulsory systems check and then they would individually change its own code to cancel out the threat. When Halley had initially been writing the code under the direction of her father and the NSA, they had no idea that an alien robot, also with its own built in super computer power, would overwhelm the control functions of the Andi Mk2s with a 'pulse energy' surge.

# Chapter twenty nine

S leep didn't come easy that night; my mind was too tormented for the peaceful recesses of sleep. I sat on the edge of my chair in the corner of the USSA operations room, my eyes reddened and leaking the gentle tears which hadn't come before.

Over the last 24 hours reports on the Andis killing spree continued to filter in from around the globe. The good news was they were not seemingly interested in the civilian population. If the Andis identified a threat, their tactical mode would take over and simply eliminate them, but if no threat was established the Andis remained passive as if waiting for new instructions.

All Andis carried the Heckler & Koch P30SKS sidearm, with ten 15 round magazines as standard. With this much ammo and a virtually limitless resupply source nearby, they could create death numbering in the millions if the civilian population tried to resist.

The use of the Heckler & Koch P30SKS sidearm by the Andis was initially widely debated amongst the world's governments when the Andis were first released onto an unsuspecting world.

When the cities began to employ Andis in policing roles the change was dramatic. Early crime figures showed the immediate reduction of violent crime was 76% in the first year and this was directly attributed to the new Andis. The crime figures didn't lie and everyone knew then, that this was the future of policing. At the time many voiced their concern about the inhuman power the Andis wielded and the potential threat they could pose. These voices were drowned out by damning statistics and constant heroic success stories concerning the Andis.

The world became used to the Andis carrying out menial tasks one minute, by moving the affected coastal cities inland, then winning a firefight between warring drugs gangs on the crime-ridden streets the next. Just like the fleets of computerized zero emission 'GOOT' electric self drive cars. The massively successful Google and Teslar joint venture, that was now truly helping save the world, and just like the 'GOOT' by 2035 the Andis had now come to be accepted as the norm.

The original fear of human annihilation was beginning to recede as the Andis paid little attention to innocent bystanders. Instead their focus was on the gold. It seemed the alien robot had given the Andis its mission objectives and now they were all working together to collect and stockpile our gold.

Reports showed that the Andis had now stolen gold from various locations around the world that the aliens had initially targeted. They were now beginning to stockpile the gold in 8 different locations. A perimeter guard of Andis was set up around each one to protect their precious resource. With every stockpile there was at least one Andi Mk2 in overall command. In command of the Mk2s was the alien robot, communicating around the world via the Foo Fighters.

Their command set up seemed impenetrable. Each Andi Mk2 was in essence a superhuman leader and combined with an army of Andi Mk1s, almost undefeatable. At present they already controlled 90% of the world's gold and therefore most of the wealth. But at any moment they could decide to destroy an entire city or country. We had to make the first move.

The remaining 132 Andi Mk2s were a massive issue, but perhaps manageable. It was the 25 million Mk1s that were potentially the bigger threat. The sheer number of them made them extraordinarily dangerous. We had to regain control of them, or just simply disable them.

I slapped my hand against my forehead. How could I be so stupid!

"Kinika!" I shouted. "What was the first task you did for my father when this whole incident started?"

Kinika thought for a split second "I created a backdoor where there wasn't one in the Andi Mk1s, so that when the aliens disabled our communications satellites we could still battle for control of them. Big waste of time if you ask me, I didn't even get to use it because we stopped that solar flare. I worked so hard as well."

I stood there in front of him, giving him a piercing stare.

"What?" he said, still typing. "Oh…"

"Will it still work?" I asked.

Kinika explained that he had left the code and its importance with his most trusted employee. One of only a handful of people that he occasionally worked with.

Halley Fisher was her name. Kinika had given her the code after the solar flare was deflected and told her to continue to work on it and continually update it in accordance with any daily developments that had occurred.

Her amateur astronomer and serial computer hacker father had named her Halley, after Halley's comet, the celestial body that is actually a short period comet.

*Halley's comet is visible to the naked eye from the Earth, returns every 75 years and will next appear in 2061. The people of the Earth have recorded its appearance since 240BC and the comet's periodicity was first determined in 1705 by the English astronomer Edmond Halley, after whom it is now named.*

Halley Fisher was an exceptional hacker. According to Kinika they had been working together for the last 5 years after she hacked into his own computer. She was young and ambitious; she wanted to overthrow Kinika as the unofficial world's best hacker. Kinika was so impressed with her talent and direct attitude that they had reached a compromise and started working together. They were now a team.

Halley came online through Kinika's monitor and explained how she had used the code Kinika originally supplied… and improved on it, of course. Kinika scoffed at this part, but with a wry smile on his face. She continued to say how she had already uploaded the code to the Andi Mk1s during their daily updates that they receive from Android AI.

"Wait. You hacked into Android AI and embedded this code into their daily update server?" I asked, a little sceptically.

"Yes." She curtly replied.

Kinika merely shrugged at me. She was his protégé after all.

Halley also stated how she had done the same thing with the Andi Mk2s but the ones who had been struck by the alien robot's or Foo Fighter's pulse weapon, were now out of her control.

"Nevertheless, you are telling me that there is a piece of failsafe code inside the Mk1s at this moment in time? And that we can access it?"

"Yes.... you want me to initiate it?"

"Wait one moment." I had a plan. I called the new President.

The bodies of the dead President and his chiefs of staff had been removed from the White House and were now awaiting autopsy and eventually their funerals. The Vice President had been immediately sworn in and was now fully informed of the current situation. She had narrowly avoided the carnage at the White House because the President had sent her overseas to meet with the Chinese President to discuss the political and economic fallout over the recent nuclear explosion in the Marinas Trench and the official explanation around the USSA's new Laser Taser device. She was aboard Air Force One on her way home when she received the news of the death of her long-term friend and mentor. She was immediately sworn in as the new Commander-in-chief.

A career politician and diplomat of note, she too was a true red, white and blue American. Most of her 30 years of service to her country had been in various U.S. government roles and she had served personally under three different Presidents in various capacities. Her subsequent nomination as Vice President during the last election campaign meant that she was the first woman in U.S. political history to hold office and she was now the President.

She wasted no time in contacting us at the Cheyenne HQ and after the required formalities and condolences we got to work. I updated her and her new team as quickly as I could about the alien robot, the Mk2s, the Mk1s and their possible plans. I then explained the amazing work that Halley had done and what we could do with it.

"Madam President we can disable all the Mk1s with this simple piece of code which is inside them. That leaves us 133 Mk2s to eliminate. We have no technology in place to do this from here so the only option I think we have is by force."

"I understand. I also see a weapon has been identified as the most effective to wipe out these machines. Give me two hours Lukas and I will get back to you."

In these two hours the new President contacted multiple nations and called in every favour the U.S. had. She needed her very best operators; they now had a mission to save the planet. After a brief call to London and within 30 minutes it was decided that the U.S. Navy SEALs and The UK's Special Air Service (SAS) would be the chosen ones. They were given their orders and immediately deployed.

*The SAS are the British Army's elite Special Forces unit. The SAS founded in 1941 during the dark days of World War 2 by Colonel David Stirling. Originally a Scots Guards officer, he was trained by No 8 Commando. The SAS exploits are legendary in the Special Forces world: they are mostly kept secret due to the highly political nature of their work. They were immortalized after their exploits during the Iranian Embassy siege that took place between the 30th of April and the 5th May 1980, in London. The 'Iron Lady' Margaret Thatcher, the British Prime minister at the time had ordered the hooded figures, clad in black, into action.*

During the 17-minute raid, the SAS rescued all but one of the remaining hostages, and killed five of the six terrorists. There was some outrage at the time about the killing of the terrorists and the 'excessive force' used by the SAS during the raid. To Margaret Thatcher and the British people, the SAS were patriots and heroes and she would have none of it.

*The Navy SEALs are one of the elite Special Forces Unit within the U.S. military. The Navy SEALs are the U.S. Navy's primary Special Operations Force and a component of the Naval Special Warfare Command. President Obama called upon the Navy SEALs in 2011, to locate and extract Osama Bin Laden from his hiding place in his compound in Bilal Town, Abbottabad, Pakistan. The men from SEAL team 6 were given their orders direct from President Obama. The rest is history.*

The President and the Prime Minister of the UK ordered the teams of Navy SEALs and SAS into action. Within 24 hours they were in place at the 8 temporary gold storage sites, set up by the Andi Mk2s.

The plan was set. Halley and Kinika would initiate the code sequence and disable the Andi Mk1s. As the Mk1s went offline the Navy SEALs and SAS would take out the Mk2s at the 8 individual gold storage sites. In total 32 Mk2s had been affected so far by the EMP from the alien robot or the Foo Fighters. Four converted Mk2s were located at each gold site. One manned every corner of each site. The SEALs and SAS had 32 highly intelligent and dangerous cyborg robots to dispatch in a matter of seconds. If anyone could do it these modern day warriors could.

The President gave the order; Kinika pressed the return key on his computer, the operation was now live. The men and women of the SEAL and SAS units, all carried the Barrett M107A1 .50 calibre long range sniper rifle along with a concoction of high explosives and other sophisticated weaponry designed to stop almost anything that moved.

The effect was immediate, the control panel at the USSA headquarters showed the red lights of the converted Mk1s shutting down all around the planet, the code was working.

The SEAL and SAS teams immediately went to work.

Special Forces units are trained to be aggressive when needed, but they are also trained to see and not be seen. They can monitor their enemies from great distances or creep up within metres unheard and unseen. On this occasion they had kept their distance and used the built in automatic targeting software on their Barrett M107A1 .50 rifles to carry out their mission.

The Mk2s at the gold deposit sites were all in plain sight.

To the SEAL and SAS teams, these things were just that, things. They did not bleed blood or feel feelings. This was a guilt free task for the hardened veterans of these elite military units. Killing a shell of technology was a lot easier than a real human.

The attack was perfectly executed. Each sniper knew exactly where to hit their targets – the fusion drive in their chests – and they did this with exacting precision using their trusted Barrett rifles: 32 Mk2s were destroyed in seconds with only 32 precision delivered rounds. Efficiency at its very best. The Mk1s stood motionless as the Mk2s fell in unison. The Mk1s continued to remain static as the SEAL and SAS teams moved in to confirm their 'kills'.

Andrew Edwards and his team worked with the SEAL team at the Las Vegas crash site to recover the gold. The Andis defensive perimeter had been breached easily once the Andi Mk1s had been deactivated. The Andi Mk2 at the Las Vegas location was Marcus's personal machine; it had stayed at the crash site under orders from the remaining alien robot and collected up all the residual gold from the spaceship with help from the converted Andi Mk1s. Marcus' personal Mk2 had worried me a little as it could have developed extra capabilities after its interaction with the alien robot, but it fell to heap on the floor just like all the others.

Andrew and his loyal team had worked with this Andi unit for some time with Marcus and had started to get used to its own sense of humour and the way it operated. It now lay in pieces at their feet, torn apart from the single round from their Barrett rifles. Tyler-Joe Bowman fired off one last round into the head cavity of the Andi Mk2 from point blank range, his smouldering weapon still reeking of cordite as he turned and walked away. His own personal act of redemption for his old employers death. He was now fully avenged.

These various military men, mankind's own elite killers stood around their dead enemy's bodies and sneered at what had become of warfare. Robots killing humans, humans killing robots, this had gone too far and become a nightmare scenario. This feeling resonated deep within most of us and was underlined as General Klein came on the radio.

"Mission successful, 32 Mk2s eliminated. Never will a robot with this much power and capability enter our human world again, I swear by this."

I solemnly nodded my head in approval.

Simultaneously as the Seal and SAS attack had begun, Halley hit the return key on her computer keyboard, disabling all the remaining Andi Mk2s. Today had been a win for mankind.

# Chapter thirty

The mission was a total success. The devastating firepower of the SEAL and SAS teams had overwhelmed all Andi Mk2s at the gold collection sites. Despite their superhuman brain capacity they were still stopped by mankind's most lethal invention, the bullet. Kinika and Halley had also done their bit by deactivating the remaining Mk1s and leaving the Mk2s exposed. The Mk2s that were deactivated by force would remain recyclable. Their core brain components and splicing technology was still there to be reused if ever the time came. For now, the remaining Mk2s were disabled, they had threatened our entire existence and that was not a risk we could take again.

As well as the silencing of the Mk2s the Special Forces units also recovered over 165,000 metric tonnes worth about $8.5 trillion dollars. The President thought to herself that it had been a very good day at the office.

The President and the Prime Minister of Great Britain had been monitoring the various missions minute by minute and released a collective sigh of relief when the good news came in. Together their two countries had saved the planet from near extinction and this drew them closer, the special relationship that had existed between these two countries for the last 150 years had again, ironically been strengthened by conflict.

They both quickly went public with the necessary announcements about the night's events and played down the severity of it with expected political ease. Their cover stories were tight, their excuses reasonable and once again the public were covered with a shaded curtain, unaware of the true events unfolding in the world.

There was however one final thing to be squashed. There was the alien robot still on the loose, evading all attempts of capture via its cloaking technique. The thinking was that while this robot was still at large we were still in danger. It could control hundreds of Foo Fighters, which could potentially cause damage and chaos once more.

"Find and kill it and this will be over once and for all," the President demanded.

For this rare and unusual search and kill mission the President called in the services of another of her military assets – the 1st Special Forces Operational Detachment-Delta (1st SFOD-D) more popularly known as Delta Force, the elite special operations unit of the United States Army. Formed on the 19th November 1977, Delta Force is normally used in hostage rescue and counterterrorism roles, as well as direct action and reconnaissance against high-value targets. With its Garrison headquarters at Fort Bragg in North Carolina, the unit was under the control of the U.S. Army Special Operations Command (USASOC). It also has another master, the Joint Special Operations Command (JSOC).

Colonel Daniel 'Dan' Prout had received his orders from JSOC and he was in control of the Delta Force tracking teams. Born to a CIA mother and an MI5 father, his pedigree for espionage and war was coded into his own DNA. Top of his class at West Point and at just 35 years old already promoted to Colonel, he was being fast tracked for his first General's star.

Dan's team of Delta Force operatives were chosen from within the ranks of the U.S. Army. All of his men had seen combat action; all were exceptionally brave but also highly trained in the art of field craft and search techniques. There had been an addition to the existing Delta Force's seven squadrons in 2027 with 'H' squadron being added to the roll call.

H Squadron was a specialist reconnaissance and combat search and rescue team, whose duties also included specialist tracking and hostage recovery. These men were mainly recruited from the existing U.S. Ranger battalions, who themselves were already among the elite of the profession compared to anyone else in the world. Rangers were ideally suited to this role and they excelled within H Squadron, Delta Force.

H Squadron had its very own role within Delta Force. If you were a downed pilot in hostile territory, they would find and rescue you. If you were kidnapped they would find you. If you were a terrorist on the run, they would track and find you. If you survived the encounter, H Squadron would then hand you over to the CIA for a 'thorough debrief' at one of their notorious 'black sites' located in various parts of the world.

In short, no one wanted 'H' Squadron on their tail. Not even an alien robot.

Chasing the alien robot was a new test for H Squadron, but the theory was the same as tracking anyone or anything. Every moving object left a trace, an imprint here, a smudge there, an odour or a trail. The robot was invisible to the human eye but its movements could still be tracked.

Native American Indians have long been the best trackers in North America. Their lives originally revolved around the lives of the buffalo. Tracking, monitoring and eventually killing them. There was an art to this existence, which was lost to most Westerners; the art of tracking a beast in the wilderness was nonsense to most, but not to 'Little Bear'.

Little Bear was by far the best tracker in Colonel Prout's 'H' squadron. Little Bear learnt his trade tracking bears in the mountains of his ancestral homeland. His father had taught him how to track and kill a bear with nothing but his senses a hunting knife and his trusted bow and arrow. From a footprint he could tell what left it, when it was left, how heavy the owner of the print was and how fast they were moving. He could tell which direction they had taken even without any signs, he would sometimes go into a trance like state and use his spiritual upbringing to feel the way, feel the energy that had been left by the perpetrator. Little Bear was the best hope of finding this robot.

Little Bear had 14 years Army service and 5 years with Delta Force, his methods were unusual and at first he was subjected to ridicule from his colleagues, but when training and he was the only one catching food for dinner, they soon realised his talent and had embraced him as one of the team.

"The depressions in the grass are only an hour old or less. They are made from the same imprint that we found at the crash site in Las Vegas sir," he quietly whispered into his Colonel's ear, his eyes still flickering around the area, always searching.

The alien robot had moved out of the Las Vegas area after the attack and H squadron was tracking it. The Colonel drew a straight line on his map from Las Vegas to his present position. It showed which direction it was travelling; this would give him a good idea of its possible final objective.

The alien robot was no fool either. It had complex command protocols programmed into its massive memory circuits. It had been carrying out standard escape and evasion techniques to try to set a false scent as to its intended destination and aims. But it was not prepared for the tracking capabilities of Little Bear and the technological advances of Delta Force and the whole of the U.S. Armed forces.

They had tracked the alien robot for the last 3 days on a compass heading west-north-west (WNW) from Las Vegas, across the Death Valley National Park, then through part of the Sequoia National Park and they were now just on the outskirts of Fresno. Dan's men were getting tired after 3 days on hyper alert combat status; they were nearing the point of exhaustion. For the robot, tiredness was not something it would ever experience; tiredness was not programmed into it. As a robot it had no comprehension of this sensation.

Despite Little Bear's skill they had not managed to make any ground on the robot, it remained hours ahead of them with no sign of slowing.

Dan Prout and his team needed to change tack, they needed to get ahead of it and cut it off. Looking at his map he plotted potential routes for the robot. They were in the wilderness, and far away from any major city. Dan Prout had no idea what the robot's plans were, he had no idea what its intentions might be but when studying the map one big complex stood out plain as day. He beckoned Little Bear over and pointed it out to him, Little Bear grunted his agreement.

The alien robot was now heading straight towards the Henry W. Coe State Park and the headquarters of Android AI.

General Klein relayed this information to me and asked what I thought, I immediately agreed. It seemed to fit, it felt right. The Andi Mk2s had been an integral part of this whole thing from the beginning. Its development by Android AI had been the reason that the command sphere had been sent back to Kepler-452b. It had subsequently malfunctioned and fallen into our hands. The Mk2s were important to these aliens, for reasons still unknown to us all.

What was it that made them so significant that they had to send a probe back through a wormhole to their home world?

It had to be the super brain technology used by the Andi Mk2s. I couldn't think of any other reason.

The radical DNA splicing techniques discovered by my Mother and then harnessed and developed by my Father were revolutionary on this planet and perhaps on another too. Once in a millennia maybe, something happens which changes the direction of mankind and brain DNA splicing was one of these moments. Perhaps it could also change the path of their future. This must be what the robot wanted; it was heading to the AI headquarters to collect information ready for its masters back on Kepler-452b.

"General Klein, I have to talk to you, I think I know what they are up to. The alien robot has taken it upon itself to steal the technology behind the Andi Mk2s and return to Kepler-452b with the DNA splicing technology. That is why the alien robot is heading for Android AI HQ; it's going to steal the research papers and the computer programs stored there. It is the only explanation."

The General paused for a moment before making his decision.

"Lukas, get your team together. You're flying to Android AI HQ as quickly as possible. Take your father's close protection detachment with you as your security escort. I will inform Colonel Prout that you are on your way, rendezvous with his team when you arrive. This ends tonight."

General Klein let this last sentence linger for a long time and kept his stare on me, in some ways perhaps he held me responsible for the death of the President. The Andis were my father's creations but I was as close as he could get to him. I nodded my response; I was as determined as him to finish this intergalactic feud.

Gus and Vicki had been itching to leave the Cheyenne HQ for some time. Both were elite athletes and being cooped up in an office for weeks was torture for them. Their muscles needed flexing.

"We're coming!" they said in unison, bags in hand. I had no choice and was thankful for it. They knew I wanted them there too, even if I never said it.

"Get your gear together lads, we're leaving in five minutes. That means you too Kinika," Andrew Edwards bellowed.

Kinika was sat in the corner of the room having a cup of his favourite Earl Grey tea and he wasn't going to hurry it for anyone.

*Earl Grey is a tea blend, which has been flavoured with the addition of oil of bergamot. Named after Charles Grey, the 2nd Earl Grey and the British Prime Minister in the 1830s.*

Kinika loved it because of its distinct flavour; it never seemed to change wherever he drank it in the world. Kinika wrote code quickly but he drank slowly, savouring the taste, letting it linger on his lips and sit in his mouth. He wouldn't be rushed for anyone. The team waited at the door as Kinika took his last sip. He slowly and deliberately packed away his things with care before finally joining us with a wry smile upon his face.

The C-20H Gulfstream jet took off into the sunset on its two-hour flight to Android AI HQ, we were all aboard and heading into an uncertain encounter with an alien robot. We were in constant communications with Dan Prout and the Colonel had a plan.

Colonel Prout planned to use a mixture of spectrometers and night vision goggles to identify the robot's location. Marcus had hypothesised that the robot may be seen at certain wavelengths and now was the perfect time to test that theory. Once identified, the Colonel expected to eradicate the robot with the same technology that deflected its plasma beam and took down its spacecraft – The Laser Taser.

The hand-held Laser Taser variant had been developed recently but was yet to be used in real combat. Every man in every squadron of Delta Force now carried it as their personal weapon. During the extensive field-testing the new weapon had proven its worth. It never lost a firefight in any computer simulation test; no other weapon had ever done this before. The reliability of the weapon, combined with the instant firepower was a game changer in weapons design.

Delta Force had been given the honour and was the first Special Forces unit to be issued with the new weapon. Dan Prout and his team were relying on it.

I instructed the lead science director on the Andi Mk2 project Jenny Chu to lock down all the computer details, file notes and research documents into the safe area. Jenny was at Android AI HQ and was responsible for everything Andi.

The safe area was only accessible to the Directors of Android AI. All these men and women had been hand picked by Marcus and the CIA. This had been a very good policy from the outset, as just about every foreign government had tried to place a spy inside Android AI in the last 10 years, with little or no success. The whole Android AI project was so top secret that the President knew of its existence only after being sworn into office. The CIA had managed to keep a tight lid on the whole project over the years. This project wasn't just 'Black' it was 'eyes only Presidential level'.

Jenny Chu worked as the Android AI liaison officer directly with Delta Force. The Delta Force teams had covertly placed the spectrometers in various locations around the Android AI facility. They had cleverly set up firing positions with their new Laser Taser's with every man having his own individual field of fire. The killing zone was laid out, now all they had to do was wait.

Jenny Chu and squadron commander Major Clamp had come to meet us in the driverless Humvee transportation. After the brief introductions Major Clamp filled us in on their recently updated position from Dan Prout.

"Colonel Prout has surmised that the alien robot traveling at its previous speeds, should be here in about 24 hours. As a tactical advantage his best guess is that the alien robot would come in at night under the cover of darkness, roughly 30 hours from now. To give you all some reassurance all Delta Force operators have also been issued with the latest Android AI night vision goggles. If it turns up here, these men will stop it or kill it, wherever or whatever it may be!"

*Night vision is the ability to see in low light conditions, whether by biological or technological means and is made possible by a combination of two approaches: Sufficient spectral range and sufficient intensity range. Humans have poor night vision compared to many animals, in part because the human eye lacks a tapetum lucidum, which is a layer of tissue found in the eye of many vertebrates, which lies immediately behind the retina.*

The latest Special Operations military night vision goggles also had a built in 3D feature to help the operator with distance and depth perception at night. It was responsible for an improvement in its 'kill ratio' of nearly 50%. No mean feat when you are engaged in life or death combat, and your new piece of hardware helps kill 50% more of the enemy!

I was a little more sceptical of the situation than Major Clamp's pep talk would allow us to believe. I knew that the alien robot had survived a crash that no human could have. I also knew that the robot had crossed heavy terrain in just over 3 days, a distance that would have taken a human on foot over 7 days without a break. They were not dealing with some normal soldier or terrorist here, this thing was on a level that both the Colonel and his men were not really trained for. I knew they would fight it and I also knew they would die trying, if they had to, I was just hoping that we could lend some scientific assistance to help them stop this thing before anymore people had to die.

Jenny Chu took me to my parent's old laboratory. As I started to look around I was suddenly overcome with sadness. My mother had been alive the last time I was here. My father had also worked here for thousands of hours, developing the DNA splicing technology; eventually what he created here would kill him. His death was still raw to me and I hadn't had sufficient time to mourn or grieve, for now that had to wait.

At times during this conflict I had questioned everything I knew about the world and its origins, I had even raised questions about my faith. I was not really a religious man but standing there in the laboratory where my parents spent their lives I couldn't help send a little silent prayer to a God I didn't really believe in. I was a scientist, I believed in Darwin, Einstein and physics.

In my prayer I asked that my parents be together now, peaceful and happy. I asked that today would be the end of it and that I could have the privilege to live out my days in peace with Vicki. In my dreary reverie I remembered the Ten Commandments that we were taught at my childhood Sunday school:

1. You shall have no other gods before me.
2. You shall make no idols.
3. You shall not take the name of the Lord your God in vain.
4. Keep the Sabbath day holy.
5. Honor your father and your mother.
6. You shall not murder.
7. You shall not commit adultery.
8. You shall not steal.
9. You shall not bear false witness against your neighbor.
10. You shall not covet.

Number 6 wouldn't haunt me. I wanted to kill this alien robot and would do it with a clear conscience. It was not human after all, it could not be murdered and even if it was, it bloody deserved it in my opinion.

# Chapter thirty one

I t was a still night. The air was silent and sharp, no wind dared blow on this night, no cloud entered the fray. The Delta Force operators lay silent and sharp, scattered invisibly around the Android AI complex, waiting for their target, waiting with just their cold still breath for company.

Sergeant Martinez from Delta Force 'B' squadron saw the digital display on his spectrometer reveal a small but subtle twitch. He had been at his post for nearly eight hours, his concentration never lapsed, never faltered. His spectrometer flickered for just a split second but that was enough to alert Martinez. He pressed lightly down on his throat mike to alert his colleagues of the possible threat and moved his eye slowly to his rifle sight.

It was the last thing he ever did.

The alien robot was in combat mode and wasn't there to play hide and seek. It was aware of all the Delta Force positions; the heat signatures emitted from the men had given away their positions in an instant. They didn't stand a chance.

The alien robot had thermal imaging technology built into its command and control systems. It saw every soldier as if they were waving a flag, and didn't hesitate to eliminate them quickly, one by one.

Martinez was a good soldier he had alerted his fellow squad members just before he drew his last breath but it would do little to help them.

The speed at which the alien robot moved in combat mode was frightening; it was like using high octane gas and being supercharged. Its body was made of an alloy not found on Earth that was both light and staggeringly strong, a single bullet would do little damage.

The robot might have been a million years old but it was from a planet that was one and a half billion years older than the Earth and some of its capabilities were much more advanced than our own Andi Mk2s, but it didn't have a spliced super brain.

Although it was a defensive robot it did have offensive capabilities. Its weapon of choice was a pulse beam similar to our Laser Taser and it tore through anything in its path. The pulse beam of intense energy struck Sergeant Martinez just below the throat, exactly at the point where his finger had pressed his mike. He was dead in a blink of an eye.

The field of fire set up by his section commander had left Martinez the weakest link in the chain to gaining entry into the Android AI building and the alien robot knew it. Its tactical planning software had composed the battle plan the moment it had spotted the soldiers. The software was so advanced it updated continuously as the firefight unfolded.

The robot's movement sensors and its visual recognition software had detected the hand movement by Martinez and had correctly deemed it as a tactical threat. Martinez's death was not without a tactical advantage to his comrades, the pulse beam had come directly from the robots nuclear fusion power cell and this could not be cloaked. The blinding white beam of light instantly betrayed its location, just for a fraction of a second.

Martinez's signal and the light from the beam was enough for the other Delta Force operators to engage. Triggers were pulled in unison and the men's Laser Taser's cut through the cloudless night sky. The alien robot was instantly on the move. It held the tactical advantage of being cloaked as the Delta Force operators fired in the direction of what they thought was their target. The onslaught of these men was utterly useless and ineffective. The robot just simply outmanoeuvred them.

The robot again fired its pulse beam, this time at two other Delta Force snipers who had taken up positions with their Barrett sniper rifles. The first pulse beam hit Sergeant Chilloski's laser sight and entered into his skull via his eye socket. The second pulse beam, emitted a fraction of a second later, hit Sergeant Fatches directly in the forehead. He was also dead before his own senses could react.

Delta Force operators were not known to panic but this was a situation none of them had experienced before. All their planning and preparation was useless against such a foe, this was turning into a one-sided massacre.

The alien robot continued on through the hail of incoming rounds and Laser Taser discharges, firing its deadly pulse beam as it moved effortlessly towards the main entrance of Android AI HQ. Major Clamp ordered the remaining Delta Force operators to disengage, this thing needed to be attacked from a different perspective.

It seemed that the aliens and their robots had missed some developments of the human race. The Andi Mk2s were one; the motion activated Laser Taser was another. They had not considered this when they tried to bomb our sun and their robot again overlooked the Laser Taser technology as it approached the main entrance to the Android AI HQ building.

The alien robot was unaware of the mobile Laser Tasers positioned in all of the entrance doorways to Android AI. These weapons were stand-alone automatic firing units and the very latest available weapons platform from within the Delta Force armoury. The design of this merciless weapon was sleek and minimal, perhaps deceiving the robot as to what lay within. No heat was emitted from these new super guns and it showed no signs of its deadly force.

One thing that mankind had become very good at over the last 100,000 years was learning how to kill each other in every imaginable way and today was no exception. The alien robot may have been cloaked and invisible to the human eye, but even it had to stop when opening doors. Physics was physics!

It had stopped in front of the entrance doors and surveyed the area, slowly scanning the entrance. We were all watching via a CCTV camera fitted with infrared night vision from within the walls of the complex. We had watched in horror as it struck down Delta Force soldiers like swatting flies. Rage had risen steadily as I saw the robot approach the doors and it culminated as it stopped outside.

"Now..." I whispered to Kinika who nodded and tapped a key on his computer.

The Laser Tasers positioned by the doorway instantly burst into life and fired a wide arc beam of certain death towards the robot. The kill zone was complete. The effect of the beam was emphatic, where the Delta Force hand-held Laser Taser's had failed, the unmanned mobile Laser Taser's had triumphed. The bright light from their two locations, initially created a small fire and a smokescreen that obstructed our view, but we could now see what we had been hoping for. The alien robot de-cloaked and lying motionless on the floor, cut in half by the mobile Laser Tasers.

We sat quietly for a minute watching the scenes on our computer screen. Part of me felt that this was another ploy, another trick by the robot. But as time ticked slowly by I could feel hope and relief rising from somewhere, mixing to form a blend of ecstasy. This might be it. It could actually be over. I looked gingerly at the others and we shared a hopeful moment.

After a minute, two Delta Force operatives and Major Clamp crept into view, rifles and Laser Tasers at the ready. They scuttled towards the titanium alloy corpse. Ready to fire if its dormant body dared move again.

"It's not dead, it was never alive," said Major Clamp to his two men who were first on the scene.

"Kill confirmed. We think," Clamp said to us over the radio.

I arrived on the scene 30 seconds later with Andrew Edwards and the others from my security detail. We were still cautious and suspicious that the robot was not dead so Andrew and his team immediately set up a defensive perimeter. After a quick systems check by Kinika, I was confident that we had fully disabled it. It was only now that the relief seemed to fill all of us, including the hardened veterans from Delta Force. This thing had been the cause of a massive loss of life, and everyone who had come near it had lost a friend or loved one in the last few days.

Jenny Chu under direct orders from the President immediately sealed off the area and took the robot away for further examination.

I was invited by Jenny to examine the remains of the alien robot. I had been given Presidential permission along with Kinika and Jenny from Android AI to investigate the robot and try to find out more about this strange adversary who had been spying on the human race for the last million years.

Jenny and I immediately agreed to move the robot's remains into the Android AI secure laboratory facility for everyone's security. Now that the danger had seemed to have passed once and for all, I began to think like the curious astrophysicist that I was. I wanted to know everything possible about this thing in front of me. The past few weeks had been so manic that my mind had rarely been freed from a combination of fear and adrenaline overload, long enough to become excited or intrigued. But here I was now, standing in front of an extra-terrestrial creation that had come from another planet and built by an alien race. A torrent of strange excitement hit me suddenly. I was still angry and in shock about my father's death but I thought searching for answers now might be the best way to help me mourn.

Jenny Chu was the leader in her field of Robotics. She had helped my mother Flo in a small capacity during her research, but was heavily involved with my father in developing the DNA splicing techniques needed to integrate the structure of the super-brains into the circuits of the Andi Mk2s. She was passionate about her work and had given the last 10 years of her life to various Android AI projects; she instantly got down to the task in hand with the same vigour and enthusiasm that was brimming inside me.

I stood over the remains of the alien robot with Jenny and Kinika. We nodded to each other and then set to work.

Jenny began her examination by analysing its mysterious alloy exterior. She wanted to know what the material was and whether it could be reverse-engineered for the benefit of the United States and the whole human race.

*Reverse engineering or back engineering has gone on for centuries and mostly has its origins in warfare. The 'Jerry can' is a classic example. British and American forces noticed that the Germans had gasoline cans with an excellent design. They both reverse-engineered copies of those cans. The cans were then popularly known as Jerry Cans. Also during the Second World War, British scientists analysed and defeated a series of increasingly sophisticated radio navigation systems being used by the German Luftwaffe to perform guided bombing missions at night. The British countermeasures to this system were so effective that in some cases German aircraft was fooled into landing at RAF bases while believing they were back on German territory. Reverse engineering your enemies' operating systems can give you a massive edge on the battlefield.*

Kinika and I were both after information. Kinika was hoping to gain a deeper understanding about the robot's programming and the code it ran on. The pulse beam it had emitted in Las Vegas also fascinated him. Kinika had studied the footage from Las Vegas and he was sure that the pulse beam was something he could reverse-engineer, if he could just gather all the necessary data.

For me, I wanted to know everything I could about life on Kepler-452b and what other advancements the aliens had made there. Even though the immediate threat from invasion was over, planet Earth was still in slow, but persistent demise. We were still steadily eating our way through our own natural resources and due to global warming running out of fresh water, but I believed I could find some answers to help us from this robot lying in front of me.

It didn't take Kinika and Jenny long to figure out where the displacement and discharge of the pulse energy had come from. The robot's fingers were the source. It came from within the tips of the robot's 10 digits; digits that we all agreed strangely represented human fingers. In each digit there was a port that could discharge both data and pulse energy.

Now all Kinika and Jenny had to do was figure out how it was done. They both rolled up their sleeves and got down to work. They busied themselves around the lab scuttling between equipment and back to the robot in almost complete synchronisation. They were an immediate team, fuelled by their insatiable appetite for information. They were so engrossed in their work and monopolized the robot so much that I couldn't even start my tests and analyses. I slowly snuck away, my mind on other things now.

For the first time in weeks I managed to spend some alone time with Vicki, we even managed to get rid of Gus for an evening. We relaxed lazily in our room; cuddled in blankets I had a glass of whisky, my first since my father's death. The whisky reminded me of my father. I had somehow managed to keep him out of my thoughts while the hunt for the robot was on, but now he came. I spoke at length about him, sharing things I never had before. Vicki listened, her eyes welling at my words that I had kept hidden for so long.

The next morning we began the dreaded process of planning my father's funeral. We had no idea what funeral he would have wanted, one thing was for certain though, there would be no Andis carrying his casket.

While Kinika and Jenny were toiling away, and Vicki and I were scribbling random funeral vocabulary, the President rang on my private iPhone number.

"Madame President?" I said.

"Lukas," she began in a soft, endearing tone, "I hear and see everything, the CIA and NSA are very diligent in their work and they even follow your conversations and report back to me. You may not know too much about this, but your father and I were friends for many years. I worked with him when I was deputy Director of the CIA. His vision and leadership of Android AI has helped the world to become a safer and better place. The Andi Mk1s have become the backbone of the world's rebuilding program. The Andis have reduced crime rates all over the world, so much so, that some countries are now starting to shut down their prisons because they have so few inmates anymore. The Mk2s were the next level of sophistication. They too were changing the world for the better, don't hold it against them, it was not their fault they were overwhelmed. Your father could never have foreseen that outcome."

"Thank you Madame President…" I muttered slightly confused at her words and why she was speaking like this.

"So Lukas, this is my proposal. I am going to hold a State Funeral for my predecessor, but I also want to hold it jointly with your father."

I was dumbfounded and taken aback by the President's offer. A state funeral was the highest of honours and I wanted the best for Marcus. This would be a perfect send off for him, I thought.

I immediately agreed with the President and she then told me that she had pencilled in the date for ten days' time. She told me that she would not release any details of my father's Intelligence work on behalf of the U.S. government and would focus on the rise of Android AI and use him as a shining example to his fellow Americans that greatness is achievable and that individuals can change the world for the better.

She finished by saying; "your father laid down his life for his country. He paid the ultimate sacrifice for his devotion and service to the flag. This country will honour and remember him."

I was greatly humbled by it all. My father had always been my hero and now everyone else would realise what an incredible man he truly was.

He would be remembered for saving millions from a solar flare attack and from ever-rising sea levels. He would be remembered for his tireless brain that ached to break boundaries and reinvent the world. He would be remembered for his Andis and for all the good they had brought into the world.

# Chapter thirty two

*The flag of the United States of America is made up of thirteen equal horizontal stripes alternating red with white, with a blue rectangle in the canton, which is referred to specifically as the "Union" bearing fifty small, white, five-pointed stars. The 50 stars on the flag adopted on July 4, 1960 represent the 50 states of America and the 13 stripes represent the thirteen British colonies that declared independence from the kingdom of Great Britain and became the first States in the U.S. There are several nicknames for the flag including, The Stars and Stripes, Old Glory, The American flag, Red White and Blue and the Star-Spangled Banner.*

My father would be buried with the flag of the United States of America draped over his casket during his state funeral, an honour bestowed on a select few. My father was loyal to his country and like so many others before him had died in its service.

Five previous state funerals have been held at the Arlington National Cemetery most notably those of Presidents William Howard Taft and John F. Kennedy and now my father Marcus and the ex-president would also be interned there.

The Arlington National Cemetery holds around 6900 funerals a year and is located in Arlington County, Virginia just across the Potomac River from Washington, D.C. Set in 624 acres, the dead of the nation's conflicts have been buried here since the American Civil War.

The President had made sure that security was very tight ahead of the funeral. The general unease among the populace had broken out into a spate of rioting and looting when the first reports of an alien invasion had been aired by some parts of the media. The President had called a State of Emergency in some cities and sent the troops in to restore order, as the Andis were not back online as yet. This had shown the President and her staff just how reliant the USA had become on the Andis.

The President summoned me to the West Wing of the White House the night before the funeral.

I arrived at the door of the oval office. "Come in and sit down Lukas we have a lot to discuss". The President dismissed her security detail and her two Aides and started talking.

"Kinika and Jenny are still working on extracting information from the robot and it seems that they keep finding new information almost every day."

"What exactly have they found?"

The President looked up at me and said, "It appears that the aliens have only about 500,000 years left on their home planet before their sun burns the surface and causes the extinction of the alien race. As you correctly discovered this is why they are collecting gold from the Earth and we assume other planets too. The issue is the time left on Kepler-452b is a lot less than we originally thought."

"The information from the robot Kinika and Jenny have extracted states that the aliens believe that the Earth could be habitable for up to 1 billion years more. This is a lot longer than their planet and it seems you were correct in your hypothesis that they were here to do a test run, to see if Earth could be inhabited successfully by their species. We humans have positively tested their hypothesis and the data suggests they are on their way here to begin the take-over.

"Their plan was to use the Andis to control and enslave the human race for gold extraction. When their ships arrived on Earth they would take the gold back to Kepler-452b and carry on with the golden sphere construction, as you predicted. However Kinika tells me that they also planned to leave a contingent of aliens and robots here to rule and populate this planet. The data from the robot suggests that the alien's know a lot more than we first imagined. Perhaps we had developed faster than they thought, or they misjudged us or perhaps it is all part of their plan. I personally believe they underestimated us and in particular the technology that your parents created."

At the mention of my parents and their work my mind began to wander again, uncontrollably. I began to think about one of my favourite mathematicians, John von Neumann.

*John von Neumann worked on the original 'Manhattan Project' during World War II and published over 150 papers during his lifetime. Von Neumann's work on the Universal Constructor is about a self-replicating machine in a cellular automata (CA) environment. The fundamental details of the machine were published in von Neumann's book 'Theory of Self-Reproducing Automata' and completed in 1966 by Arthur W. Burks after von Neumann's death.*

It was more and more likely that the aliens had discovered how to create self-replicating robots and that is how they had managed to spread out across the Universe. It was also highly likely that this is what the aliens were doing here on Earth, and they were also doing on countless planets, in other Solar Systems. This was the benefit of self-replicating robots. They could be sent out into deep space, communications could be lost for thousands of years but you could be confident that they were completing the task as instructed. The more I thought about it the more I thought that this must be what we need to do, we need to create a self-replicating Andi Mk2 for deep space exploration. We needed to emulate the aliens' plans and spread the human race throughout space too.

Would we then do to other races what these alien robots have done here? Would we become the invaders and killers of fathers? Perhaps we would just repeat the process of what had happened on their home planet. Perhaps that's what they wanted. Perhaps it was in our DNA to explore and conquer.

In 2035 you can now buy a laptop computer with more computing power than the human brain for $1000. Computers and machines really did rule the world now, not humans. We may have reached a point in our evolution where computers don't need humans anymore. Humans were now surplus to requirements, survival of the fittest meant that humans' time was limited unless we could adapt and evolve ourselves.

I was falling down a rabbit hole of questions without answers and I had to force myself back into the room, back to the here and now.

"As I mentioned the other day Lukas, this is now a very important time for us all and I need you. I need you to predict when they will arrive on Earth and what we can do to ensure our survival. I know this is an ominous task and one that will drain you but you are the best person for this job. You need to carry on the work your mother and father started, only you can do this. What do you think?"

I knew the scale of the task that I was being asked to undertake and I knew that the outcome was likely to be bad but I was strangely excited. There was a bubbling in my stomach and a tingling in my fingers. Despite the recent devastations, I had never felt so alive. My mind was tested and pushed to its limits and at times I had been responsible for protecting an entire race. The feeling was something I never expected to experience and never expected to enjoy, but I did.

I locked eyes with the President and firmly told her how committed I was and that I would not fail her. She smiled and seemed relieved, not many would have accepted the task I guessed.

"I have one final thing to tell you Lukas..." she paused briefly. "The Medal of Honour is the United States of America's highest military honor Lukas. Usually the President, in the name of the U.S. Congress awards the medal to a serving member of the U.S. armed forces.

"Lukas, tomorrow I am going to award your father posthumously 'The Presidential Medal of Freedom' the highest civilian award of the United States. It was originally established in 1963 and replaced the earlier Medal of Freedom that was created by President Harry S. Truman in 1945 to honour civilian service during World War II. Your father will be in exalted company."

"Thank you Madam President," was all I could muster. We said our goodbyes and I left.

Morning broke; it was a chilly January day. I walked with Vicki and Gus surrounded by Andrew Edwards and his security team. They were not there for security purposes but to pay their own respects. They all loved and respected my father and they carried a heavy burden of guilt after his death. Even with constant assurances that there was nothing they could have done they were still bitter that my father had died. In their eyes they had failed in their duty to protect him.

Days earlier I had read my father's will and had felt slightly dizzy at the scale of the fortune I would inherit. I had a task ordered by the President, but I also wanted to do more. Vicki and I agreed we would commit 50% of the inherited money, and our futures, to helping those in need. I knew my parents, especially my mother, would appreciate this gesture.

The hearse carrying the President draped in the Flag of the United States of America led the way, my father was a respectful 200 yards behind the President's car. It reminded me of him during his life, always in the shadow of the leaders he had served. He had thought about standing for the Presidency some years ago but after the torrid and bitter Trump/ Clinton Presidential campaign of 2016, he had chosen to remain in the shadows when it came to politics. Marcus's reasoning behind this was simple, he could influence the world a lot more by being creative rather than destructive and that's what had spurred him on back in 2017 to form and develop Android AI with the backing of the CIA.

The funeral service was as one might imagine – grandiose but respectful. The prayers and speeches were numerous and every possible respect was shown. I delivered Marcus' eulogy, with words I don't really remember; my lips moved independent of any conscious thought. All I remember from it was Vicki's eyes; they helped me through, guiding me home.

The day after the funeral the media was back to speculation about the past events. The U.S. government had indeed spun web after web of cover stories and it was a massive task trying to conceal the truth from the increasingly investigative media and truth-seeking populace. The initial cover story given was that a perpetrator had hacked into and had taken control of the Andis and tried to use them as an army for their own ends. This mixed with the space flight crash was difficult for many to swallow and I knew that the secret of life beyond our planet was soon to come out.

It was only a matter of time.

Nevertheless all the Andis would be back in circulation within a month. With updated systems and the latest security protocols but stripped of any weapons. They would be back helping the city relocation scheme not policing the streets; human influence had definitely taken control again.

Although the data and statistics backed up the Andis use there is a non-removable bond between humans. Even those we don't trust we can relate to, this is not so with the Andis. Despite all their qualities and relentless help, they will never be human. They will never be flesh, bone, sweat and tears; they can never share emotions or secrets. They will never have a soul and for me that was that.

Humans were back, for now.

# Chapter thirty three

A week later at 6am my phone abruptly rang, wrenching me out of a deep sleep.

"Hello?" I mumbled. At first all I could hear in response was a slurping noise. "Kinika?"

"Come to the lab now. You need to see this."

I clumsily pulled on my clothes, which were dotted around the room after the night before. Vicki lay there on the bed sound asleep, wrapped in just a sheet. I watched her for a moment before heading out the door. As I walked down the long dreary, grey corridor to the lab I wondered if I had neglected Kinika and Jenny slightly. I had taken a bit of a back seat in the last few days; they were the expert analysts on robots after all. I only got in the way. That's what I told myself anyway.

I walked into the laboratory and sealed the doors behind me. Kinika and Jenny were sat down, chatting in an excited manner. Kinika had his extra-large energy drink and was slurping it through a long straw whilst Jenny sat nursing a mint tea. I rubbed my face as I sat down next to them.

"You find something?" I yawned as I poured myself a coffee.

"The President is calling soon, we'll explain everything then," Jenny said between sips. We sat in a calm silence, sipping our morning drinks, staring inquisitively at the robot's remains.

The President appeared on the big screen a few minutes later, looking remarkably awake, I guessed she'd been awake for an hour already.

"Morning all. Golden Goose?" The President said.

"Golden Goose indeed," replied Kinika.

I looked from one to the other, totally lost. Luckily Jenny was there to explain. The President had issued her with a code word 'Golden Goose'.

*The German fairy tale the 'Golden Goose' is by Jacob and Wilhelm Grimm, better known to the world as the Brothers Grimm. They were storytellers and are best known for their book published in 1812 about Children's and Household Tales.*

The Golden Goose fairy tale had nothing to do with what was going on here, the President just loved the fairy tale from her childhood and she was aware of the storyline and the effects gold can have on people who touch it. She thought it was symbolic in some way, but it all seemed irrelevant to me.

"Ok... So you've found the Golden Goose?" I asked.

The President spoke again. "Ladies and gentlemen, we are the only four people on the Earth to see this information contained within this alien robot and I intend to keep it this way. You are only ever to discuss this information between the four of us, or anyone else who follows me into this office. You are never to discuss its contents with anyone else ever, is that perfectly clear? That also includes your wife Lukas. She does not have the security clearance." We all respectfully nodded and then verbalized our agreement with the President's request.

She then told Kinika and Jenny to continue with their briefing.

Kinika and Jenny looked at me excitedly.

Jenny began, "Madam President, this robot is made of an alloy not available on Earth. It is remarkably light and flexible at the same time. Well it's much, much better than that really. The alloy body is not only a conductor of heat and electricity, but it's also a massive piece of computer hardware. The whole body itself is one large computer and memory chip, all rolled into one. Its engine and power source is a tiny little nuclear generator and it's fully intact. Its generator is only emitting very small doses of radiation and is not harmful to us at all, whilst it's intact. The engineering involved in creating this robot is quite beyond anything we have achieved on Earth up to this point, with the exception of the DNA brain splicing of course." Jenny threw a quick glance at me.

The President nodded her head in approval and before she could reply Kinika spoke up loudly. He was extremely excited.

"Have you read my initial four page report Madame President? Because the information we have extracted from this thing is a game changer."

"I've read it Kinika."

I gave Kinika a confused look, I was lost again.

"What report?"

"Lukas, your fathers friend Kinika Lawal, may have just rewritten our history books."

The President stopped, shook her head slightly in a sign of disbelief and then refocused.

"Lukas, the command sphere that you found in New Zealand didn't quite give us the whole story. Kinika - please enlighten us."

Kinika began explaining the process they had used to extract the information. He explained that he had painstakingly formed a code that infiltrated the robot systems and then this allowed him to extract every single piece of information that was held within the robot. As Jenny said earlier the robot was one huge memory stick, so every bit of data that it had collected over the millennia was stored inside. The process of extracting all this data and then decoding it must have been excruciating, I thought to myself.

"Why didn't you ask for my help?" I mused.

Kinika and Jenny shared a look, a look that you couldn't mistake. They couldn't stop their mouths rising in a slight smile and their eyes glistening with emotion.

"Oh..." I muttered behind my own grin.

"Now for what we found," Jenny continued with a slight blush on her cheeks. "As you previously discovered Lukas, the alien robots have been here on a mission for the last million years to collect the gold for their defences against their own aggressive sun, which over the last five million years has been gradually burning up their home planet."

I nodded my agreement.

"But here is the astonishing truth; the robots have also been here on Earth secretly watching our progress as a race. You see, they have a very intimate interest in all of us, Lukas. It transpires that we are built in the image of the aliens back on Kepler-452b, we have some of the same DNA."

I let that sink for a moment and then said, "How can you be sure?" My voice was surprisingly calm.

"It's all here, it's all explained within the metallic cells of this robot," Jenny said reassuringly.

"They have been testing and probing the human race for hundreds of thousand's of years. Those alien abduction stories you hear all the time, well they would seem to be highly accurate."

Kinika paused then took another deep breath. "Most of the robot's work has been around manipulating the human DNA code, especially the thalamus area of the brain."

*The thalamus is a small structure within the brain, which is located just above the brainstem, between the cerebral cortex and the midbrain, and it has extensive nerve connections to both. The main function of the thalamus is to relay motor and sensory signals to the cerebral cortex. It stimulates the cortex of the brain.*

"That's why the alien robot was heading for the Android AI HQ building, it wanted the technical data on the super-brains developed by your parents. Your parents had between them exceeded anything the aliens had previously developed on Kepler-452b and now they wanted their secrets," the President chipped in.

I looked at Kinika, Jenny and the President in turn – my jaw was hanging on by a thread.

*Francis Crick and James Watson discovered the existence of DNA in 1953; they were geniuses of their time. Crick's seven-page, handwritten letter to his son in 1953 where he explains his discovery, sold at Christie's New York on the 10th of April 2013 for $6,059,750, still the largest amount ever paid for a letter at auction.*

My mother's work on DNA splicing was inspired by an article written in 2013 by two scientists - Dr. Vladimir I. Shcherbak, a mathematician at the al-Farabi Kazakh National University of Kazakhstan, and Maxim A. Makukov, an astrobiologist at Kazakhstan's Fesenkov Astrophysical Institute.

Their theories at the time were accepted for publication in the prestigious planetary science journal the 'Icarus'. Their work focused on the mathematical code within DNA. They argued that human DNA was mathematically based and not random. They argued quite convincingly that the complete layout of DNA was too precise to conform to standard random logic.

Crick, the Nobel Prize winner and co-discoverer of DNA, along with Leslie Orgel proposed that life might have been purposely spread by an advanced extra-terrestrial civilization based on the theory called panspermia.

*Panspermia is the Greek word that literally translates as 'seeds everywhere'. The panspermia hypothesis states that the 'seeds' of life exist all over the Universe and can be propagated through space from one location to another. Some believe that life on Earth may have originated through these 'seeds'.*

"You know very well what this theory is Lukas; you yourself wrote extensively on the subject whilst completing your PhD in astrophysics, yes the CIA catalogued everything you wrote, even then, your father read your papers with interest. For everyone's clarity can you please elaborate to Kinika and Jenny your current understanding of this hypothesis?"

The President knew her facts but she wanted me to explain. I told Kinika and Jenny exactly what my hypothesis was based on.

I began by listing my three favourite versions of panspermia for Kinika and Jenny. The President listened intently.

Lithopanspermia or interstellar panspermia is impact-expelled rock from a planet's surface, which serves as transfer vehicles for spreading biological material from one solar system to another. Self-explanatory really.

Ballistic panspermia or interplanetary panspermia is impact-expelled rock from a planet's surface, which serves as transfer vehicles for spreading biological material from one planet to another within the same solar system. Again, self-explanatory really.

Directed panspermia is the intentional spreading of the seeds of life to other planets by an advanced extra-terrestrial civilization or the intentional spreading of the seeds of life from Earth to other planets by humans. I pointed out to everyone that our recent visit to Mars could be seen as the start of this process from a human perspective.

The fact that every member of the human race was directly linked to alien DNA came as a complete shock. I'm a scientist and if you put all the pieces of the jigsaw puzzle together, as hard as it was to swallow, the facts, the evidence and the assumption all added up to the same conclusion.

"Is this why they are here..?" I asked myself aloud. "If they purposely sent their DNA here and watched the human race grow, populate and successfully live off the Earth, maybe it was a test. Perhaps we are just rats in a gigantic galactic lab experiment…"

"Go on Lukas…" said The President.

"My father had a plan to send the Andis into space for exploration of other planets and surely he would have done the same. Sent human DNA with them and watched to see if they could survive on the planet. Then when we had finally squeezed this planet off everything it has, we could move there. Is this not exactly what the aliens have done here? Our plan is their plan, they just simply had a 1.5 billion year head start on us."

There was a momentary silence in the room as we all absorbed this information; only the occasional slurping from Kinika could be heard.

It was an impossible situation because we were at the mercy of a civilisation way more advanced than us. We had fought off their first attempt at taking our gold and perhaps trying to inhabit our planet but it had come at a cost and I wasn't sure if we could do it again.

The President took control of the conversation again and her priority was on more Earthly matters.

"I understand that all this is rather hard to comprehend and for that reason I think we need to focus on managing the current situation here on Earth with our citizens before we worry about another attack or another colonisation attempt."

"At present we have a massive containment situation to control.

The White House and the U.S. military have layers upon layers of cover stories that we have fed to the media about the whole situation. So far some of the media have had reports of alien spaceships crashing in Las Vegas. As you know after the spaceship crashed in Las Vegas, we issued a joint statement with the Chinese President telling the world it was a space exercise with the Chinese that had gone horribly wrong."

The world's media had bought into the story, because it was the only story. The statement explained that the China National Space Administration (CNSA) and NASA were working on a secret joint space venture to Mars when there was catastrophic equipment failure. This destroyed one of our new top-secret spaceships, the remnants of which are now being collected in Las Vegas and the surrounding desert. The city of Las Vegas is still under Martial Law whilst the remains of the spaceship are completely recovered.

The President continued "The Chinese President knows of the alien spaceship and of the alien robots, we have had to explain to him giving full disclosure on the current situation. He now understands fully, why the tactical nuclear device was used in the Marianas Trench and he has subsequently stood down all his armed forces in an attempt to ease the political tension around the world. He now wants to work with us at all levels. He agrees that there would be a worldwide meltdown of civilized society if the truth were actually released to the masses. He has also agreed to a new secret joint space venture, with a view to combatting any future alien threat and that we would jointly fund it with the profit from the new gold reserves we would unearth."

"So with the media under control to a degree and the Andi invasion now thwarted, can we assume that Kinika and Jenny can continue to reverse-engineer this robot?" I asked.

"Lukas here is the final outcome as I see it. The Chinese know about the gold and the alien plan. I have told the Chinese President that the robots were all destroyed in the crash in Las Vegas and he believes this. The CIA has even released a fake top-secret memo to this effect. Any double agent working within the CIA would have passed this document on to their Chinese handlers. There are only a few people in the world who have seen the alien robot. The Delta Force operators on duty the night of the attack on the Android AI HQ complex thought they were pursuing a rogue robot. The Delta Force operators that actually saw the robot, and there are only three of them in total, including Major Clamp, have all been told personally by me that it is the latest Chinese combat surveillance robot and that we have destroyed it. This is where their story ends. I have also told the three of them personally never to ask another question about it and never to discuss it with another soul, as long as they live. I have also had the same conversation with Andrew Edwards and his team. There are no pictures of the alien robot in existence and all the information we have on it is stored securely where you are now, in Android AI HQ."

The President spoke with total confidence and clarity but I was still dubious that the entire population would believe these cover stories. A lot of unusual activity had happened in the past few months and it wouldn't take a genius to discover that governments were trying to conceal information. Nevertheless, that was the President's problem and I trusted her to manage it in the best way possible. She had some pretty clever people working for her and they would go to any lengths to keep the true story suppressed.

For now I felt a little bit surplus to requirements, even a little out of my depth. Kinika and Jenny would continue to work on the robot and extract any more information they could that might help us and continue with their reverse engineering project.

"What can I do Madam President?"

"Lukas, I want you to use the data that Jenny and Kinika provide you with to try and discover what these aliens will do next. What will be their plan and how can we beat them again."

I rubbed my hands together as I envisioned the grand task ahead.

# Chapter thirty four

Beckham Andrew Levi Linsky was born into a simmering world on the 14th July 2035. Vicki deliberately made his initials spell the word 'BALL', her love for the game knew no limits.

The Fédération Internationale de Football Association or (FIFA) was formed on the 21st May 1904 and was now 131 years old. FIFA, despite its past corruption scandals, was the equivalent of NASA for any footballing fanatic. I remember the moment clearly when Vicki received the phone call. Her face dropped at first, her jaw hitting the floor before rebounding up into a huge smile, FIFA had offered her a job. With her ambassador experience with the 3-2-1 Football Academy and with a child named Beckham, no one was more suited to the role.

Vicki was in disbelief for a while, working as an ambassador for FIFA was her dream. It made me smile that we were both working within our dream companies. I tried once to tease Vicki that the reason she had been offered the role was because she was married to one of the richest men in the world. The look she gave me would have turned Medusa herself to stone. I never made the joke again.

Around the world things had settled down. Sections of the world's population still didn't buy the cover-up story the governments of the world had spun but there was almost nothing they could do. The establishment held all the power and manipulated the media and reported evidence however they wanted. The 1% controlled everything and all the rest of the world could do was have their opinions and beliefs and then get on with their lives.

The President and her advisors had settled on a sufficiently dramatic and elaborate cover-up story that didn't fail to whet the appetites of the media and the general population.

The President released joint statements with the Chinese government that a rogue Russian spy and computer programmer, Sergei Valenkov had been the sole perpetrator.

He had worked for the Sluzhba Vneshney Razvedki more commonly known as the (SVR RF), the now defunct Russian external intelligence agency. Local Russian police had found his dead body in his Moscow basement apartment after a mysterious tip off.

Valenkov was found with a Smith and Wesson .44 Magnum, the world's most powerful handgun, lying by his side. He had blown his brains out, quite literally the remnants of which were all over the wall and the surrounding flooring next to his lifeless blood soaked body. The door was locked from the inside, no signs of forced entry and only Valenkov's prints on the gun. Simple suicide.

His execution was actually a staged suicide perpetrated by the CIA. The CIA had worked in tandem with Bill Fisher and his team from the NSA to plant the computer complete with all the details of the Andis codes to incriminate Valenkov beyond any doubt. The NSA's Back Door Entry team had been hard at work for the last 4 months making the evidence into a compelling cover story and then planting it into Sergei Valenkov's own offending laptop. The past-his-sell-by-date ex-Russian double agent just happened to be the perfect cover story.

Brett Hall the Moscow CIA station chief supplied the final touch of genius. He booby trapped Valenkov's apartment with stolen Russian military-grade plastic explosives. When the local Moscow police officer turned the handle of the apartment door, he triggered a simple trip switch, which blew up half the building, conveniently destroying some, but not all of the evidence in a massive fireball. The local Moscow CSI team and his old SVR RF colleagues were at a loss on this one. There was no suicide note or any real reason they could find why Sergei Valenkov would be involved in such a treacherous act, apart from the fact this rogue ex-agent wanted to steal the world's gold!

# Chapter thirty five

T he tenth and final remaining alien robot had escaped the depths of the Marianas Trench explosion seven months earlier via one of their underwater recovery vehicles. Each robot had been allocated their own vehicle, which they all individually maintained. Today was its scheduled maintenance day. The nuclear explosion had destroyed the others.

There was a certain amount of luck involved in the robot's escape. The remaining underwater vehicle was located the furthest distance away from the epicenter of the explosion. The escape tunnel being five miles long, gave the robot just enough time to leap into the vehicle before the shockwave and blast arrived. The vehicle made from the alien titanium alloy could withstand the water pressure at those depths and was more than adequate to protect the robot from being blown into a thousand pieces by the nuclear explosion, that had been detonated a few seconds earlier by Star.

The remaining robot had initially made its way to the nearby island of Guam from its underwater base. It had camouflaged and hidden the recovery vehicle in a cave 400 feet below the surface. The robot had then cloaked itself and made its way ashore. It then boarded a plane via the cargo hold for the 5798-mile trip to San Francisco. Once in San Francisco it made its way to the Android AI research laboratories where it was now holed up observing from a distance Kinika and Jenny Chu's daily movements. The alien robot knew it was they who had access to the remaining destroyed alien robot.

Kinika and Jenny had not realized it yet, but built into the whole frame of the destroyed alien robot was a signal being emitted by cloaked Nano robots that were hidden within the shell of its lifeless host. The security alert code that was now being transmitted by the Nano robots was a fail-safe, which had alerted the last remaining robot to its exact location. This is how thousands of years earlier, the alien robots had been able to collect the remains of their savaged fellow robot from the clutches of Alexander the Great's men and more importantly for them at the time, retrieve Alexander's lost gold.

# Chapter thirty six

As usual, there were a handful of sceptics and rightly so, but after a while everyone moves on. News broke, new scandals arose and that allowed the alien invasion to be shunted onto smaller and smaller columns of the press and eventually to be all but forgotten. Editors could be bought and influenced, just the same as politicians.

We had all settled back into our new work regimes and we were now back in New Zealand. I was working on a new alien invasion strategic defence plan for the President, Vicki had started with FIFA and baby Beckham was doing his best to exhaust us both. The nanny really did help.

I worked closely with Kinika and Jenny back at Android AI HQ as we used the data that they uncovered on a daily basis to try and create the best defence strategy possible.

The Andis were now back in action and the faith in them was starting to be restored but this would take time. The new Andi Mk3 was in its early development stage with deep space exploration its sole purpose. Jenny and Kinika were now working hard on developing their self-replicating capacities after their initial reverse engineering of the alien robot, so the Mk3s could begin their own space adventure.

Of course, even with all these events going on around me, I still made time for my beloved telescope every night at the Linsky observatory on top of the Pisa Range. And that was the first time I noticed the anomaly – through my telescope.

The lustrous Southern night sky had been shimmering with a light show provided by the Aurora Australis, the southern lights. I had been observing the exit point of the wormhole located in the far distant reaches of our own Solar System.

To understand the distance to the wormhole you need to understand the size and make up of our Solar System. As you travel past our own outer planets you reach the Kuiper belt, which is a circumstellar disc extending out from the orbit of Neptune. It's similar to the asteroid belt and consists mainly of Small Solar System Bodies or (SSSB's) which are remnants from the formation of our own Solar System, billions of years ago.

Beyond the Kuiper belt is the Oort cloud, which is interstellar space. This region of the Solar System is named after the Dutch astronomer Jan Oort and its outer limits define the cosmographical boundary of our Solar System. The Voyager 1 space probe, launched from Earth in 1977 is currently traveling through the Solar System and will reach the Oort cloud in about 280 years and will take about 30,000 years to completely pass through it. The Oort cloud is a massive region of space.

The aliens had used the wormhole located within the Oort cloud to send the plasma bolt through space. I had been watching it for two reasons. The President had asked me personally to give her a full report on whether to expect another alien attack and the USSA were on a constant state of high alert to repulse any further attempts by the aliens to send another plasma bolt screaming across our Solar System with our own sun as its intended target.

The second and much more interesting thing from an astrophysics perspective was that up until nine months ago wormholes were just theoretical, but now we knew they were real. My work now involved the realization of Einstein's theories and I set about writing a paper that I hoped would be seminal in the world of astronomy and astrophysics.

The anomaly was not easy to see at first, it seemed the light in the area around the wormhole had changed in its density and clarity. I ran a diagnostics check and reviewed the complete operation of my telescope, but the figures just didn't seem to add up. I re-ran the calculations through my computer and the only thing in space I could think of that acted in this way was a black hole.

The thing is – there were no recorded black holes in our Solar System! The light that surrounded the object was being diffracted by something.

I enlisted the help of my newly found friends at the USSA. I had emailed General Klein with my concerns but he was on a cruise off Hawaii having a well-earned vacation on board the new superliner 'Global Sunshine' operated by Royal Caribbean, the largest cruise company in the world. The 'Global Sunshine' with its 8000 passengers and 3500 crew was an astonishing sight to behold and an awesome feat of modern shipbuilding engineering. The superstructure was enormous, the elegant futuristic design epitomized everything that modern day cruising had to offer. The rich and elite were having a ball.

I eventually got through to General Klein on his personal iPhone. He snarled, "This better be good Lukas, I'm having a beer and watching the football". I was aware by now that his bark was worse than his bite. Some of his young USSA recruits lived in fear of him, but it was just an act. Tough love was his management style, but he was ferociously loyal to all his charges and deep down they all knew it.

I began to speak, "General have you read my report on the anomaly at the entrance of the wormhole the aliens used to shoot the plasma bolt at the sun?"

"Lukas," the general replied, "My top people are on this and they can't seem to see anything unusual with any of our assets."

"Well General, it's the way your people are looking for it that seems to be the issue here. My telescope at the Observatory has the very latest equipment required to observe the anomaly and I'm telling you something is out there and my new calculations tell me that it's moving through the Oort cloud in the direction of the Earth".

That's when it suddenly it struck me.

"My God General," I swallowed hard and took a deep breath. "It's them, it's the bloody aliens. The anomaly, it's not a black hole, it's them, they've cloaked their Mothership and they are coming back for their Gold!"

I took a deep breath and said…

## "Call the President and do it now!"